"Once you've experienced a true Dominant, you are never the same. They ruin any possibilities of anyone, and anything else."- E.L Discipline

THE *Seduction* OF Discipline

E.L DISCIPLINE

authorHOUSE®

AuthorHouse™
1663 Liberty Drive
Bloomington, IN 47403
www.authorhouse.com
Phone: 1 (800) 839-8640

Published by AuthorHouse 06/08/2017

ISBN: 978-1-5246-9603-0 (sc)
ISBN: 978-1-5246-9602-3 (e)

Print information available on the last page.

CONTENTS

INTRODUCTION

What is the real definition of the acronym, 'BDSM?' We know what it stands for, Bondage and Discipline, Dominance and Submission, Sadism and Masochism. But what is it really? Many different people engage in many different things. Some may engage in S & M, which is just Sadism/Masochism and there's no Dominance. No Discipline or bondage. Some engage in Bondage/Discipline and not S & M. Some engage in all four. Let me break down each one for you.

Bondage; is physically restraining your partner along the lines of tying them up with a tie, a rope, hand-cuffs or pinning them down with your own hands. Bondage can be psychological also. **Discipline**; is psychologically restraining your partner with rules and rituals they must abide by along with forms of punishments that are enforced if the partner is not compliant. Dominance is complete excellence. It's Overpowering. It's Dominant. One who exercises control in everything, everyone, and every aspect of their own lives. They know how to get in people's head. They know how to seduce, and they know how to take charge. **Submission**; is yielding to something overpowering. A "submissive" is one that relinquishes all control and at all times, or for a short period of time. **Sadism**; is an act of inflicting pain for sexual pleasure. It can be physical, psychological or emotional. Along the lines of; verbal abuse, humiliation (private or public), spanking, hitting, penetration. **Masochism**; is the act of receiving pain for sexual pleasure, along the lines of humiliation (emotional or physical) pain. **Soft limits**; are things that are discussed between a Dom and his sub. These limits are a list of things that you don't mind to do sexually and in public. Fantasies that you would love to have fulfilled. Things you are unsure of or that you are nervous about trying but always wanted to engage in. **Hard limits**; are list of things that are absolutely non negotiable with the sub. Things she will never try perhaps because they are scared, or repulsed by a certain act, or through a childhood drama, they don't like a particular thing i.e spankings, basically anything that doesn't not turn them on or something they hate. Last but not least: **Safe Word**; is the word to be respected by both parties, this word needs to be worked out prior to any sexual play. When used, it is a code word to stop any and all activity immediately and at any time the person feels unsafe or uncomfortable. Remember, trust is the foundation of this lifestyle. There is more trust, more openness and more security found in this lifestyle, than any other basic traditional relationship.

There are so many misinterpretations of this lifestyle. I've heard them all.

"You beat the woman".

"You treat her like a slave".

"Oh my goodness, how can she like to be tied up like an animal".

"Oh they're all freaks".

But this lifestyle is nothing like you've heard or seen. The movies have it wrong, the rumours are wrong. You see if you are not part of this lifestyle then you are losing. What you are about to read in this book will break all the boundaries and all the moulds that exist around BDSM (BDSM). It's not just hard-core sex. There are so many intricate levels to BDSM. If you've been in a BDSM relationship and it didn't blow your mind, then you were in an average one. If you didn't have a proper Dominant (Dom) to guide you and nurture you, then I feel sorry for you, you were ripped off. There are many different types of Dominants and different levels and dynamics. There's Dominants that engage in BDSM 24/7 and then there are the ones that are just sexual Dominants. This means that they only engage in the lifestyle in a sexual environment, however, this particular Dom is desired by most women. I'm not a switch. I am a 24/7 Dom, inside and outside the bedroom. My word is law, and if my submissive/s (sub/s) do not adhere to this, yes, they will be punished. But also if they are good, then I treat them like the queens they are. I help in their growth as a woman and build their confidence and strength. Some Dominants like weak submissive woman. However everyone thinks that to be a submissive it makes a woman weak. What they don't understand is that when a woman submits to a man, she is stronger than any female in the world. She has the confidence to let go of everything and know that her Dom will look after her and protect her. She might be powerful and strong in all aspects of her life, but for a strong female to submit their "being" to another human makes them the most prized gift in the world. I like the alpha submissive, a strong powerful woman who can bow down to me, her King. That to me is priceless. In order to obtain what I have, in order for me to provide what I do and am, comes with a price, tax included. I don't come cheap. What I provide as a Dom is worth more than money. My Dominance is the most prestigious thing in this world. Everybody talks about the gift of submission, but what about the gift of Dominance? The gift of your Dom accepting you for who you are and seeing what you could be? Loaning his strength when you are weak, elevating you like no regular man can.

Am I too good to be true? Yes I am. If you are unwilling to give me everything, I will gladly take nothing. I don't fucking negotiate with that.

This is my world. I live it daily and this book is here to educate those people that think this lifestyle is a "fad", a "joke", "not real". I will introduce you to the many levels of

BDSM and smash any misconceptions you have. This book will have you fascinated and even tempted to try something out. But it will also educate you and open your eyes a bit into this lifestyle. You may scoff at what has already been portrayed to you in TV and in books and think "oh my God, no way in the world would I ever crawl on my knees to a man, no man is worthy". But have an open mind. What I do, what my lifestyle pertains is something far beyond what you could ever imagine. Keep reading if you want to educate yourself a little better into a lifestyle that is fulfilling and satisfying for both parties. However, don't say I didn't warn you. You might laugh and toss this book aside but you will be awakened, and there is no turning back from that.

CHAPTER 1

The Man Behind The Dominance And The Crown

You may think you know me from what I allow you to see on my social media pages or when you see me in the street. But don't be fooled. Only a select few know the man behind the tattoos, the man behind the whips, the man outside of the boxing ring. Only a select few are allowed inside my inner circle. I keep things tight. If I don't want you to know anything, you wont. It's that simple. If I don't think you are worthy, you won't be addressed. To those that know me well, I go by many names. However if I don't know you and you don't know me, you will address me as 'Mr Discipline'. Whatever you think you know about me, I can guarantee you, you are wrong. Don't let my gangster exterior fool you. I am a gangster however; I am highly intelligent as well. I think deeply and my heart is pure. I'm the realest soul you'll find. I'm not into BDSM because of some sordid secret from my past. My lifestyle choice is my passion. I live and

1

breathe it. A true New Yorker, born and bred, I come from a large family who were full of Dominant males and Alpha females. I grew up in a family that if one kid got in trouble, we all got punished. We learned pretty quickly that we had to band together like a team. I had very strong male figures in my life; my father, grandfather and brothers, all of us strong males would occasionally bump heads. My father was quite strict in every aspect of my childhood; there was punishment for disobedience. Physical and mental punishment. Most Caribbean households are pretty tough, however mine was on another level. I was also blessed to have had amazing strong females to help guide me. My older sister. My late grandmother(who died in August 2011) was an inspiration to me. She saw the potential in me and made sure she bought it out of me. She was the one that would constantly tell me to "Man up".

"Take control".

"Look after yourself and those around you" and; "Always protect those that are your family, those that belong to you". Of course at 14 years old, I didn't understand the truth depth of what she was trying to explain to me. It wasn't until I reached my late teens did I grasp her words and made them my code of ethics. Her words, I still live by to this day. My Grandfather taught me a lot about life. He was the one that, at 11 years old, taught me how to tie my own tie. My grandfather also taught me that aloe vera heals a bee sting.

He showed me. When I was 7 years old, I was playing outside my grandparent's house I was stung by a bee. I ran crying and my grandfather pulled me, told me to be quiet in his native language and before I could even get one word out to explain to him what had happened, he picked me up in his strong arms, put me on his knee, and without one word, he opened up a jar of the aloe vera he had in the kitchen and applied the gel over the sting. I could feel the instant relief from the cool gel working it's way into the bee sting. My grandfather was silent, and as I hung on to his strong shoulders, I too was silent, just watching him. He was calming and reassuring and quite gentle with me as I was quite young. I watched him move in silence to quickly heal me. In those moments I learned a few things. One, that aloe vera heals bee stings. Two, I could read people very well without having one word pass between us (which is a talent I still have to this day). Three, my grandfather and I were very similar. He gave me more than any man in my life could have given me. His strength, guidance, love and support built me into the man I am today. It's one thing to be smart and know a lot about one specific thing, we are all smart, educated on a specific topic, but to be intelligent, to know a little bit about everything is on a different level. An innate understanding is not something you can teach. Phenomenal art comes from great struggle and diamonds are created from intense pressure. Many people have memories from their childhood, good and bad, some they want to remember, some they really want to forget. But the bad parts are always remembered, the good vanish out of your memory bank. My mother was an exceptional alpha woman, she taught me to never allow a woman to control me and who I am. My father always taught me to Dominate in every situation. I excelled in school, but I thrived in sports. This is where I began to find my true self. I could see that if I worked hard and practiced daily, I would succeed. My coaches became like my mentors outside of home and they constantly pushed me to become better than I was the day before. The confidence of continually winning and become the best in all areas I played, grew in me and awakened a sense of pride, and confidence. I loved the exhilaration of the challenge, the challenge of beating my old self. I loved proving to people who said I couldn't do it, just how wrong they were. I loved proving to myself just how great I could be. Sports taught me that with Discipline and hard work, you could be the best there is. This is where my passion for Discipline grew and shaped me into the man I am today it gave me the ability to master my mind and my body. It starts with that. The confidence I have built, the self-development I have gained, has been the epitome of being able to develop others. What I do, what I engage in, how I engage in it; means my life is not associated with inadequate development. You gain a purpose coming into my lifestyle and you have an ultimate goal, and with that goal, you could enter as a 'little' and leave as a 'Queen'. There are levels to this lifestyle that can be obtained with guidance and Discipline and everything will be explained.

CHAPTER 2

What To Expect From A King

Choose your King wisely because he represents you. You know when you've met a real King because, his energy Dominates you and his energy Dominates the entire room. You can feel it and you can sense it. Your whole demeanor changes, your behavior alters and you act accordingly. You are drawn to the realness. You want to be part of it. You are pulled towards the aura of a real one. You gravitate towards it not knowing at first what its all about, but knowing that you need to have it, to taste it, feel it, touch it. A King will teach you and guide you in all aspects of your life. You will never lack anything. He will make you feel strong, sexy, safe, supported and loved. He will make you fall in love with yourself all over again. You will become more confident in yourself and your abilities. You will be more comfortable in your own skin. You will feel alive again. I believe that 'a woman that has the courage to crawl, has the potential to fly'. Your King will help you fly. He will set you free from what constricts you. Help spread your wings and grow. His goal is not to force you to kneel to him; his goal is to make you proud to kneel for him. He will inspire you to fall to your knees, as you kneel at his feet, to worship him as he worships you. He will give you complete sanctuary to explore and embrace your sexuality, your womanhood with no judgment. The 'freeDom' of release you will experience is beyond anything you can imagine. He will cultivate your mind and your body. No matter your past, your King will fully accept you as you are. He will help you flourish into greatness. Your trust in your King comes easily. It is given freely and willingly. You know that you are not giving your trust to someone who is unworthy. You are giving it to someone who will treasure it and respect it. His ability is great. You will willingly surrender yourself over to him, to give him your all, to allow him to take control of you, and your life. To follow him blindly into whatever he leads you into. Knowing that he has your best interests at heart. He will never lead you astray, will never abuse the trust and faith you have in him. He will cherish you and all that you give. Your complete surrender will be the sweetest reward. He will train you in all aspects that a King trains his Queen. Through Discipline, trust, patience and time. He will mold your mind, your psyche and your character. You will be trained to please. You will be trained to receive pain and then pleasure. Then trained to give ultimate satisfaction to your King. Through it all, you will find complete fulfilment in knowing your King is satisfied, content and happy. Your King is your friend, your lover, your teacher and your punisher. He is everything to you. He is your world. He will be the man you think of when you wake up, when you go about your day and when you go to sleep. He will be your main priority. He will be your number one. Putting him first and making sure he is completely looked after and cared for in all aspects of his life, will be your reward. Knowing you have achieved this, you have achieved his happiness, his contentment. Feeling and knowing that he is content, you will reap many benefits. If he is not guiding your mind, assisting in your growth, he is failing as a Dom, and as your teacher. However, a true King will never fail. His magnetism makes everyone around him thrive to be great, to do better, to be better, to make him happy, to make him proud. As a King, he wants to see those under his wing, grow and be amazing to flourish. You must remember that you are a team. You must work together; otherwise it just will not work at all. Your complete and utter obedience will be rewarded in more ways than one. You must remember a sub is a true reflection of her Dom. What you do reflects on him, on his teachings, his guidance and commands. Working together is the only way to succeed. Once your souls have touched, no matter where you are in the world, your souls will always be bound to one another.

You will be linked in a bond that is unexplainable to the outside world. Outside relationships do not go as deep. Their connection is not firmly planted in their souls. The Dom/sub relationship is something out of this world. Your love is deeper, more intense, more stimulating and more passionate. He offers you freeDom. He offers you protection, he offers you Domination, he offer you Discipline, he offers you life like you've never seen or lived before. What he offers you is the best, the very best of him. If he touches your soul, you will be his forever. Once you're his, you are protected. A King is territorial. Overprotective even. What's his belongs to him, and he does not share. For your complete submission, a real King offers you this, and more. Together you can access an emotional, psychological and physical level, which transcends the limits of a basic relationship. If you are ready to fly, prepare to surrender. Many women may view themselves as a Queen, however, a King crowns you at the end of the day. A woman that knows her place, never loses her position. You carry yourself to the highest degree. That includes your mindset, attire, and your energy. In a game of chess, the king is the most prominent piece, however, the Queen is the most powerful. She can maneuver positions on the board, like no other piece can. She may have bishops, knights, rooks and pawns around her, but she's aware the King is the most prominent piece. She learns how to cater, worship, and protect her King. She is aware that if the King is captured, then the game is over. If you wish to view yourself as a queen, do not resemble a whore in public or on social media, where a man will lose interest in you quickly. It's fine if you have an enormous sexual appetite or libido, but leave a little mystery. Guys thrive off the hunt, the chase. Hard work not only builds character, but it makes them appreciate you more. However, do not play games, you could potentially chase away your soul mate forever. Be open, honest and communicate efficiently. When it comes to myself, I am rarely disappointed, because I know what to expect. I demand things from the beginning. Which consists of your hard work, devotion, dedication, loyalty, willingness and honesty. If you are unwilling to provide that, I'm sure there is someone willing and able to take your place. Never forget this is a power exchange relationship. When you give him the gift of your submission, he grants you the gift of his Dominance. A woman needs to be taught how to be a Queen and through his proper guidance, his energy, his spirit, it will inspire your growth. Your mind set will be different. The way you dress will change; your behavior will be different. Your demeanor will be different. The way you speak will also be different. When you are with a true King your entire being is elevated. You are who you are from your past and current relationships. Who you surround yourself; all this will determine your character and what you attract and do not into your mind, body and soul. This will determine the person you become tomorrow, so be careful who you welcome into your psyche. Basically, if you cannot tell the difference between a King and a pawn, stick to checkers.

CHAPTER 3

Sub Standards

One look into your eyes and I know. I will study everything about you very meticulously. I will stalk you mentally and emotionally, to see if you are worthy enough to enter my world. You will not know what I am doing, as I will sit back and take everything about you in, while I assess your worth. I will decide if you are worthy enough to be part of my world, and my life. You see, I only allow certain women into my life, my world, because it is not for the weak. If you haven't been invited into my world, it should tell you what I think of you and where we stand. However in this moment, I have carefully decided to invite you in. Now I must warn you, this is the most dangerous place on earth. Why? Because it's a jungle, and jungles are dangerous. I am the lion and you are my prey. Everyone knows that the Lion is the King of the jungle. Let me make my intentions perfectly clear, you......are.....going.....to.....serve me. If you come into my world, you will prioritize serving me over all others. The completion of my tasks will take priority over all other things. You will focus on pleasing me; you will cater to my needs, fulfil all my darkest desires, be there when I want you and need you; to fuck, to suck and to kneel. Your loyalty, dedication, devotion, hard work; I don't crave or desire these things, I fucking demand them! When we come together, we won't 'have sex' or 'make love'. I will completely Dominate you and your total existence. I will fuck you until you feel your soul lifting out of your body, and connects with mine. I will tantalize and seduce your mind, and will abuse your body to the core. You will submit to me in all your entirety. I will make you beg, scream, crawl, cry and moan, and this makes me dangerous, because I know who and what I am. You should never become complacent, because you will never know what to expect from me. All you need to know is that I will never mislead you. But I will make you feel more alive than you ever have felt in your entire life. I will make you feel sexy, desired, secure, safe, loved and protected. The added bonus of being fucked by a master is my daily gift to you. But don't mistake all that I offer as anything more than what it is. I am not your 'boyfriend, baby, honey, boo, bae'. I am your KING, you are my sweet baby girl, you are my Queen, but behind closed doors you will be my little whore who will be fucked senseless. In the BDSM world, my world, one does not 'create' a submissive (sub). If you are unwilling to give everything to me, I will then take nothing at all from you. A good sub is a result from having a great Dominant (Dom). When a sub submits to her Dom, she then binds her soul to his. As my sub, you not only represent yourself, you are a representation of me. What you do, reflects on me. This is why I do not allow my sub/s to conduct themselves in any kind of way that reflects badly on both of us. A true sub will conduct herself appropriately on all levels, socially online and socially in real life, whether her Dom is present or not. I always say, if you do not behave as your Dom's true sub at all times, then you are wasting both your time and your Dom's, and clearly do not deserve a true King. You are not truly 'owned', you are just pretending. Some Dom's like to role-play, I don't. I don't expect my sub/s to role-play either. My relationships with my sub/s are all psychological, mental and emotional. We are connected on all levels. I've said it before and I'll say it again. This is life. This is my world. This is not a game. I take my role as your Dom very seriously, I do not abuse the trust or power that is bestowed upon me. I cherish it, as I do my sub/s. This lifestyle is not a part time thing either. To me (and my sub/s) it is 24/7, 365 days a year, in and outside of the bedroom. This is the way of my world. Being submissive doesn't make her a freak, a whore or kinky. Just because she is submissive doesn't mean, she'll be YOUR submissive. It's not about just rough sex, being tied up, choking, enduring great pain, displaying aggressive behaviour, spankings, none of that. The act of submission happens in the mind first. The submission comes from a psychological need to submit. She has slavish tendencies, but she is not a slave. Submission happens way before the bedroom. It's all about trust. It thrives and remains consistent outside of the bedroom. I believe ninety percent of women in this world are 'bedroom subs'. Once inside the bedroom, that's when the power exchange takes place. They relinquish control up to their Dom. Man. Boy toy, etc. Once they are out of the bed, or sexual environment they go back to their vanilla (regular) roles in life. If the woman runs the relationship, whether she wears the pants, makes the decisions, etc, then they go back to doing that. To some subs they only feel loved when they are being controlled.

The Psychological Sub:

With a psychological sub, the act begins in the mind first. She does not necessarily need to be in love with her Dom first to submit. The act happens in the mind of the sub. It is a need to surrender; the act of submission is a psychological event. She gives herself to the Dom, she can give as little or as much as the psychological sub wishes or needs to give. Then it would become the responsibility of the Dominant to determine her choices and direction. With a psychological sub, the surrender of the power is the driving force. Once the psychological sub surrenders, she can simply become nothing. She can abandon herself completely to her Dom trusting in the Dominants strength, thus the power exchange is complete.

The Bottom:

The bottom is the person who in the BDSM lifestyle enjoys pain. They wish to be on the receiving end of the flogger or the paddle or the whip. The bottom maintains the control. The act of 'bottoming' is not always sexual, but most of the time it is. The bottom does not release control to the top, it's more of a mutual partnerships. Some examples, those that are into the spanking aspect of the lifestyle, I have met spankers who will tell you they don't have a submissive bone in their body. They are in this for the sexual pleasure of the pain. The bottom is more of an act than a state of mind. The bottom is a lot different than the psychological and the sub with the slave's heart. The bottom does not necessarily need to engage 24/7, and this may only occur in a sexual environment. A bottom can also Dominate from the bottom. If you're in a relationship with a man, and you both come to certain agreements about what the dynamics will be. All of a sudden you witness her doing the opposite of what you have agreed upon and she is undermining, overstepping her bounds, challenging you constantly and making it seem like you have to answer to her, checking up on you, etc, those are little subtle types of behaviour of Dominating from the bottom. This is a good example of Dominating from the bottom. This is perfectly fine for some men if they are a "switch", because sometimes outside of the sexual environment the woman takes the switch role. For example, the woman may make all the decisions and the man is very passive, but when they are in the bedroom the man takes control and the woman becomes submissive, so they are "switching roles".

The Slave:

Unlike the submissive, the slave surrenders complete control to the master or mistress(yes a slave there is no gender specifics. It can be a male or female, but in my case, female because I do not swing both ways). I am not saying the slave has no limits, however I believe we all have our limits, whether they are moral or cultural. I believe those limits do exist, and I believe a good master will respect the limits of his property; the slave, and take care of the slave. The slave has an undying need to become 'owned'. She gives complete control. She is willing and able to do anything for her master, and for her mentally, physically and emotionally she has no limits. Her only desire is to please him. No matter what.

The Bedroom Sub:

The next type of submissive is the bedroom submissive and the best way to portray this type of submissive in every aspect of life is similar to the 'bottom' or 'vanilla (non BDSM relationships)'. Now here's the best part, when the bedroom door shuts, the roles drop and she or he submits to the Dom. In the bedroom is where the power exchange takes place; it is also where it stays. This is almost always sexual. In the bedroom, the act of submission is complete. However when the bedroom door is open, the bedroom sub returns to her "vanilla role" in life. The difference between the bedroom submissive and the bottom is: control. The bottom is in control, however the bedroom sub gives control, but only in the bedroom.

The Masochist:

The masochist is not submissive; he or she is just in it for the sexual gratification or humiliation. Whether it is emotional, mental and physical pain. They thrive off of pain, and it becomes a necessity. He or she needs consistent Discipline and is incomplete without it. These individuals normally gravitate to Sadists. This relationship becomes very efficient as they engage in S&M (Sadism and Masochism). There are still agreements that are discussed between both parties, however most of this act is usually in a sexual environment.

The Submissive With A Slave Heart:

This level, is the deepest level of submission, the submissive with the slave heart wishes to surrender without becoming a slave. Unlike the psychological sub, with this submission comes the psychological need to submit. The heart is a different matter because the love of the Dominant is craved. The submissive with the slave heart desires to give her heart as well as her submission to the Dominant. Like I said prior; the psychological sub does not need to be in love to submit, however the submissive with the slave heart has the need to give not only submission, but also love with that submission. The submissive with the slave heart is at the threshold of completely surrendering herself to her Dom. The level of trust is greater in the submissive with the slave heart than the psychological sub.

Every sub needs to know who they are and what their identity is, as per above. For example: the masochist will not match with a 'daddy' because the masochist can't 'play' well with the daddy. The 'sadist' will not play well with the 'little.' The 'slave', may be a little bit too much for the Dominant and I say this because it's 2 people, but 1 relationship. Even though it is an unequally but balanced relationship, it still is one relationship and that's what gives it balance. The sadist feeds the masochist and the masochist feeds the sadist. That caring daddy caters to that needy clingy little, and the Daddy Dom knows how to protect that baby girl. What tames women and their attitudes is; good loving. Also certain Disciplines that is quite efficient. Masochists, if they feel they are not getting punished enough, they will manipulate you to get what they want. The masochist is usually a woman, and a woman can't

Dominate herself. However, she may behave a certain way to get you to Dominate her. The key is to never give them what they want; you need to give them what they need. If you are giving them what they want, then they start falling in love with 'more'. More attention equates to more want. You give them gifts and they want more. This is not conducive to what you are trying to build. They seem to forget who they are, who you are, and what your relationship entails. The reality is they will not learn to appreciate the rightful things. When you keep giving to someone, they will never appreciate it. When you relinquish complete control, you will get everything you desire. You will begin to trust in his strength, his power, his decisions, and his authority. Now he becomes her strength in all things. She follows his lead. Every Dominant is different, and there are different types of Dominants. Myself, I'm all about 'TPE' (Total Power Exchange). For me, the only submission is complete submission. The only negotiations I will go through with you are your 'hard/soft' limits and safe words, but everything else I have control over. A man can fuck a woman, that's easy, but to invade her every thought, to touch her without touching her and for her to surrender completely, now that's when pure servitude takes place. That's the challenge. If you're not ready to be 100% committed in a D/s relationship, do not attempt to start. They are both equal in servitude. Ultimately, a sub needs to be wanted and a Dom wants to be needed. Show me your dedication, show me the hard work you do for me, impress me with your loyalty and I promise, I'll reward you with Discipline.

The submissive is commonly referred to as the Sub, Bottom, Slave, Little, Pet, or Bitch. The Submissive passively participates in a BDSM relationship; they consent to the relinquishment of their physical and mental control to the Dominant. All submissives are masochistic by nature; they embrace to some extent, mental, emotional, and physical pain. The degree to which they submit, and the nature of their masochist desire is reflected in their taken name. BDSM relationships are founded on the exchange of power between two individuals: the Dominant and the Submissive. This page discusses the role and nature of the Submissive in this power exchange. A Submissive relinquishes a degree of control for either a specified period; be it short term for a session, or long term as part of a BDSM relationship. The bottom receives physical sensation from the Dominant or Top. However, a Slave relinquishes total control, also known as total power exchange (TPE), over one or more aspects of their life. To ensure that all activities are safe, sane, and consensual, the Submissive is given a safe-word to ensure the unequivocal ceasing of activities if their hard limits are met. Contracts can be used to formalize rules and expectations; and to signify the commitment between the Dominant and Submissive. However, it is not likely. This lifestyle begins with trust.

Therefore, there's no need for contracts. Additionally, the collaring of a Submissive by the Dominant, communicates the status of their relationship. A submissive is not weak and self-hating; on the contrary, a submissive is strong willed, fearless individuals, willing to face their own mortality. There is great strength in vulnerability; the giving up of one's desire, body and mind requires immense trust, honesty and intimacy between two individuals. The act of submission signifies the human desire to kill the ego and transcend their own individual existence. This submission strips the individual of their false or pre-conceived self; they strip away all social conventions, and stand bare, ugly, pathetic but pure before another soul. It's at this point that BDSM becomes a spiritual experience; one in which the individual connects with the power of the universal unconscious, and their opposition, the Dominant. For the Submissive, this place is referred to as subspace. Most submissive girls and women are shy. Not all of them, but most of them. They do not like being in control. They have a difficult time making decisions. They're laid back, and quiet. They are reserved. You're not going to see them plastering themselves with copious amount of makeup. They think twice, three maybe four times before they make any decision. They're not very loud when they speak. They show you very little of themselves, physically and emotionally until they open up to you. Until you eradicate those walls, and guards they work so hard to keep up.

Now an alpha submissive is more confident, bold and assertive. Even if she's not a boss in her work, or life, her idiosyncrasies show her leadership abilities. Most alpha subs are alone, or in relationships that bore them. The reason is they find it difficult for a man to feed them or are stronger than them, emotionally, physically, and mentally. But can you blame a man? Yes, a smart, strong submissive is a prize to a Dominant. However, it is a turn off when you are consistently trying to 'one up' him. Whether it's beating him in an intellectual conversation or argument, on a board game or calling him weak is just an excuse for your poor behaviour. If you want to be a woman, or treated like one, you must act like one. Allow him to be the King, to be the man. However, a true Dominant man is not going to Dominate you either just because you are begging him to. He has to want to engage in it also. When it comes to Dominant men, if you're begging or asking a sub to submit to you or be yours, then you've lost. Lost power and all control. You are now the submissive. Subs, they tend to have the most innocent faces but they don't fool me. The sexual sub has the most artistic minds when it pertains to sex. They do not like to make eye contact much. If stared at too long they get anxiety: "Why is he looking at me, do I have something on my face, what is it. How do I look", etc, the list goes on. Shy females will always gravitate to bad boys, or alpha men. Why? Because, they are the most confident, and adventurous and shy females crave to be like that. If you go through power struggles everyday, trouble letting go, letting go of pride. Then this life is not for you. You need to re-evaluate yourself and what it is you're actually looking for. Because most of you women just want to be Dominated sexually. The women who are happiest in this life, have let go a long time ago. Maybe this life looks attractive, fun, intriguing, enticing, adventurous, phenomenal and once in a lifetime experience. However, so is a jet, but it doesn't mean you can get one, or afford one.

Let me break it down for you.

You.
Belong.
To.
Me.

I can do what I want with you. Even in public, especially in public. If we are out, I will touch you wherever I please. I don't need permission either. I don't care who is watching. I don't care what people think, and neither should you. If we are out for dinner, and I want you to feed me, you will. If you struggle with this and are ashamed and embarrassed to do this simple act, you are not a true sub. You have not given me your soul. No matter what I ask of you, you are to do it. No questions asked. No back talk, no nagging. If you are not ready to be 100% committed in every aspect of my world, don't waste my time. All of my subs are good and if they get out of line, I put them back in line, however, if my sub is a lost cause, I let her go. This is something I hate to do. I do not like to lose. It is not in my blood or in my vocabulary. I believe what is mine is mine for as long as I wish. I don't play for fun I play to win. I am not going to offer you me if I don't have all of you.

Total Power Exchange (TPE). That's the catch. The Dom/sub relationship should be peaceful and calm and serene in all aspects except when we fuck. This is where I will destroy you and put you back together. 'Daddy, Sir, Master, King' or whatever your Dom allows you to call him, knows what is best for you. If he is a true Dom, he has and always will have your best interests at heart. Now with me, you should always trust my judgment. Never doubt my decisions or actions, as this shows your doubt in my ability to lead you. The only thing I will allow you to assume is the position. Every Dom is different and has different rules, but with me, I will not Discipline you for the same thing twice. This is not a game. What are you learning? I do not play games and I don't play with people who do not know the rules or blatantly disobey them. If you deliberately set out to break rules and boundaries just for 'punishment', we will not last long together. I don't play.

Most of the world does not understand the world of BDSM. This lifestyle is not just about 'rough sex', getting tied up and spanked. It's not about grabbing a woman and taking her by force. It is a lifestyle of philosophy, trust, fulfilment, sacrifice and a challenge beyond the physical. Your body is mine to violate and destroy. Your mind is mine to cultivate and discipline. Your soul is mine to love, Dominate and protect. I will do things to your mind, body and soul beyond your wildest imagination.

Submission is difficult. It takes strength and courage to be the one that must let go. Submission, I mean complete submission is beyond the body. What I want with my submissive women is *complete* submission. Just because you have a desire to serve or please does not make you mine. Submission is strength. It is not for the weak. It takes strength to stand-alone, to give control to another. Courage to kneel for the one you trust. It takes honesty to open up, trust to allow someone access inside your mind, body and soul. Your secrets, your doubts, your fears, your dreams, your pains, your pleasures, your insecurities, your imperfections. To be comfortable to communicate efficiently and articulate your emotions and desires is hard work, but once you let go, and are accepted by the one you trust, love and yearn to please, its invigorating. It is a heavy weight, that is lifted off your shoulders. Nothing eases a woman's mind more than a man who is comfortable in being assertive, a man who can take charge without hesitation. A submissive requires more than the average woman. More structure. More rules. More security. More focus. It is a lot to take on, but then again, a woman gives a lot. Once you're able to open all these things then you have unlocked a door forever where only you possess the key. Her wants become her need. There's nothing more intimate than OWNERSHIP. It is intense. It is invigorating when one gives themselves to you. When one owns you. Everything feels massive. Physical gifts and objects are mundane, but memories are a lifetime. Each sexual experience is not just craved. Each conversation is not just to converse. But is needed so badly that sometimes the body aches in anticipation. Each word either cuts deep, or soothes your soul. I am extremely intense, and passionate. I can manage different set of tasks efficiently. I love hard. I Discipline hard. I punish hard. I fuck hard. However, It's not alway the biggest, flashiest that speak loudest in this lifestyle. When they come consistently and effortlessly, it's the little things that make a huge difference. It's moments where not just her actions or voice screams, "I submit," but whispers of warmth that carries past your eyes and melts directly into your hard, cold soul. This is the beauty in submission. Power is given and power is attractive. To own is precious. Her eyes have their own vocabulary. Her mind is quiet when you're around. Her begging pussy is wet as soon as you place a hand on her. Trust, it's very expensive. Money cannot purchase this. Witness the alternation of her mind, soul and body. The places it's never been will be breathtaking for you both. Complete submission! This is my life and you are now part of it. You are mine. You're welcome.

CHAPTER 4

Damaged

I told her to strip for me. Start with your fears, doubts and insecurities. I want you naked on the inside. I believe everyone in some shape or form is damaged, some more than others. I am no exception. There many ways to be damaged, but the three main ones are: mentally, emotionally and physically. You can suffer from one, you can suffer from two and sometimes you can even suffer all three forms of damaged. You will find that most damaged individuals gravitate towards each other. It's similar to a string that links us all, connects us all. You can feel that pull. That energy. It's like a sense of purpose, you feel secure when you connect with another kindred spirit. You feel it and you need to be around that person, to touch them and feel them so they can bring calm to the storm that rages inside of you. You feel the need to be released from that, which holds you captive in your psyche. Damaged individuals always tend to turn to what damaged them. When you're in a relationship that person's energy intertwines with yours, whether it's good or bad energy. Damaged people are unique. They love hard and they laugh loud. Their screams are ferocious, they fuck harder and they feel things so deeply. Overcoming what you have been through is a big deal. But, what does not kill you, makes you stronger like the cliché saying. Now, articulating it and speaking of it is powerful. Most people preach they are strong. But if you're unwilling to confront your past then you're not there yet. Pain is love and love is pain. What are you afraid of?

Trust?

Loyalty?

Hard work?

Dedication?

Love?

If you are afraid of these things then you are not strong.

I can tell a lot about a person with not much but just a look. It's like a sixth sense. I constantly feel the need to protect and nurture damaged and broken things. I do not seek these people out. It's in my character. My fierce energy has a fierce gravitational pull. This is especially true with shy women. A shy woman will always gravitate towards someone like me, a strong alpha male. She feels that my confidence and strength will give her the power to be strong like she so desperately wants to be. She wants to be confident, but doesn't know how to start, doesn't know where to begin. She will always seek out that stronger figure to help guide her and protect her. A woman that loves or craves danger is another person who gravitates towards a man like me; dark, dangerous and wild. She feels at home with him because she likes the thrill. She can unleash her inner wild demon with no fear of judgment or confinement. Knowing she can get the thrills she wants from a man like that, will always connect these types of souls and keep these types of women coming back to the 'dangerous' Alpha male. I love the challenge to fix these damaged souls. To help set them free. Why? It's something that's instilled in me. I was raised to be the man of the house, to protect the women. To protect what's mine. To make sure they were always safe and loved and because I know what it's like to be damaged. I know what people need to become better, to thrive in themselves and in the life the want to live. Innocent faces get me. The face that looks so angelic in the day, I want to have that face twisted in ecstasy at night. These are my favorite souls to corrupt, that sweet innocent face of a shy, sweet, timid, nervous type of girl. They may look innocent, but I know deep down what they want and what they need. Their need to become my own little whore. Come stand before me, baring not your body, but your soul, all your emotional and mental wounds. Let me fix you, because I know what you need. I know what you crave and what you desire.

There is no substitution for hard work, and these women are all hard work but, as you know, I love the challenge. I welcome it. A damaged soul is nothing simple, it's not as easy as 1-2-3. I will take this woman under my wing and I will strip down her defense, her insecurities and her imperfections until she kneels before me, not ashamed but proud of whom she is and all that she will achieve with me. I will embrace everything about her and who she is. Her past, present and future. Give me your damaged soul, and I will cherish you. All that is demanded in return is your loyalty and dedication to all that is Discipline. When you're in a relationship with me, we will feed off each other's energy, so we need to have it right from the beginning. You will give me everything and I will take it all. In exchange for your soul, you will have all of me. This world is all about balance and control. I will balance and control you. You don't need to worry about your past, because I don't care about it. I don't care how damaged you think you are. It only makes you more beautiful in my eyes. I take a lot of pride in making those around me prosper and flourish. I make sure of it. If you're on my team, you will win. With me, it's all about development. What people do not understand is that BDSM is way beyond the bedroom. It's all about trust, once I have your trust, your obedience will follow. When it comes to submission, it's all psychological. It begins and ends in your mind. I always say; if you kiss her mind, her body will follow. If you water her body, you nourish her soul. What got me through my dark times were lots of things;

excelling in sports, reading, educating and bettering myself. But once I got my first tattoo, I knew I had found something that could reflect what I was feeling on the inside and take the pain away from me. The needle did not hurt; I was numb to the pain. I kind of liked it; it was like my therapy, my escapism from the darkness that haunted me. It articulated my pain with words that I would not speak, could not speak of. I knew that I was addicted after my first one, and decided to express myself, my thoughts and passions through the art of tattoos on my body. Each and every tattoo I have is something that was thought about, researched and considered very carefully, very meticulously. I could tell you about each and every tattoo that I have and the meaning behind each one, and you might be able to understand me a little bit better. Some people turn to drugs or alcohol to get them through their dark times, but this is how my damaged soul is calmed and silenced. Through the art and poetry of the stories that are inked into my skin and my soul. *DOMINANT* all my life. It is what I am. What was instilled in me, what I was born to be. As a child it just didn't resonate. I am a DOMINANT as well, not just Dominant. It's who I am. *KING*, it's the life I've lived (I've never had a woman I was with that didn't treat me like a king outside of the bedroom. All my life, I fucking demanded it and still until this day). Sometimes, you must remind people why you are king. I'm different from what society condones. I'm not here to take part, I'm here to take over. Reign supreme. Powerful. ALPHA, natural born leader tendencies. Everyone wants power, titles, or to be in charge, but no one knows how to properly lead, inspire, motivate or coach. *SADIST.* Sadistic. Cruel. Savage. I am a Scorpio after all. You could have done me wrong 2 years ago and never made it right, and I will punish you for it today. My punishment will be calculated, methodical, strategic, penetrating and slow. You will not see it coming. I have a memory like an elephant. The ones I care for I'm over protective over. I love to give. BEAST, conqueror. DOMINATE, it's what I do. In all things, forever, not just sometimes, it's not something. Not an act. I look back, and realize all this was my calling. Just begging me to realize it. Regular, traditional relationships were mundane. The Limitations, the disappointments, the dissatisfactions. "Why didn't you text or call me? I need your attention". Demand, demand, demand, blah blah blah." See, I don't answer to anyone. I'm a Scorpio I don't do anything you tell me. We like to move when we want. It's more genuine. If I give you attention because you beg for it, I just did it to shut you up.

I didn't get any:

"Did you eat?".

"Did you make it home safe?".

"How can I please you?" etc etc.

Hold on one second *click* dismissed, cancel that bitch. She's selfish. She's needy for the wrong things. Needy for the thing you provide her, and not you. Was this really life? When it comes to the bedroom also:

"Ouch(that's not a safe word)".

"Stop, get off".

"Not so rough please".

"Wait, you're going to stick that big, huge chocolate dick in me? You'll kill me".

"You want to do what? Try what? Hell no, I'm not trying it, or doing that".

Not just the whining, but the looks. Confusing, the looks as if they drank spoiled milk.

"You're crazy, a freak, this is not normal, what's wrong with you?".

"You must not have respect for women".

So I bottled up my darkest desire just to keep them from running away. What did I get in doing that? They were happy with mediocre. I was not fulfilled. Now I want them scared, yes run away. It just keeps the wrong people away from me, and that's good. Run you scared little kittens, the wolf is loose. The lion is on a mission. He loves the fear in your eyes, the look of worry and nervousness on your face. The boring, unadventurous the "just get on top and fuck me" looks. The fakes who called themselves "freaks" but their idea of freaky was 2 major positions. "Choke me, but not too hard, spank my ass, pull my hair". She's getting the best sex of her life, because most women are terrible in bed, and the men do the minimum because they are lazy. So that's the most amazing thing for them to experience, or their past lovers just gave them the norm. But boring to me is phenomenal to most women. So boring is what they are used to. Familiarity becomes safe. Comfortable. But it's really just all mental. But for me, there was no fulfilment. My creativity was stifled. My passion was not sustained. My intensity was bottled up. I was like a painter with no paint, a sculptor with no clay. I am great, not just good. I am phenomenal. Mind. Body. Soul. Not ordinary. So why would I settle for mediocrity? I found the real me. He was always inside me. No more compromises, no more settling. This is fulfilment. Forever, and vanilla (regular) was gone forever. I'm an asshole, a freak, a savage and a beast. Crazy? I've accepted all this a long time ago. So in bed, shut the fuck up bitch, I'll do as I please. Do not tell me, 'harder, pull my hair, spank me!' I know what I'm doing, you follow my lead. When I want you to fucking open your fucking mouth, ill say so. Until then, remain quiet. The only thing I want to hear is when you're begging me to cum whore. "Daddy, may I cum please?" Other than that, shut up. Do not even moan, unless I say so. If it's a hard limit of yours we can perhaps throw it out the window (depends what it is) but I'm in charge (in and out of the bedroom). If I want you to speak you will, otherwise shut the fuck up or get gagged. This is my world and you just live in it. This is the best experience you will ever receive. You have been cordially invited to the jungle, my jungle. You will be preyed upon. Devoured. Ravaged and you will love it. So kick back and enjoy the ride. If not, there is someone else that would love to take your place. Discipline and punishment doesn't adjust to anyone, we all adjust to Discipline, pain and pleasure. Get with it, or get lost. That's not negotiable. You can't stand the heat? Then stay out the fucking kitchen bitch. It hurts? Tell someone that cares because I swear I don't. You know what my life entails and what comes with me: passion, intensity, Dominance and power. I fuck hard, Discipline hard, punish hard, train hard, teach hard, gaze hard, love hard and Dominate hard. Who are you? A mother fucking King. What are you? Dominant.

Where are you from? The land of Dominance.

What do you do for a living? I FUCKING DOMINATE. Are there more mundane questions? No? That's what I thought.

CHAPTER 5

Life Of A Dominant

Most of us live this regular life that society offers. However behind closed doors perhaps we are different. I do not condone in the mild pleasures that society offers. I do not offer mild pleasures that society condones.

Most Dominant men are high ranked men in the world. Whether in life, finance, in a group of individuals or in the bedroom. In this world, there's an epidemic of Dominant men. However, there are only a few Dominants. There's a major difference. People get Dominated by your energy and aura. Men want to follow you or be like you. Women want to be around you or be with you. A Dominant exudes strength, confidence, wisdom, pride, resiliency, courage, honor and power all without having to say one word. His hunger is the most potent thing on this earth. You witness it in his eyes, in his actions, his energy, his passion, his hard work, and his love. He has a confidence that is contagious. He knows he's great at whatever he does, therefore he is. He thinks positively all the time. He's proactive. He's a master of the mind as well as the body and the soul. He has emotional intelligence through the roof. A calmness to him he controls and can turn up the noise at ease. He has the spirit that innately commands yours. He is the epitome of control. When he walks into a room, you automatically feel his energy. He is approachable. He is able to walk into a group of people and not appear Domineering but more charismatic and confident. He listens to your words, but knows when to take charge in the conversation, or in the group in general. Self-confidence is the difference between feeling unstoppable and feeling scared out of your whits. It's something I have in abundance. Being Dominant is not part time or something you do on the side or when you're bored.

It is life. My life. It is all day, everyday. Soon as you wake up, as soon as you open your eyes, you're on. You take control. You get up everyday and know you are the best. You live and breathe your passion. Your perception of yourself has an enormous impact on how others perceive you also. The energy you give off, our cells in our being pick up on. If you know you're the best, others will know it and they will feel it. Perception is reality. What you think, you become. The more self-confidence you have, the more likelihood you will succeed in anything you do. It's all mind over matter. You must be Disciplined in your mind, body and your emotions. You need to have the strength to be able to control all three. Discipline is the prime factor of Domination. It's not 20% Discipline. It's 100% Discipline. If you are Disciplined in your focus, you can Dominate in all that you choose to do. You cannot just switch it on or off either. It's ON, all the time. You either have it or you don't. There's been a discussion for years if you're an alpha, or beta type? To a lot of people that don't know the characteristics of an alpha male or the traits of a beta male, they assume an alpha male is just a jock or a jerk. The type of men girls say, "you're so annoying, or you're such an asshole. I hate you". All translating to: "you make my panties wet." "Fuck me hard" and "I love you." This is the alpha male.

Confident. Alpha males tend to think very highly of themselves. They aren't always right or perfect, but they always believe in their own ability and themselves no matter what.

Not embarrassed easily. Alpha males don't worry too much about other people's opinions. Masculine. Alpha males are men. They come in all shapes and sizes but have common traits: leaders, Dominant personalities, comfortable around the opposite sex, etc.

Take What He Wants Attitude. Alpha males are not jerks or rude but they believe they are entitled, this allows them to do things and request things an ordinary person would not.

Direct and honest. Alpha males are not afraid to speak their mind. If they need something they will tell you. They don't hide behind a lot of fluff when they are talking to you. They tell you things you might not want to hear. Social. Alpha males have a dynamic personality that allows them to connect with all types of people.

Take Chances. Alpha males are risk takers (big or small). They aren't afraid to fail because they know that success comes from taking chances.

Beta Males Are Nice guys. Beta males are some of the nicest people you will ever meet. They help you when you need help; they are courteous and pleasant to be around.

May Question Their Ability. Beta males lack the confidence alpha males have. There are times that beta males will second guess themselves or make excuses to not do something even though they are fully capable. They just don't always realize their potential.

Worry About What Others Think. Beta males are usually restricted in life because they care too much about what other people think. This includes family, friends and strangers. These external factors limit what a beta male does and the choices he makes in life.

Puts The Needs of Others First. This isn't a bad thing, but beta males put the needs of others ahead of their own. They are very giving people and unselfish. Secretive. Beta males don't always make their desires known to others. Beta males have secrets they keep to themselves including their career aspirations, dreams, and sexual desires. This is usually due to not wanting to be judged by others and may be due to lack of self-confidence.

When it comes to Dominant men, or Dominants, they are Alpha. Alpha males have always captured the admiration, even jealousy, of men and the love and lust of women. Men want to be them; women want to be with them. These are the guys who act as if the world is theirs. They are always in leadership positions, in both their personal and professional lives. They often have swollen bank accounts. They always seem to be surrounded by vast amounts of beautiful women. Confidence. In the song, "One More Chance", Biggy Smalls said: "black and ugly as ever, however, I stay coogi down to the socks, rings chain and watch". He was saying, you don't have to look cute or handsome to get a woman. If you have confidence. Smell nice, dress well, have money, you can get women. Guys use to come up to me all the time, and say, "I have to get a lot of tattoos like you. Have to get a six pack like you. Have muscles and workout like you and I'll have all the ladies". Wrong!! Beauty is of no relevance when it comes to confidence. You can have money and be desired. Some women gravitate to the ball players, the rappers, singers, men who are in control of Fortune 500 companies. These men perhaps are assertive in life, but not in the bedroom. Then again you have different type of women. You have some women who are sapiosexuals, where they find intelligence sexy. They require a connection so deep, that it exceeds the limits of what a basic traditional relationship has to offer. Intellectual conversations will have their feverish, begging pussy lips at your mercy. These alpha males, they refuse to conform. They're the type women tell their friends about, then their friends tell their friends about him. They are unconventional. They are Dominant. They are badass. They are everything that a man could wish to be. The root of the alpha male is his mindset, his unshakable confidence, mental strength, and masculinity. Or, in slang terms, he has balls. All of this having balls and living life like a badass comes from within. It's a mindset. Being an alpha male is an attitude. It is from this mindset this inner alpha attitude that everything else flows. The exciting lifestyle. The money. The women. The world. Even if he doesn't have the money, he is Dominant or in charge of every aspect, everything or person around him. All men envy and desire to become alpha males. Alpha males have balls. In the movie, "Scarface." Al Pacino playing Tony Montana said, "the only thing in this world that gives orders is balls." Alpha males exude power and authority, both in the boardroom and the bedroom. Their very presence commands respect and leaves others in awe. I have witnessed a dramatic decline in masculinity. Whether it's on social media or life. Men are becoming increasingly emasculated and less assertive, less Dominant, and much less manly. Men are beginning to behave more like girls than they do men. At the same time, men are becoming more and more emasculated and womanly. Men are finding themselves increasingly hopeless around beautiful women, working jobs they hate, being walked all over by others, and becoming increasingly depressed. This is why, when women today stumble upon an (increasingly rare) alpha male, they are left in awe. So let's dive right in and learn to adopt that awe-inspiring alpha attitude. I've always remembered that every time I have been at the club, a party, or social gathering, I noticed how when I walked into the room, every woman automatically turned to check me out. It didn't matter if she was married, had a boyfriend, was engaged, or in a "kind of, sort of" -relationship, they all stared. What is it about men such as us that arouse the curiosity of the opposite sex? I'll tell you. Two words: Body language. It's not just women. Often you'll find that men turn their heads to snatch a glance also. Some men are able to hold themselves in such a way that they bring with them an incredibly powerful presence. They are alpha to the core. Everybody turns and looks. Every time I walk into a room, people will stop what they are doing and look up and seek eye contact with me. They can feel my energy, my Scorpio aura, and the royalty in me. They can sense the wild animal in me that is caged within my body just waiting in patience to come out. They sense the electricity in the air because they know a King has walked in. Instinctively, you sit up a little bit straighter, you fix your hair up, you smooth down your clothes or straighten up your tie. You automatically want to be better when you're in better company. My confidence is key. Confidence is how you act; it's knowing you're the best but never being overly cocky. The way I wear my clothes is a sign of my confidence. It shows I am proud of who I am and what I look like and of the vibes I know I omit to those around me. No one is more conscious of your own physical appearance than YOU are. If you don't look good, you will not feel good, and those vibes will also ooze out of you. It's simple, dress how you wish to be addressed.

Life as a Dominant is all about finding out your strengths and weaknesses and sharpening them to perfection. There is always room for improvement, but never focus too long on flaws. Acknowledge them and fix them and move forward. Don't let negativity hold you back. If you start to drown in negativity you'll start to focus on the bad and not the good. This is redundant and does not help in your growth or the growth in those around you. As a leader, you need to be strong, and determined. You need to have the strength and confidence in yourself and for those who don't have those traits, so they can seek you out and know that you can support them in abundance.

Fitness is a huge part of my life, and it's also a huge part of self-confidence. You work out, you feel great, you act great and you are great. Working out makes you feel powerful, untouchable, magnificent. No matter how tired you are, you have to be stronger than your mind, and you need to be Disciplined. Keep focused; working out is an integral part of everyday living, especially for your health and for your mental wellbeing. It all comes down to how mentally strong you are, and how much you want something. If you want something bad enough, nothing and no one will ever stop you. I don't accept excuses I accept results. Keep working on you. Only you can do you, no one else.

Preparation is key. Always strategize. Always plan your attack in your daily life. If you are prepared, then you will succeed. Be methodical and meticulous in how you approach things, with how you spend your time. Don't waste it on shit that will get you nowhere fast. I always make sure that I am doing something to make me better every single day. The only person you have to beat, is the person that you were yesterday. You are your own competition. Between work and clients, and my busy daily schedule, you will always find me reading, or writing or finding ways on how to improve something that I am not 100% happy with. I don't waste my time. I make time. Time is money and wasted time is wasted money. You can't get that back. Only boring people get bored. To keep someone motivated, and I mean yourself included, you need incentive. Ask yourself, what you want the most, and set goals to achieve this. You need to make sure the right people surround you. People that inspire you, that push you to achieve those goals. Hence, why is it that those wanting to better themselves, always congregate around a Dominant/alpha male? You must always appreciate the good people you have around you, and you should always want to impact those around you. If you surround yourself with the right calibre of people, you will not want to disappoint them. It's a good form of motivation to make sure you hold yourself accountable for all that you do. How you treat people, is a huge representation on yourself. If someone has done something good, show your appreciation, compliment him or her, and make him or her feel worthy. A true King knows how to make those around him feel like royalty.

The life of a Dominant is one full of success and growth of power and control. It is not for the weak. The weak never survive. But the King of the jungle will always be King, and you want to know why? Because he knows he's the best.

CHAPTER 6

Seduction Of Discipline, The Power Of Conversation

Seduction is a thing of anticipation. Waiting is a form of bondage. Time is a chain in itself. Many women yearn to please a man, and I'm not talking about what's between her legs or with her mouth. Many women crave to cater to a man. Serve a man. It's in their DNA. They are inclined to being submissive. However, many men are not Kings. Why are they not Kings? Because, they were never taught how to lead, and what is the result of them not being able to lead? The woman will never be able to follow. Why doesn't a woman follow? Because there is simply no trust. Not every woman wants flowers, candy, and money. Some women want to be spoiled with attention, time, affection, moments, memories, bruises, bite marks, welts, and amazing fucking orgasms. I will spoil you with pain. Spoil you with pleasure. Spoil you with this fat, long chocolate cock. Not every woman can say they engage in sex. Most of them are just fucked, but they don't engage in intimacy. Intimacy doesn't have to be physical. Intimacy is conversing. Sharing an efficient conversation. Laughing, holding hands, cuddling. Discussing how your day was. Money doesn't mean much to some women, especially if they have it.

In the past, I've had rich sport star wives that were dying to please me. Rich, famous women and I did not even have to spend a dime to get their attention. What people don't understand is "the power of conversation." I mean affairs don't start in the bedroom, they start via conversation. This is effective because, women are more emotional. They desire more. They become bored easily. Especially if it's the same old shit, same old guys, doing the same old thing. Most women don't feel desired, loved, or appreciated enough. Weak men will never understand this, women are not meant to be understood. They are meant to be loved, pursued, taken, protected, conquered and devoured. To be at his feet. To be his. But, how do you get to that point? It's all through conversation, not just conversing to converse for the hell of it, but to converse efficiently. Most women (not all) do not care for the superficial. The petty mundane shit. They get older, they desire more. The time you spend and the effort you put in is worth more than you know. They don't care for fame. They just want to feel like the only girl in the room for the time being. The little things make a huge difference. They don't ask, they just desire to please. In my opinion, women that do not ask for anything, deserve everything. I teach and I make individuals around me better, especially women. Women love to learn, and they will always love a man, that can teach them a little something. I never give them what they ask for, only what they earn. When you work for something, you appreciate it more. It's all psychological

To have power does not require total transformation in your character or drastic improvements in your physical appearance. Seduction is of psychology not beauty, fame or even money. It is within the grasp of anyone willing to master it. All that is required is that you look at the world differently. Seduction is a process of penetration. Penetrating your target's mind, which is the first point of defense. Once you've infiltrated their mind,and have them fantasizing about you, it's easy for them to lower resistance creating their physical surrender. Like a good general; they plan and strategize. What will seduce the person is the effort on your behalf, by showing you care and allowing them to see what they are worth to you, through your eyes. Falling in love is not a matter of magic but of psychology. Once you understand your target's psychology and strategies to suit it, you will be able to cast a magical spell.

Your mouth is the tool to conquer your mind and another individual's mind. When you put, 'I AM' or 'BEST' in your mind, you start to become that. It's like when you converse and you speak, you're sending vibes to the universe. Words are a woman's weakness. I am the master of the seductive language. It's all about word choice, your mannerisms and how you are present yourself. Before you attempt to try to seduce, you need to put in your head you can get her. No woman is out of your league. Whether she is rich, powerful, Dominant, submissive, etc. No matter her race or nationality. When it comes to a woman, it's all about the connection. Women are the most emotional creatures on the planet. Anyway you touch her emotionally, she will gravitate towards you. People don't know how to converse anymore. There is so many different forms of technology now. Technology has evolved, and it is killing the power of seduction. Everything is at our disposal and our fingers. Most women can't take control in a conversation, which is not expected and most men are lost. The men, they have no idea how to begin a conversation. Good sex is physical, but great sex is mental. Yes, physical attraction is big. Bodies connect. However, the allure, the intimacy, the fulfilment is all mental. In order for the seduction to be successful, you need to be able to lead it to where she follows. In order for her to follow, your conversation will say a lot about you. Whether you're assertive, confident, bold, shy, whatever it is. A woman will throw hints at you. For example, you meet a woman at a social event. She may smile, wink, twirl her hair, while she stares at you. Normally, she's not going to make the first move, but she will test to see how long to take you. When you do approach her, you need to be able to penetrate her mind efficiently, and her body will follow successfully. Find the weakness and the strength in their mind, and you can use that to your advantage. Not in a manipulative way. You need to put 100% focus and complete undivided attention on her. Eye contact is more intimate than words will ever be.The main key things are:Firm eye contact. Word choice. A little body contact. You don't want to overdo it. You don't want to seem too assertive, because it drives people away. Roll with the punches assess your target. Whether it's verbal or over the phone or face to face, spoken communication or through technology. It begins and ends when you want it to end. You don't want to give everything of yourself at the beginning, leave some anticipation and leave them wanting more. I don't meet a woman in person and say, "hi, my name is so and so, I am a Dominant." That's just weird. Clark Kent didn't go around metropolis or the daily planet, where he was doing his vanilla(regular) gig telling all the employees, that he was SuperMan. All I'm saying is, people love anticipation. Suspense. Give a little, you leave them wanting more. If you get feedback follow up on that. Make a connection. If she's shy, and not giving you any feedback, you're not connecting, because even if she is shy she has to give you some feedback. If it's just one sided, it's boring, it's not right. Make sure you're face to face because body language will tell you all you need to know. Suss out her facial expression, especially her eyes. All this plays a major factor. Make sure you make it about her. Shake her hand and greet her respectfully. "Hi, how are you? What's your name?" If she's interested she will ask you your name. But don't volunteer to give out information. Make her your main goal. Your main focus. Show her real interest, because women love attention. If you're showing them attention it means something, and it shows them you're interested. Most men take whatever they can get. I don't date, if I like you, and I want you, I will get you, because you're already mine. Yes, we can go on dates, but I never have been the type to say, "you want to be my girlfriend?" I see it, I want it, it's already mine. Confidence is everything, women gravitate towards confidence. Confidence correlates with strength. Women gravitate towards strength. They are subconsciously designed, to be attracted to the stronger genes. It makes them feel confident in themselves.

Confidence is:

Assuredness.

Assertive.

Dominance.

Alpha.

Charismatic.

Leadership.

Confidence leads to decision-making and planning for moves. If she can't pick a place to eat, he will pick it. Don't give her the option. Be a fucking man. A man that loves to be in control, makes it easier for indecisive women; it's less pressure for the woman. Women have changed, as they have gotten older, from my experiences. What girls didn't like about me in high school, or even middle school, they love about me now. You can teach it, it has to be in you. In order for you to develop someone, you must develop yourself. You must be developed mentally and emotionally. Then you will know what you're looking for. Especially when you have certain standards for yourself, you're going to put the same standard on others. You are coaching. You're not going to settle for excuses. Only expectations from yourself will be set to high standards, whether you can exceed them or not. People are going to change to meet your expectations. Everybody is trainable. I've learned as I become older, people are fickle. It's just about practicing what you've learned. Sometimes to be taught a lesson you need to experience it. I can touch you in many different ways, without using my hands. My power speaks volumes and it reaches from afar. The deep bass in my voice will make you melt. My words will resonate in your mind. The steel in my eyes, will stop you dead in your fucking tracks. It will touch your soul. My intimidating and authoritative presence will give you chills. My firm gaze will make you want to kneel to me. My energy will inspire you on so many different levels. My Dominance will ignite the fire in your heart, resulting in you relinquishing all control to me. I will invade all your thoughts, where I am all you want. When you're at work sitting at your desk or in the car driving home, the slightest thought of me will leave you drenched. I will mark your mind so aggressively, you will beg me to mark your body viciously. Once I've captured and touched your soul it will bind yours to mine, and no matter where you are, you will know where you belong.

CHAPTER 7

When Your Words Make Her Wet. Touch Her Without Touching Her

What makes my methods effective? My passion and intensity. When I speak and you look at me, you look into my eyes. You see the passion in my eyes. If you want inside my mind, you're going to have to earn that.

I am a man that works off of the emotions of others. I react to energy and high vibrations. In order to have a great relationship, I require a deep connection. I have never coerced a connection or chemistry. Some people just have a great sexual chemistry, but not an emotional connection. Some have a great emotional connection, but no sexual chemistry. This is what leads to "friends with benefits", or one-night stands and miscommunications. Both parties have no idea how to engage in an efficient conversation. I attack a woman's emotions. By doing so, I am able to pleasure her efficiently. I know if I can make her feel safe and get her to trust me, her sexual desires will never be confined. She will do her best to please me; however, whenever and wherever. Sexual desires will ooze out of her. Only a foolish man assumes taking off a woman's clothes is the only way to get her fully naked. A naked body is beautiful, but a naked mind is amazing. The vagina is not the only way inside a woman. Women only respect men that can Dominate them. Respect is equal to obedience. Women are already thinking of sex more frequently than us men, if not more. However, she wants to see how you handle her outside of the bedroom. If you can't handle her outside of the bedroom, she will never trust you to be able to handle her inside of it. Remember, you have to be able to talk your way to the bedroom. Most men who are viewed as being assertive in life, are often viewed as being assertive in the bedroom. I'll reiterate, affairs do not start in the bedroom, they begin via conversation. A woman will always love a man she is able to learn a lot from, over a man who spends a ridiculous amount of money on her. The body is the servant of the mind. Stimulate her mind and her body will do what you want. Your words can have her touching herself. You can push her up against the wall, rip her clothes off, kiss her into a sweaty heaping tangled mess, penetrating into her soft yielding wetness and call her a slut, bitch or whore, and if she's into that, it can be fun. But you will only truly claim her, when you have invaded her every thought. How do you invade her every thought? Sometimes you have to go deeper and she will still feel you after you're gone. The deepest penetration is of the mind. Once you've penetrated her pituitary gland, there are now endless possibilities. Body language: You know she is being receptive to the conversation, when there's a lot of movement on her end. By the way she moves. Twirls her hair. Where she puts her hands. If she touches your shoulder. Laughs at your fucking corny jokes. These are all signs that she's into you. If she's meticulous, she will be able to know that he's into her also. As long as he knows that she's into him, that's all that matters. My goal is to be in control at all times. The handshake is a very formal, cordial introduction of one's self on their first encounter. It's the best way. If you touch someone other than their hands at the first encounter, you could make him or her nervous or anxious, causing anxiety for someone that doesn't know you or hasn't been touched by you before. It doesn't matter where you are, your soul will be bound to mine. I'm far from prince charming. I will not wake you up with a kiss, but I will fuck you savagely to sleep. I will put you on my plate and make you do the dishes. I will suffocate your thoughts to the brink of asphyxiation, as I feel the blood rushing throughout your body. My words will make your begging, wet pussy throb, and my Dominance will inspire your fear and desire. My energy is so strong that when you're in my presence, you will relinquish control willingly. I will take your mind to places it has never been before. Places you never thought possible in and outside of the bedroom. The deep bass in my voice will feel like there is a vibrator on your throbbing clit, stimulating your inner organs and your mind. You will be completely romanced. I will excite you intellectually; by entering your mind using my intuitive capabilities, reading your body language. Words are very powerful, but actions speak so much louder. Body language is huge. Stimulate her mentally and cover her spiritually. By knowing her thoroughly; the connection becomes spiritual, energies entwine and it's like there is a link connecting us. Complete intimacy. Before satisfaction or engagement of physical intimacy, there must be Discipline. One must have patience to stimulate her mind,body, and soul and be Disciplined to enforce her Discipline. Control of her body to control her body. Reading your mind allows me to read your body and vice versa. Most women need to build a connection with a partner in order to stimulate their body. Majority of women shut their eyes when they climax, so their eyes don't pop out of their head like when you sneeze. Just joking. They do this when it's so intense. When it's so fucking amazing. Think about, not eating all day, and you're starving. Take that first bite, I bet you shut your eyes when you do it. I will touch your subconsciousness and those repressed desires shouting out for liberation. I will learn your weakness and use it to my advantage, giving you just enough to fiend for more. When you keep her in suspense, you will keep her wanting more and she will always crave you. You will always be in control. You will ponder my words. You will create images in your head of my body, and of my touch, and of the moments I will give you. You will feel it in your dreams. I will ignite your libido. I will be your eye candy, your chocolate addiction, your favorite sin, your drug of choice, your structure and stability, your balance. If I touch your soul, you will love me forever. I love honesty. Where there's a vanilla relationship, there's limits. It becomes stagnant, regular and boring. It's not passionate or intense or real like a BDSM relationship. With BDSM, you're allowing a person access into an emotional, physical and psychological space that belongs to you. It's very rare. With vanilla, there is a fear of inadequacy in trying to meet expectations. You can't teach passion. It has to be instilled in you already or someone has to ignite it. When a woman observes a man that is intense and passionate, they imagine how he will be in bed. Women pay attention to things like that. Women are very emotional creatures. They react off impulses. Women being emotional, it causes them to want things like deep emotions connections. They love sex immensely, because of the intimacy it creates. Once you are connected, it's like a psychological bondage. Discipline is psychological bondage. If you give her certain rules to abide by, in and outside of the bedroom, then she must follow through. You must train her mind to be a certain way to please you. That's the Discipline. I think people mistake Discipline as punishment. Linking both words together, but that's quite misconstrued. Discipline is just really structure. It's all I know, especially growing up in sports.

I believe 95% of women are bedroom submissive. But, that doesn't mean that they engage in BDSM, and it doesn't make them a sub. Outside of the bedroom, they transform or take on the role of being the boss in the relationship. For a sub to willingly relinquish control, she has to feel it in her heart, and in her mind. Her mind is where the psychological shit comes into effect. You can meet a domineering, tough, controlling Dom, but you won't get any growth from that. You're only getting a tyrant, you aren't getting any kind of fulfilment. It all goes back to the connection with the subs.

The hard and soft limits, and the negotiation process and building that connection. BDSM is not associated with inadequate development; it's a lifestyle of fulfilment, trust, sacrifice, fulfilment and challenges beyond the body. If you have a Dom that is not in control of himself, how can he control anyone else? It's all about self and mental Discipline. It's like people who are attracted to BDSM, probably have a high need for rules, boundaries and structure. When you're in this lifestyle, there are plenty of rules and boundaries. For example: no smoking and no excessive drinking. You may drink, but not excessively. It also depends on the beverage. I'll always approve of wine though. Wine is good for the heart. Anything that is detrimental to your body and your health, I will put a stop to it. I will eradicate this habit. With me, fitness will definitely be instilled in their lives. Once you start conversing with someone and interacting, you're building a relationship, building a rapport. Everything in this world is about relationships. Business relationships, bedroom and marriage relationships. Sometimes you will see couples randomly incorporate bondage into their sex life. This might be a phase or a fantasy. People will start role-playing "Oh let's try something different. It's Valentines Day, lets try something new baby." It's not like that with BDSM. It's a connection, it's a bond, it's about building their trust to allow someone to have power to do damage to you, but trusting that they won't. I've never been able to have a "fuckship." If you don't know what that means, it's two people who just meet up, and fuck. There is not communication. It's not even a, 'friends with benefits.' My body reacts on energy only. If I'm not stimulated mentally, I'm not going to be physically stimulated. BDSM emotions are so strong and intense. You see that 'fuckship?' It doesn't last too long, because someone catches feelings. Women are fickle; they can never make a decision. A woman's actions always betray her words. They say they're not in love but they are. Their actions betray their bodies and their minds as well. It's all a big game about power, it's all a mind game. That's their power struggle. Their walls go up and they don't want to give anything away. Dom and sub love is unconditional, and they are both equal in servitude. If you're not willing to commit 100% you shouldn't even attempt the relationship. You are going to be wasting each other's times. BDSM is all about the philosophical. If a Dominant force encounters a steadfast and unmovable force, it will yield. There are two types of people in this world; the ones that have the strength to control, and the ones that have the strength to yield. A Dominant woman is a switch. They require a special type of man, because not many men can tame these types of women. These type of women are special, very loyal and only a special type of man can tame them. Once they eradicate those walls, they will be dedicated to their Dom.

CHAPTER 8

Look Me In My Eyes When I Fuck You

"Hello there" I stop in mid walk and stared at the most amazing woman.

"Excuse me miss", I look at this amazing woman as she's sitting down at her table drinking her coffee, and reading her book. She is paying me no attention whatsoever. Clearly she is aware of her beauty. I try a different approach. "What's that like?" I ask. Her doe like eyes quickly flicker up towards me, looks me in my face but even quicker. They flicker back down to the book she is so deeply immersed in.

For a second, I assumed she was going to ignore me. But I see her body slowly lean in towards me, and I know. Clearly I have intrigued her. Without taking her eyes out of her book, she murmurs:

"What is what like?"

"Your mind, what's that like?"

She doesn't reply for a few seconds, as if she's trying to work me out in her head. "Let me guess, you say that to all the women?" She questions me, still not looking at me.

I laughed. "Why would you worry about other women? Are you bisexual?" She looks up sharply and stares at me, a little taken back at my bold approach, and shakes her head. "No, I mean the line you're using, you use that on all the women you ranDomly meet?" Her eyes go back to her book, but I stared squarely at her. "This isn't a line, and you're clearly not just a woman. That is not what I'm witnessing in front of me. What I see is a Goddess, an intellect." I watch as her beautiful lips turn up in a shy smile.

"Oh, so now you know me?" she playfully asks."I know what I see", I stated firmly.

"So you're a psychic? Tell me what else you see in my future." I could tell she was enjoying our little interlude. She felt comfortable enough to joke around with me. I shook my head. "That one was a freebie, the next one you'll earn," I promised cryptically. She seemed a little lost with the meaning, but she laughed anyways. She was so pretentious; I could tell that I was already fucking with her halo with just my eyes alone. So I thought to myself, let me gas her up a little bit more. I leaned down over her. I rested one arm on the back of her chair and the other on the table, so she was locked in on my embrace. I whispered in her ear;

"If you were that book, I'd read you all day. Gaze at you and your words firm and long, as my strong, muscular fingers flip through those exquisite pages, as you give me head.... excuse me, I mean, as you give me knowledge and stroke my cerebral aggressively. Your cover supporting a block of pages, backed up by your spine. As I run my hands all over your chapters. Every single line will be a whole new experience, striving to reach the depths of you and to find the beginning and end of you. I would of course take my time. It would be exhilarating, invigorating, climatic and euphoric. Orgasmic even. I would read more of you, and fill you up....... with words of course, consume your thoughts as I go deep, deep, deep into thought and...." My voice was low and hummed over her. She had sat frozen during that whole speech, spine tighter than a rod, hands holding onto that book for dear life, her eyes staring blankly into that damn book. I felt her sigh loudly. "What's wrong?" I asked, feigning concern. I knew exactly what ailed her. "Nothing", she replied stoically. Her eyes remained locked on her book. She's playing it off, I thought. Does she clearly wants me to think that fucking book is way more interesting than what I was saying. Bullshit. Fuck that, I'm not buying it. I continued on, "However, you're not that book are you? The book is way more important than you are anyways." "Hey!" Her head snapped up, staring at me flatly, she shut the book. She looked at my face for a few seconds. I stared back. "What's your name?" She asked. I gaze into her eyes firmly and said forcefully "Discipline."

She giggled. "What's funny?" I asked. Clearly I knew what was funny. She wants to act as though my words were of no significance. I was going to play along as well. "Clearly, you have a real name. Your parents obviously gave you a name." She said. I smirked. "Names are irrelevant. Why is knowing my name so importance to you?" She shakes her head. "Because, that's what "normal" people do when they meet someone."

I chuckled. "Normal you say? If you're good, you will learn my name. But you have to earn it." She giggled again. I don't know what the fuck she's laughing at, I guess I was really funny today. If she were a regular girl, she would have walked away or went back to reading her book. Said some shit like, "you want to play games", or "forget it", as though she would want me to chase her. No not her, she was fucking something else. "Earn it huh? Earn your name? Who do you think you are?" she demanded. I gazed into her eyes, didn't smile or blink, and took a few seconds before I replied. "You'll earn that as well." Cryptic again. "So you said, if I'm good I will know, right?" I smiled at her. Showing my teeth this time. "Tell me miss, how bad can a good girl get?" I pulled up the seat next to her and sat down. "Well, Mr. "DISCIPLINE", I wouldn't know. I'm a good girl… All the time!" she huffed. "You're learning already." I laughed. But I knew she was lying. The right person would break her. Her innocence was so precious just waiting and begging for me to corrupt it. "What is it about you mister? You have this mysteriousness about you. That look in your eyes….it's quite…powerful, scary even." She said as she stared into my eyes. My beautiful brown eyes stared back at her. My menacing tone of voice ignited her curiosity, and I could tell. "Why do you feel you need to have all the answers? Have you ever felt the need to just let go? Release?" I questioned her. But there is no answer from her. She avoids this subject and tries to change it. "I still want to know your name. If I don't know your name, how will I give you my number?" she sulked adorably. I said to her, "Two things. One, this isn't a fucking negotiation. Two, who said I wanted your number?" I stand and watch her beautiful face. Her eyes shocked wide, and her gorgeous mouth left stunned opened. Perhaps she's used to men bowing to her feet. Her luxurious hair, and pretty lips and eyes had power of their own. I could see a ordinary man giving her anything she wanted. Compromising himself even, just to fit her standards. That's probably the type of power over men she had, but not with me. "Have a nice day Miss." I started to walk off, but before I could take one step, she softly whispered under her breath, "You sure have a way with words mister." "What was that?" I asked. I had heard her but, I wanted her to say it again, loud and clear. "Nothing Mister Discipline", she snapped back. Walking away, I could see out the corner of my eye that she continued to stare at me. Staring at me like I was food, and she had been starving for years. She looked so sweet and innocent sitting there in stunned silence. I wanted to hold her innocence deep in the darkness of my shadows. Spread her mind wide open. Stroke her thoughts aggressively. Watch how her body spoke. Wanted her bound by my words and voice, and wanted her frozen with compliance. I wanted to ignite her deepest desires. I could see her hunger; fuck that, I could feel that shut. It was evident in her eyes. I could tell. She was already mine; she just didn't know it yet. She couldn't have known what I am and what I do, but if she found her way to me, she would belong to me completely. She will come to me. This I knew. She'll find me one way or another. The chase is on...............

I arrived at a club and greeted the bouncers who I'd known for years from back in the day, when I always frequented the club scene. It was rare for me to be out in this scene now, but sometimes I would head back to the club only when I felt the need to dance. Music was in my blood and I loved to dance. The owner was a good friend of mine and I greeted him as I entered. I headed over to the bar and was greeted by the bartender, who clearly remembered me and before I could say anything, she asked me if I wanted my usual. I nodded my approval. I watched as he poured my vodka and cranberry. I was never a heavy drinker, more of a social drinker than anything. I've always monitored my drinking and always limited myself when it came to alcohol. Being Disciplined like that came easy to me. I turned to survey the room. It was bumping. The music was invigorating, and the atmosphere was beautiful. As usual, I scanned the entire room and I notice a woman that looks familiar to me. I gazed because I never forget a face; I was blessed with an amazing photographic memory. Then I thought to myself: "Could it be her?" It was. Miss "face in her book, hello miss what's your mind like." There were so many women in the club tonight. What are the odds that I would see her here! She had my undivided attention. I watched her as she stood laughing and drinking with her friends. My energy must have Dominated her, and she gazed over in my direction. I knew my aura called her. She felt me. She smelt me. I watched as she looked around, obviously feeling my eyes boring holes into her. I watch as she looked around and finally her eyes land on my face, our eyes meet and lock. She smirks, like a cat that's licking cream out of a bowl. I watch as she shuffles her friends to move a little closer to me. She's extremely inviting as she stares and then looks away playfully. Inch by inch she moves closer until finally she is standing next to me. I had turned my back to face the bar as soon as we had made eye contact, but watched her from the side of my eye. The pull between us was magnetic. I know she can feel it because, I could feel it with my whole being. I ignore her while I sip on my drink. I could feel her standing next to me, her pheromones seeping out of her skin and directly into my soul. I turn my body to face hers, and we are standing face to face, her little petite face staring up into mine so boldly. I watch as she opens her mouth to speak to me. "Hello there mister, what's that like?" She asks me while batting her beautiful eyelashes at me. I look down at her and lift the side of my mouth into a smile, and look at her lips for a full 10 seconds, before lifting them up to look directly in her eyes."What that like? Oh this is vodka? It's good. It's a clear liquid containing water, ethanol which is purified by distillation from a fermented substance, such as potato grain or sugar beet molasses. The cranberries are antioxidants", I finish off my sentence and take another sip. She let out an exasperated breath and tilts her head at me."No, I mean, what's your MIND like? I'm not talking about the drink!" I laughed at her; of course I knew what she meant. But I always like to toy with my prey before I go for the kill. I indulge her petulance. "Well hello miss", my voice is like butter.

"Fancy meeting you here", she playfully hits my shoulder.

I smirked "So we meet again." Her smile widens. "Yes, Mr. Discipline, indeed we do." Her dark hair was long and sleek. She had her hair down. Last time I saw her, she had it tied in a pony tail. She was wearing a tight long black dress to her knees which hugged her waist, and her toes were blessed with some sexy black stiletto's. I looked back to her waist and couldn't help but imagine if her panties were lace. I Dominated her with her gaze, and my gaze traced every curve of her body discreetly. I did it so swiftly that she barely noticed. At least I didn't think she did. I asked her, "what are you drinking tonight? Perhaps something light like vodka? Or perhaps we should get something strong, and dark inside you like Hennessy".

She took the banter.

"Nah, tonight, I prefer sex on the beach." She flipped her hair over her shoulder and touched her collarbone, and looked up at me flirtatiously. I then said......

"Well I was going to ask you to dinner first, but I'm sure we can make that happen...."

She giggled placing one hand over her mouth and her other hand softly hitting my shoulder. I turned and ordered her drink. The bartender nodded to me, indicating, that this one was on the house also.

"You don't have to buy my drink," she said.

"I insist. Plus don't worry about it, that round is free". I literally meant it was free, but she took it out of context. As if I was giving her a pass. She doesn't need to know that I'm well known here. I mean would she treat me differently? Better? Perhaps worse? I wanted to see if she wants to know ME, and not the 'idea' of me. I mean after all, she still doesn't know, that I am a Dominant or that I engage in BDSM.

"Listen Mr Discipline, I buy my own," she declared independently, as she reached for her purse. I smirked.

"I understand that and I respect it. Sometimes a woman that asks for nothing deserves everything," I told her.

"I thought you weren't giving freebies?" She said asked.

I chuckled as I leaned into her.

"Oh you remember that, do you? You've good, it's been several weeks and you still remember most of our conversation from our first encounter. I'm impressed, good girl." I stated genuinely. I watch as a blush covered her cheeks.

Most women give hints, obvious hints when they like you or find you attractive. They laugh at your corny jokes, they become nervous, they may twirl their hair a lot, their body language changes and how they touch you becomes more evident.

"Even from the last time, every time you say 'good girl', I get this weird feeling, I can't describe it. Anyways…." she changes the subject and her blush intensifies.

"You must come here often?" she enquired. I could tell she was totally interested in my answer. I locked eyes with her.

"I use to, in my party days. I come now once in awhile, because I love to dance and the music is great".

She laughed

"What's so funny" I asked, "Clearly I am very amusing tonight."

She smiles, "My apologies, but you don't seem like the dancing type! You're so serious and stern; I'm surprised to even see you here. You actually seem really boring", she again touched my shoulders, laughing and tilting her head to the side and leaning into me. The audacity of her, but I can't lie, that was pretty funny, as I'm laughing inside. I could smell her perfume and it turned me on. Everything about her turned me on.

I said two words to her before I grabbed her hand.

"Let's dance". I didn't ask. I didn't look for her to lead either. I didn't seek her approval, I just fucking grabbed her. I grabbed her like she belonged to me. I was going to shake her world. We danced to everything you could possibly think of. Every music genre: bachata, hip hop, reggae, merengue, reggaeton, salsa, soca, dance hall. We were body to body her hand clasped in mine. I told her to stare into my eyes and do exactly as I say. The irony about this whole thing is how intense our eye contact was, how intense we were. In our first encounter, she would barely look at me. But now, she couldn't take her eyes off of me. Reggae came on; I turned her around, my hands discreetly and slightly went around her neck. I didn't squeeze, at least not yet. I pulled her into me. Her ass was meshed to my pelvis. I turned her head so I could whisper in her ear. "Remember our first meeting? Remember I asked how bad can a good girl get?" I could feel goosebumps come out of her skin on her arms, but I also felt her melt into me.

With her leaning back into me, I could see her face, her eyes were shut but I could hear her response loud and clear.

"Yes I do" she murmured.

I whispered back forcefully.

"Let me show you just how bad…."

I swung her back around into my arms, and held her close as we molded into one as we danced. We danced all night. Nothing could tear us apart. We went back to the bar, and she had a couple more drinks. Her friends come to her and tells her they're leaving, but at this point I know she is extremely intoxicated. I watch as she tells her friends that she's not ready to leave just yet. Her and her friends argue back and forth and I decide to intervene.

"Listen, tonight she's under my protection, and I'm going to make sure she gets home safe," I exclaimed to 4 very confused faces.

"Excuse me, but who are you? We don't know who you are!" They turn to their friend. "Girl do you know him??" they ask skeptically.

"Yes of course I know him" She reassures them and she insists on leaving with me for the night. Her friends hesitantly leave as it's getting late. They make sure that they tell their friend to message them as soon as she gets home. She reassures them that this is exactly what she will do. She turns to me and smiles. She stumbles slightly and I know it's time to take her home. I then told her, "we're leaving."

"But I don't want to go home yet, I want to have more fun", again the bottom lips drops out and she looks super adorable. But she's drunk. Super drunk.

"Listen, you're under my protection tonight, so that means you're not making any decisions tonight. I am, and I said I'm taking you home. I don't give a fuck what you want to do, this is what you will do." I walk her out the club, grabbing her jacket on the way out and placing it on her shoulders. I walk her towards my car that the valet has driven around, and I open the passenger's side door and help her in. I strap on the seat belt across her body and make sure she's locked in nice, tight and secure. Without having to ask, she supplies me with her home address and I enter it into the gps. She must have dozed off, because not a word was spoken until we arrived at her house, some 30 minutes later. I pull up in the driveway and walk to her side, open the door and help her out. I walk her up the stairs and grab her purse and grab her keys. She's leaning on me for support now. She mumbles the direction to her room, and I take her there. As soon as I open her bedroom door, I pull back the bed covers of her queen size bed, and sit her down on the mattress. I take off her stiletto's and lay her down, not touching her anywhere else. I cover her with the blankets, and watch as her eyes open up, and she reaches out towards my forearms and grabs them pulling them towards her. She stares me in my eyes and I watch as she places my hands on her luscious breasts. Damn, she had my big chocolate dick hard as a missile, as her nipple were as firm as my big dick. Her pussy was drenched. I know what she wants. I wanted it more than her. I wanted to taste her. Suck on the luscious breast. Tug on her hardened nipples. Taste those lips and inhale her scent. But not like this. If anything was going to transpire between us, she was going to be 100% sober and sane and it was going to be 150% consensual.

As much as it killed me, I stopped her hand movements immediately.

"Listen, it's not about to go down tonight. My job is complete for tonight. I made sure on my word, and you are home safe. I am a man of my word and I stand it. Your safety is of utmost importance to me," I whisper as I watch as she sticks her bottom lip out again in disappointment.

"But sir, I wanna have fun tonight", she looks seductively up at me. I place a finger against her lips and the only sound that comes out my mouth is a low "shhhh".

"I have spoken and I will not fucking reiterate," I stated firmly. I tuck her in, kissed her forehead and told her to sleep tight. She watches me as I grab her phone and get her number and put it in my phone. I also open the messages that were coming through from her friends asking if she was okay. I responded for her, with a, "I'm fine, home safe and sound. I place her phone next to her on her bedside table. She's fast asleep before I walk out the door. Even though she's asleep, I say out loud.

"I'll contact you in the morning to make sure you're okay." I take one last look at her as I turn the door open and close it behind me. I leave her house, making sure she is securely locked inside safe and sound, and head towards my car for the long unsatisfied drive home.

The first thing I do in the morning is send a message to make sure she's okay.

I look at her response and can't help but smile.

"Who is this?"

"It's Discipline, I'm messaging you to make sure you're okay from last night. How are you feeling?"

"Arghh I have a huge headache"

"I can only imagine. You were out of it by the end of the night"

"Oh no! What happened, I honestly don't usually drink that much! I hope I wasn't too out of control".

"No you were fine, just very drunk. I took you home because you didn't want to leave with your friends"

"Oh my God, you take me home? and I allowed that? You could be a killer! A stalker! A rapist!! What was I thinking?!"

"Well if I were all those things you'd be in bad shape right now."

"That's facts, you're right… Thank you! I truly appreciate that you had my best interests at heart and getting me home safe."

"Not a problem. Now sober up and shower. We're having lunch in 2 hours." It was noon. I expected her at 2pm.

"Wait, what?!" I hung up immediately.

I finish off texting her by giving her the address to the café that we were to meet. Texting her after I gave the address, to "not be late. I don't want to have to come to you now."

I'm already seated as I watch her enter the café. I smiled as I note the time. I told her 2pm and it's exactly 1.59pm. I watch as the waiter walks over to her and greets her.
"Hello miss, how can I help you?"

"I'm meeting someone, a gentlemen…" she tries to find me in the café with her eyes. She can't because I'm reading a book and I had my face buried in it.

"Ah you must be Mia?" the waiter said matter of fact. Her head snaps back to him.

"Yes, how do you know my name?" She looks confused.

"Oh Mr. Discipline advised me you are coming, and he is already here, please come this way".

She arrives at the table, I placed my book down, and I look up at her. She looks fresh and a wave of lust washes over me.

"How'd the waiter know my name?" she asked me still looking slightly confused.

"Whoa, where are your manners lady. I didn't fucking sleep with you last night. You greet me accordingly. "Hello, Mr.Discipline, now how did he know my name?" I point to the seat with my index finger, "sit down now." "I'm not sitting down until you tell me!" He knows, because you know, and how did you know, because I didn't tell you." She's so bright. I loved that about her. Always analyzing shit. Seeking all the answers. "Let me fucking tell you something, this is not a negotiation, you will fucking sit your ass down, or you will receive nothing. She sat down immediately. "Good girl. Well, you know the answer to your question already, I told him".

"How do you know my name? I don't even know your name?" she looks frustrated.

"Well that's for me to know and for you to earn. Now relax."

As she settles into her seat, my mind wanders.

She was like honey and I was the bee, yearning to sting her at ease, to shut her eyes as I slid my big, muscular chocolate man hands around her throat. I could feel her breath escape her lungs and leave her body, meticulous with her body, it spoke to me, she didn't have to say a word, I read it well. It's like for a moment, she was dependent on my touch for survival. I leaned in for a kiss and paused close to her lips, her eyes were shut, and she moved her head towards me, awaiting my kiss. In that moment, I fucking knew she was mine. I knew her body craved me in ways she didn't know possible. I kissed her roughly and passionately, as I explored the depths of her pretty mouth. My tongue in complete Domination, I paused and pulled away as I whispered, "look at me".

I gazed so firmly at her, I watched her squirm under my gaze.

"No one has ever looked at me like you do. Looked into my eyes like that. Looked at my body so thoroughly either. Looks can kill but your eyes contain a much greater power. I feel as if you're looking into my soul. Like I'm exposed. I'm this confident, bold and proud woman, but around you I become shy and nervous." All her words are rushed without a breath. I place my fingers over her lips to shut her up.

"Don't you every display shyness in front of me again. We will eradicate this little tendency you have," I said.

I removed my finger.

"I'm sorry Mr. Discipline. It's just that, when you stare at me, it makes me feel alive. Like I'm the only woman in the world, the only woman in the room and that scares me." She whispers at me.

I smirk.

I spoke softly but forcefully, "I like your fear. But enlighten me, why are you afraid?"

She turns her eyes down, but I grab her chin with my index finger, and anchored it up to allow her gaze to meet mine, I said forcefully "Why??"

Her eyes were wide open, she replied; "I'm scared because, I haven't felt like this in a long time." I could sense her fear, I watched as her pulse beat furiously at the base of her neck. I wanted to lick it. But I looked back into her eyes.

"Forget about your past, this is your present and your future. You will come in my world as yourself and leave as mine. You will never be the same again. and you will never view regular men the same again." She stared into my eyes, and we didn't say one word for a good minute.

She breaks the stare to look at her watch.

"OMG look at the time, we must pause this and resume this later please, I must go, I have an appointment." She started to reach for her bag.

I grabbed her by her thigh firmly.

"I'll allow you to leave, because I know you have prior engagements. I hate to see you go, but damn, I love to watch you leave," I murmur seductively.

She shyly giggles, stands and looks down at me; "Have a nice day Mr. Discipline."

I watched her walk in rhythm, her ass cheeks moved up and down, her heels giving her these gorgeous calf muscles as she brushes her hair over her ear, she stares back to make sure I'm checking. I wanted her to witness my stare; I wanted her to witness the hunger in my eyes. Oh yes indeed the chase is on.

CHAPTER 9

The Beast Will Feast

I watched my phone ring and her name lights up my screen. I answered on the 3rd trill.

"Hello" I spoke clearly.

"Hello Discipline, I wanted to call and apologize for leaving so abruptly the other day." She spoke so quickly there were no breaks between her words. I could tell she was nervous.

"Don't worry," I laughed, "you'll be making it up to me. Meet me now", I tested her. To see exactly how honest she would be with me.

"I can't Discipline, I'm out jogging now," she still sounds nervous.

Good, she wasn't lying. I knew she was out jogging. I knew all of her moves. Especially her morning cardio. She wakes up every morning and jogs around her block.

"You have 1 hour to be dressed and ready to go", I ordered. I heard her start with her questions, but I had already hung up the phone. I could already picture her racing home to get ready, throwing her clothes off and jumping in the shower, because she knows when I say 1 hour, I mean 59 minutes.

But today, I've decided to switch things up. Today I'm going to test her further. Not even a wait, that twenty minutes later, I'm standing at the front of her door. I don't even give her a chance to get dressed, I hammer that doorbell and start knocking on the door. Now normally, people will scream out, "hold on", while they get themselves ready. But I continued with my hammering. Hoping the noise was such a nuisance, till she has no option but to jump out of that shower, and race to the door and frantically ask

"Who is it?"

"Me". Instantly, I know she recognizes who I am. I can hear her catch her breath. I picture her standing there frantically, looking around and clutching at her towel. Does she dare be disobedient and not open straight away for me? I deliberately did not give her the hour I advised her, because this is how I wanted her. Disheveled, raw, naked, exposed, vulnerable with nothing to hide behind, not even make up. This is when I see her beauty, her natural, honest beauty. This is what I want the most. This is what I crave.

I know I looked dark and dangerous, because I'm dressed all in black, and I know I must scare her slightly because of my dark, and intense stare that never wavers from her delicate face. I know the strength of my intensity. But again, she needs to see this; she needs to feel the hunger in me, she needs to see the beast in me. I see the fear, the need and also the anticipation in her beautiful eyes, as soon as she opens the door and looks at me in my eyes. Without anymore words,

I move in as she silently steps back, to allow my entrance, and I kick the door shut with my foot, not even bothering to turn around, but satisfied when I hear the door successfully close behind me. I take in her beauty. Freshly clean and still damp from her shower, the only thing protecting her was her big towel, which she grasped so tightly between her fists just above her breasts. Her long wet hair trailed down her back, and I could see the glistening of water still on her beautiful skin, because she had no time to dry herself off, when I was pounding at her door. I grab her roughly by her long, lean upper arms and pushed her up against the wall next to the doorway. I leaned in towards her neck, as if I'm going to kiss her, but instead, inhale her scent and rub my face against the softness of her delicate skin. I rub my hard body up against her soft body, and just stand there for no more than 30 seconds like the calm before the storm. I take her all in; breathe her essence into my soul, as if it is giving me fucking life. I place my forehead against hers and note that her eyes are closed. I look down towards her hands still clutching at the towel. And with one swift move, I rip the towel away leaving nothing but her nakedness to come between us. Her eyes whip open and look directly into mine and I can tell her breathing is heavy, I can see her little pulse beating frantically at the base of her neck. Just like a delicate little fawn right before the lion jumps in for the kill...I grab a fist full of her long curly hair, curling inward with my big, muscular chocolate man hand, and angle her head for my kiss. The kiss is rough, savage because I need her. I need to fucking feel her tongue. Her submissive lips. Her kiss.

"I know I gave you an hour to get ready", I say as I break away from the kiss, "but I couldn't wait for you any longer. I need to have you now. You left early the other day during our brunch, but I'm still hungry and what I'm hungry for right now has nothing to do with food. I didn't want to wait to have you. I want you right now, not now, but right fucking NOW. I want the entirety of you." I whispered into her face as our foreheads touched, and my hand still angled her face from the grip I had on her hair, my other hand grasping her ass. "I want to feast on your soul, your body, your mind. I'm going to bite you, spank you, choke you, slap you and eat you up. Tonight, I'm going to take your soul and put it into my body," I growled.

I turned her around roughly so her hands were on the wall, and her legs slightly spread. I grab her hair again and anchor her head towards me, bringing her ear to my mouth and whisper:

"Tonight, I devour every inch of you. You are my prey, and I am the most fearsome Dominant predator. You ignite my fiercest appetite and tonight the beast will feast," I growled. She bought the animal out in me.

I slap her round ass with my massive hands so hard, her tits vibrate from the sensation. I move my hands from her hair to her throat, and her head drops back, her eyes close and her beautiful mouth opens wide. I reach down and unzip the zipper on my jeans and take out my already hard and throbbing thick chocolate dick. I slide it between her ass cheeks, down towards her pussy and can already feel the wetness seeping out of her. My hands tighten against her throat, and I can feel her body relax more. She pushes her ass back trying to grab more of my dick, which turns me on even more. I turn her around, lift her up and wrap her legs around my waist, as I slam her up against the wall, like she was a masterpiece. She was a work of art. I penetrate into her wetness. I slide so deep in, our chests are fused together, I search for her lips once again. I find them and our tongues start to wrestle again. Her arms wrap around my neck, and I can feel her tight walls accepting and accommodating my girth. One hand on her ass holding her up and the other hand sneaks around her throat to a chokehold. Her eyes close in pleasure. I start to thrust. Viciously. The harder I thrust, the harder I choke her. I can feel her walls closing in around my big dick and I know she is ready to cum. She starts to beg me for permission. She has already pleased me immensely tonight, so I allow her pleasure.

"Yes baby girl, you can cum." I feel her walls tighten, and her body clench in anticipation of her climax. I keep thrusting, never stopping, driving her wild, kissing her lips, her neck, grinding my hips into hers, she whimpers her pleasure as she releases her sweet juices down my big rock hard cock. She collapses in my arms and I hold her tightly. I cradle her gently and whisper into her ear, "I'm not done with you yet, that orgasm is the first of many tonight, go get ready". Slapping her ass firmly.

I walk us over to her bed but change my mind. There's no time for rest. It's time for round 2. I walk towards the shower, baby girl still resting comfortably in my arms.

"Come on princess, let's clean up," I say as I help her stand up. She looks slightly dazed and confused, as she watches me turn on her shower and take off my clothes. She notes my big rock hard erection still and takes it in her hands, while looking me directly in the eye. I chuckle, "I know baby girl, it's okay, we have all night, now get that ass into the shower", I playfully slap her ass again and she squeals with delight.

The water is cool and soothing on our bodies, and I take my times in washing her down with soap, making sure I don't miss any spots. I lavish all my attention on her body, and rub my hands up and down her wet supple body. The water raining down on us, I again turn her around and enter her from behind. I kiss her neck as I pull her head back roughly and slap her ass. I drop her hair and grab both hands, and raise them above her head. I hold them there with one hand. I spread her legs, I run my fingers over her pussy lips to make sure she's ready for me. Her groan assures me that she is. I need to explode. The tension in my body is too much. Soon as my big dick enters her sensitive pussy once more, I allow myself to release. It's quick and powerful. This triggers her climax. She takes it all.

She stands there and watches as I clean myself off and I assist in washing her properly. We get out and dry ourselves off with some fresh towels, and finally head towards the bed.

"Lay on the bed" I commanded sharply. I look around for something to tie her up with. I find some bed sheets in the cupboard and take them out. This will have to do. I tie her hands up and connect them to the bedposts.

"No matter what I do", I say "Don't fucking move. Got it?"

"Yes, I got it." She answers me. I drink in the sight of her. Lying naked, hands tied above her head and her legs spread. I've never seen her more beautiful.

"Good girl" I murmur. "Tonight I'm going to reward your very good behavior. Tonight, you can moan as loud as you want to. You can even scream. But if you scream, you have to scream out MY name. For now, I'm Daddy. This is how you will address me. As I rip into you, scream my name. Oh, you're going to moan from pleasure, whimper as scream from pain, but no other name will come out your mouth but me. Don't call out for god, he's busy. If you curse. I'll be the fucking reason. As you tear up, scream my name, got it baby girl?"

"Yes daddy", her eyes have already closed in anticipation and I watch her body as she writhes around in pleasure, her body so highly strung with tension that if I touch her, I know she will explode.

I walk around to the base of the bed, with the view of her pussy. I bend down and place her legs on my shoulders. As soon as I started walking, her eyes opened and she tries so hard to follow my gaze to see what I am looking at. I look at her from the angle between her legs, and stare at her in her eyes and slightly smile at her before I bend my head and kiss her flesh. I rub my face between her thighs and inhaled her woman's scent. She starts to moan and tries to grind her hips into my face.

I stop what I'm doing.

"I said DON'T fucking move." I slapped her breast mildly rough. Then severe, just to show I'm not fucking around. She gasped. I grab her waist with my hands and hold her in place. I go back and part her pussy with a lick of my tongue and head towards her clit. My tongue traces a 2, 4, 6 and 8 on her clit, side-to-side, flickering up and down. Her moans were louder, she tried so hard to not move her hips. I noticed her body had cracked a sheen of sweat all over from the pressure of holding in her movements. She was going insane. But I didn't stop. Her moans were even louder and louder, they drove me insane. She was on the brink of cumin, I stop and climbed up between her legs, slid my body up her body and covered her mouth with mine. She can taste herself from my lips, and she sucks on my lips and tongue and drinks her juices. My body is hard as a rock again. She is so open, so trusting in me, she has me going wild for her. I make love to her passionately, but savagely. I run my hands over her breasts and up towards her face to hold her head still to receive my hard brutal kisses. I know I'm rough, but my passion for her is intense, and I can't control myself. I bite on her lips and pull her hair.

"You're mine," I growl like a wild beast.

"Yes daddy, I'm yours," she sounds so breathless as she takes the poundings from my big muscular dick into her tight body. She was a dripping mess. Our bodies were covered in sweat and her moans got louder as her hips rose to meet each and every powerful thrust I harshly delivered. I covered her mouth and her eyes open and stare deeply into mine. I don't blink and so she doesn't blink, she follows my lead.

I run my hand down to her clit and massage it, as I continue to thrust into her pussy. Instantly her body tightens up and her release gushes all over my big dick.

"Daddy", she screams and her hips buck up. Hearing my name on her lips in the throes of her ecstasy, spirals me out of control and pushes me over the edge and my orgasm erupts like a hot messy volcano.

I untie her and order her to shower and get dressed. While she's in the shower, I walk into her walk in closet and pick the dress I want her to wear. I walk out holding a little black dress and hand it to her and advise her:

"I want you to wear this", I hand her the dress and am proud when she doesn't argue or question me, but says "Yes daddy", and takes it over to her bed and lays it on there while she gets ready. I walk into the shower to clean up and get ready.

I open the car door for her to get in. I shut the door and walk around to my side and get in, place the key in the ignition, and start the car. I pull out of the driveway. I look at her sideways and admire her beauty, I look down at her hands resting on her thighs and reach over and grab one, intertwining and locking our fingers together. She looks at me a little shocked at the intimacy, probably assuming that I don't have it in me.

"What are you doing Discipline?" she asks me.

"Unless something is a hard limit of yours, never question my moves. But let me explain something to you. When we are together. We walk together, side by side. Hand in hand. What you need to understand now is that you are a reflection of me. There is much I must teach you, but as of now, you are my submissive, and a sub is a reflection of her Dom. This is why you will now dress a certain way, and conduct yourself a certain way. So I hold your hand because you mirror me. You are in my protection now; I protect what's mine. I walk on the sidewalk closest to the road to protect you."

During my talk she is silent and by this time we have reached the restaurant. I park the car and walk to her side to open her door, and hold her hand as she exits. We walk silently towards the restaurant.

The waitress approaches me and asks, "table for two." In my mind, I'm like, 'duh bitch, no, let's get a table for one.' I stare at Mia, and then back to the waitress, "yes, table for two.

However, I want us to be in a booth. No exceptions, see we want to feed each other." Mia, had her head down, giggling, and by the look on the waitress face, I made her blush.

We reach the booth, and she slides in. I can tell she's shocked when I slide right in next to her.

"Again, I want you next to me at all times. I won't sit opposite of you, how can I touch you from across the table? Smell you? Feel you? If anyone needs to get to you, they have to go through me first" I explained. "I don't do that regular shit. Perhaps you're used to the traditional way, well fuck that."

"That's perfectly fine Daddy, I like this" she flutters her eyelashes down and a soft blush covers her cheeks, as I know my aggressive and possessive behavior is turning her on. "I'm sorry, am I allowed to call you, 'Daddy' in public? I smirk, "yes, I actually prefer it. You may address me as only two things, Daddy, and Discipline for now." She was so appreciative, "thank you Daddy."

The waitress comes over and hands us the menu and asks us if we would like any drinks. We place our drink order, and she leaves us for a few minutes, as we decide what we are going to eat.

I lean over to her and whisper in her ear.

"The panties I picked out for you back at the house." She looks squarely at me, "yes Daddy?"

"Well, take them off, not now, right fucking now." My voice is low so only she can hear.

Her big eyes look up to me, very confused. "If you have to go to the restroom then do so. But I want them off now. I don't want anything between you and I. Nothing between what's mine", I state casually as if we're talking about the weather.

She looks at me for not even half a second and nods her head. She wiggles around slightly but manages to remove her panties with no one none the wiser but me.

"What would you like me to do with them?" she asks me.

"Give them to me."

I reach under the table and grab them from her hand and put them in my front pocket.

"You'll get them back, when I want you to get them back",
I tell her.

I place my hand on her thigh and slightly massage it
under her dress. The waitress has come back to our table
to take our order, and I keep my hand on her thigh as I
gave the waitress the details of what I wanted to eat. The
waitress couldn't see what I was doing, mostly because the
table covered everything, but I also made sure that my body
was covering anything else from any wandering eyes. I allow
her to give her order and as she does my hand slides to make
direct contact with her pussy. I could feel the juice, the instant
my fingers slid down her slit. She gasps and I turn and look
at her and stare at her blankly. The waitress had to ask her
twice. I kept rubbing her pussy up and down and slipped one
finger into her very drenched entry. I was proud of her. She
managed to give her order, albeit with a very jumpy voice. I
turn to thank the waitress and watch her leave with a very
confused look on her face and that makes me smile.

I turn to look at her face and can see she's closed her eyes
in pleasure. I instantly pull my finger out. You will not enjoy
this. I will tell you when you can enjoy this. This is for my
pleasure right now. Maintain your fucking composure now.
Her eyes open and I smile.

"Good girl. Now we are ready for the appetizer." I said.

She nods, already knowing it's not food. I give her my finger and watch as she took it into her mouth, and tasted herself on me, licking and sucking my whole finger. My big dick was instantly hard. I had to fuck her now.

"Go to the bathroom and wait for me there", I demanded gruffly. I get up to allow her to get out. I stand as I watch her leave in the direction of the bathroom. I give it 20 seconds and follow. Luckily no one is in there except her. I pull open one of the stall doors and drag her by her neck into the toilet stall. I slam the door shut and lock it. I push her up against the wall, and mesh my mouth to hers in a hot rough explosive kiss. It was all tongue. Oh it was nasty, it was delicious, it was wet, it was passionate. I grind my big hard dick into her soft, tight, torrid walls and grab her head with both my hands roughly. She moans so loud I was sure that they could hear us outside. She's moaning loud. My strong muscular big black man hands cover her mouth. "Shut the fuck up, I told you I will tell you when you can enjoy this my whore." I'm thrusting, and abusing her with my massive chocolate cock from behind, yanking her hair. I hiked her leg and thigh up, with my arm, and held it there. My foot on the toilet seat. Thrusting in rhythm, dancing in her delicious, tight, submissive pussy. Through her begging, sweet pussy lips, like there was music and I was doing a new dance to the beat.

I hear the door open and I instantly stop. Oh but I was still inside her. She looks confused and dazed, obviously unaware that someone had walked into the restroom. I haven't moved my body an inch and I watch as she squirms on me wanting more.

The person who entered, hearing noises, asks "Everything okay there miss?"

I raise my eyes to stare directly into hers. I uncover her mouth. I haven't moved a muscle. I indicate with my eyes and whisper in her ear, for her to answer.

"Yes I'm fine thanks. I'm just constipated." she said breathlessly. I smile and whispered, "good girl." That person left abruptly. She made me laugh. Mia laughed following my laugh. Now, back to business…

I kept grinding my big chocolate dick into her pussy so she could feel all my hardness.

I wait to hear the door close as the patron leaves. My hand pulls up her dress again and I find her pussy. It was saturated. It was throbbing, it was pulsing. I rub my palm over clit. She was on the brink, I could fucking see it. I could feel it. One little touch on her clit and she was gone.

"Pleaseeeee Daddy, pleaseee can I cum?" She was begging me. I stop what I'm doing. I loved to watch her beg, I loved watching her squirm as well. It was a fucking turn on for me. But I had the control, and she needed to know that, and understand that.

"No. Not yet. You have to understand, your orgasms now belong to me. They are my gifts to you, and I can withhold them when I want. Why? Because I can. For my pleasure." She came already before we got her. She needed to understand, "I am the one in control here, not you" I grunted out, my forehead resting on hers.

I pull back and unbuckle my belt .

"Now get on your knees and finish off your appetizer", I pull out my big throbbing cock. It was ready to explode. It only needed to feel her beautiful mouth around it for a few seconds before, I exploded into her mouth. She took it all and swallowed every drop like a greedy, little child eating ice cream.

I buckle up and my pants and help her up off her knees. Her body is so tightly wound, but she holds her composure and it fills my heart with joy.

I kiss her lips and playfully slap her ass and tell her to walk out first.

Back at our tables, it's like nothing had happened in that restroom. We ate and drank and talked. I whispered in her ear all the things I was going to do to her later, and I knew she was just one tight ball of nerves. I reached between her thighs and didn't even have to touch her pussy to know, she was wet because it was all between her inner thighs.

I watch her mouth as she eats and it makes my big dick harder. It seemed like I was constantly on semi arousal around this woman.

I throw my napkin down.

"Fuck this shit, fuck this place, I'm fucking horny and I want to fuck you again." I throw enough money onto the table to cover the bill, and help her off the seat as we head towards the car. She's so obedient I note. She was amazing.

I drive, and my hand is rubbing her thigh playing with her breasts. She lays back and squirms ready to explode. I deliberately avoid touching her pussy because, I want to keep this exquisite torture going for as long as I can.

She pulls my fingers into her mouth and sucks on them hard. This tugs on my big dick and my erection is about to burst through the seams of my pants.

We reach her house and we unbuckle our belts.

"Come here now" I demand. I couldn't wait a second longer. She climbs on top of me and rips open my belt buckle and pulls out my throbbing dick. I rip open a conDOM and quickly put it on.

"Put it inside you now", I command. I watch as her face lights up as if I had just told her she had won a million dollars. Her wetness, allows my big dick to slide right inside her. So deep. So very deep. I grab her hips and pull her down further. It felt so fucking good. Her pussy was so tight, it gripped my dick and sucked me in further. I pull her down to kiss her mouth and suck on her tongue. I buck my hips to give her a jump-start and she starts grinding up and down. I reach around to her ass; our lips still locked, and spread her ass cheeks apart and smack her ass Hard! I slide my middle finger towards her ass and slip my finger inside. Soon as I did that, she let out a guttural moan and almost as if possessed, she asked me if she's allowed to cum. I kissed her in response and thrust my dick into her pussy with an explosive thrust. She erupted like a volcano onto my dick, which brings my dick to explode and we cum down together. I busted more powerful than a desert eagle magnum .44 pistol. She was left drenched like Niagara Falls. Squirting like she was a busted fire hydrant.

She lays on my chest as we catch our breath. I embrace her into my arms and hold her tight, kissing the side of her head. She did good. I was proud of her.

"I'll call you tomorrow", I say and pull her back so that I can give her a soft kiss on her lips.

"Thank you sir", she replies so meekly my heart grew warmer. I help her climb back into her seat and watch as she walks out the car and into her house. I clean myself up and buckle my pants back up, start my car and begin my very pleasurable drive home.

CHAPTER 10

When She Is Acting Up

woman that constantly begs for attentions will always love attention and not you. Many women beg

for attention in many different ways: crying, misbehaving, back and forth, power struggle, nit-picking, complaining etc. Most men are thought by many, to be the more assertive partner in the relationship, but in many cases, it is the woman who is the stronger assertive one, especially in this day and age. Women show controlling behaviors, along with serious levels of threats, intimidation and physical violence when in a relationship more often than men. Constantly checking up on you, jealous and possessive. People will behave however you allow them to. If you don't nip it in the bud, the pattern will grow and patterns turn into habits, as habits turn into behaviors. If you don't know how to keep her in line, she will run circles in front of you. All around you, and behind your back. If she's an alpha wolf and she smells a scent of your weakness, she will eat you alive like deer. Control can even be disguised in a way like, manipulation. Allow me to explain: instead of demanding her way, she will utilize unfair arguments, use emotions, cry, complain to get what she wants, the reality is women only respect men that can Dominate them. Whether it's physical, mental or emotional. Show me a woman who doesn't want to be Dominated, and I'll show you a liar. Women do not respect or trust men they can manipulate. But man, do they go crazy over a man that can man-handle them. As a man, if you can't control your woman, you are the woman. I'm just keeping it real.

If you're scared of your girlfriend or wife, you are the bitch. You are the girlfriend or wife. Women are not built to control men. It's not in their DNA. There is a strange feeling of being helpless that turns women on. Knowing that they can be overpowered, whether it is physical, mental or emotional. It is a common sexual fantasy. Women have desires, which will only come out when there is complete trust. No trust = no respect. No respect = no attraction. No attraction = no relationship, at least not a real one. I'm telling you now don't give her good dick every time she acts up. It goes like this: when she acts up, and you give her good dick to get her to calm down, it's all good. But then when she acts up again, you give her good dick once again and it's not breaking any cycles. She learns that by acting up, she will get good dick. She has no respect for you. Perhaps only for what you provide her. Do you see the pattern you've created? You think you're doing something great, meanwhile she has you wrapped around her fingers subconsciously. You have now become the sub. She's never going to learn because she knows how to manipulate you. Her bratty tendencies play a factor to get what she wants. My advice is next time she acts up or gets wild and goes crazy; grab her by her pretty little throat or her hair and speak in a calm tone voice, or whisper in her ear and tell her, 'shut the fuck up.' This is going to throw her psyche completely off. All the adrenaline coursing through her will be kilter. If she continues to rattle you, bend her over your knee and spank her ass. She wants to behave like a child, treat her like a fucking child. Truth be told, if women are familiar with anything, it's pain. When she attempts to sit down the following day, when she's shifting in that chair, It will be a constant reminder for her disobedience. She won't act up again unless she's a masochist. She will learn to appreciate her Dominant and therefore behave as you wish. Tell me if you keep giving a spoiled brat everything, how is she ever going to learn? Her attitude is your fault. Her bad behavior is your fault. Don't complain about how she is because you have allowed and created it. You are the enabler. You must set the tone as her Dom. A true leader sets the tone. A queen or princess always follows her king.

A good sub is an example of a great Dom or Daddy. If she's a brat I can guarantee you her Dom is letting her get away with anything and everything. There's more to being a Daddy, a Dom, an alpha or a king. Just because you think you can spank, tie or choke a woman up, doesn't make you Dominant. Most people misconceive BDSM with aggression, savagery and brutality 24/7. But this is a lifestyle of fulfilment, development, love, trust and obedience. This isn't a hobby for me and punishment for me is not fun. However, how else are you going to learn? This is not a fad, this is not a movie, this is not Cinderella or prince charming. I will show you what being a real princess is all about and its nothing you've ever seen on Disney. Most men that want to engage in this lifestyle and the women that want to comply with it, they have to understand that being a sub is not forced; it is earned. You cannot force a person into this lifestyle. You can't bully them; you can't ask or manipulate a person to be in this lifestyle. You both have to agree upon this. Like I said before, there are 2 people in this but it is 1 relationship. In that relationship, both parties have responsibilities.

CHAPTER 11

What Dominance Is Not About

Any man can force a win. It's so simple. Any man can take a woman by force. Any man can shout orders. Any man can rip a woman's clothes off, toss her on the bed, pin her up against the wall. But that's not true Dominance. An example of Dominance is staring at her so firmly, it's like you're looking into her soul. A look so piercing and magnetic it inspires emotions. She willingly wants to drop onto her knees and worship you. A soft tone, a gentle touch that can make her remove her clothes methodically piece by piece, relinquishing her control over to you. The integrity of Dominance is in the inspiration of submission. A woman will submit to a man who is powerful, because of financial security, physical Dominance, emotional Dominance or because of a big Dick. But the majority of women are not being satisfied physically. Women love danger even if it appears like it might kill them. A woman will submit to a man that has those attributes. What allows her submission to stay consistent and thrive? It's his character. How he holds himself to a standard and how he holds her to the same or higher. Be a man worth submitting to. He will hold her accountable for her actions. He needs to be Disciplined in order to enforce her Discipline. It's not just physical, it's all aspects. You can Dominate someone with your mind as well as your mouth. Intellectually, not just physically. Psychologically. This is what you are and who you are. It does not control you. Don't sell your soul to make the money and don't allow the money to make you. Make the money and remember you define who you are. True confidence doesn't come from alcohol. Dominance and confidence correlate together. Your energy introduces you before you even speak. You control you. Psychological, it's 65%, and 35% it is physical and emotional etc. Be influencing and inspire someone else. A true master inspires, motivates and encourages. They thrive to make others excel. They have an intuitive capability in making others around them better, they know what motivates people. When you can connect with people, there is a 75% chance you're always going to have that great relationship, great results and people will come to you constantly for advice. It's always good to inspire and motivate those around you. Now ask yourselves this question, would you still want to be a Dominant even if there were no sex involved? If you honestly cannot separate the sexual aspects from the Dominant lifestyle, than perhaps your reasons to wanting to be one is just superficial. I thrive off the power. Employees come to me on personal and professional levels. I just like being needed. I always take pride in being great and making others around me great. I personally take extraordinary pleasure in coaching. The power turns me on more than anything else. This isn't role-playing. This isn't a 'thing', a moment or an act. This is instilled in me. This is something I was born to be. This is now, then and forever. Part of Dominance is being able to influence others. Men are many things but masters of nothing. I exercise control in all things. Whether it's mental, physical or emotional. I claim ownership and no matter what I do I put my mind, body, heart and soul into it. I have passion, drive, Discipline and dedication. When it comes to Dominant and transformation, I have a tendency to do both with positive results. You have to possess this type of intensity. It's either that or perish. Dominance is something that is influential. It influences power. Power is something that lures you and gets things accomplished. But it's like control and allows it to remain consistent. Control is about making things go your way. I've impacted so many people's lives and always motivate others to be better. Dominance and real men go hand in hand. Why is it that many of times women get into arguments? She's clearly not getting something fulfilled. Remember, she follows you and you lead her. You wear the pants, you're the man you take control. She needs to know what her role is. In that establishment, she has to know what her role is. You have to hold her accountable at all times, as it is detrimental to your dynamics, if not. Most women who know how to do their job will become masters. At the end of the day, a sub is a strong individual seeking another stronger individual to compliment them. If you don't follow the rules, then I don't have an issue replacing you. It's really that simple.

CHAPTER 12

Relinquishing Her Gift

Everyone talks about the gift of submission, but what about the gift of Dominance? The gift of accepting you as you are, but still seeing you for what you could be. Giving purpose beyond your presences, offering you access in a safe place to articulate your fears, desires, your doubts without worry or judgement. Offering peace, love, guidance, deep connection, security, and Discipline. If there is a fear of resentment or judgement, there will never be a gateway to freedom to openness.

He loans you strength and courage when yours fails you. In order for her to relinquish her gift, she needs to feel these things from you. The type of man you have to be. At the end of the day, a sub has the freedom to do whatever she pleases. However, with that freeDOM, she chooses to kneel. Her gift is her submission. Trust comes before obedience. So the gift of submission and the gift of Dominance go hand in hand.

This is where TPE(total power exchange) takes place. Once she relinquishes control then you have the power, now you're giving her a gift back and I call that the gift of Dominance. The thing about women is when they start opening up about certain insecurities, and fears, you have to try and figure out a way to maneuver it to make it a strength. Because, if she tells you her fear and you mock her, she will not open up to you anymore, in fear of resentment and in fear of being judged. That's why most basic relationships are boring. There may be honesty, but genuinely, you're afraid to tell her or him what your true desires are. Mainly, because of the fear of resentment, the fear of judgement. The fear of him or her feeling inadequate. Inadequately, unable to perform or fulfil your desires. Inadequate to provide you with protection or a deep connection. Passion. Intensity. Security. There is way more freedom and openness to it. It is one of the things I offer my submissives. I never met a bond more passionate than a passionate Dom, and a loving sub. To cultivate your mind, body, and soul. Your title as Dom or sub is irrelevant without power. It's how you use your power that holds value. The ones that engage in this lifestyle, we are just a bunch of deep, passionate and intense individuals. We grant each other access into a psychological, emotional and physical space that transcends the limits of what a basic relationships have to offer. Myself, I love hard, I punish hard, I Discipline hard, I Dominate hard, I fuck hard. It is a bond and connection at the end of the day. It's like when I write. I say certain key words where the reader can connect with me. When you read my words you feel me from a distance. Show me 50 different BDSM couples and I'll show you 100 different ways and styles of BDSM. Once trust is established, there is no one-way to display this lifestyle. My subs love me unconditionally, because I'm more than just looks, more than just money, more than just materials. What I give them is priceless. As I earn you, you will earn me. If you're not 100% committed in this lifestyle don't even attempt it. Why? Because each party is equal in servitude. So as you receive you give back. That's the power exchange. Most women love a man because of what he has and what he can provide. Most men are use women for what they have and what they can do. We live in a world where we are visually controlled. We react based on what we see. Men react to what they see and women react to what they hear. For example, a woman wears excessive make up and the result is the man thinks you're so beautiful. So he sees what he likes, he's may say, "that's sexy, that's hot, you're beautiful." Now, women react to those words, and now she wears that make up, because it's a conscious habit, that the excessive make up, is very inviting. Women are more emotional. Women want to hear those words that trigger desire. These words allow the woman to open up to feel they are wanted and desired. However, what one man loves, the other may dislike. I personally don't care about your outward appearance. It's a bonus. How you impress me is with your imperfections, loyalty, devotion, fears, doubts and flaws. I don't want to see what society sees. I want to see the ugly, the bad. I want to see what you're afraid others will turn you away for. I want to know what you fear others will not love you for. I want to see all of you. Not everyone deserves to see all of you though. Only those that are worthy. When women use that cliché that 'all men are the same' it means they clearly have never encountered a true, educated Dominant man. A woman will relinquish control only because of trust. If you are genuine with people and not just women, they will respond to you in a positive way. They learn to trust you. People react based off emotions. Especially women. Women react based off impulses. Most Dominant men are so confident and they really are so alpha, they don't care what you think of them. That's why they will say whatever they want. Most men are afraid of laying shit on the table. Doms are not scared if you run, stay or leave. They will be strong with or without you. They don't chase women. They try to excel in life and accomplish their goals and if people don't want to follow them it's not detrimental to them or their life. So most of these guys are clear with their intentions. They don't sugar coat shit and are very straight forward. Women can appreciate that. Most Dominant men are so blunt that some people view them as being arrogant self-centered or assholes. Normally, if a man goes up to a woman he likes and they are connecting on most levels, and he says to her 'I want to make my intentions perfectly clear, you're going to please me'. She might laugh at you. It's nothing she's ever heard of before. Normally, that comes off as arrogant. Who the hell does this guy think he is? However, you're already his before you realize it. This is why he speaks like this. This is why he states these demands. As a woman you don't know what's going on. He knows what he's ultimately going to give you. You're not use to this you're use to the ordinary, vanilla, mediocre type of male. You will yearn to prove yourself to me constantly and you will happily submit, because of my confident, measures authority. Willingly be ready, able and eager to prioritize serving me over everything else. For if you're not willing to give it all to me, then I will take nothing, give nothing. For me the only submission is complete submission. I want it all. If you are mine, it doesn't matter how you were in the past or what issues you've had, I am ultimately looking at the bigger picture. I am not inadequate. I know what I posses and what I give. I know what I bring to the table ultimately. I know what my capabilities are. I know how far I can take you. Women are the way they are, because of inadequate guidance and non-Discipline in their lives, so it's not a concern to me to push you. I take pride in being great; I am the best in the world at what I do. I'm the alpha of alphas. The strength of a man is from a woman, and a man needs a woman. There are things a woman can do that men cannot do.

A man needs a woman that is truly his. A man thinks that when he shows emotions or communicates, it shows him as weak. A Dom knows this is not true and in fact the opposite is the truth. It makes him strong.

He knows the strength that comes from opening up to his woman. When you love a woman and not enjoying her presence, her physical, her mental, the entirety of her, it's like having vodka in your fridge and you never drink it. Drown in someone! The entirety of them. Love them hard. Fuck them harder. Why would you want mediocre love? Mediocre pain? Mild pleasures? You want to drown in someone and vice versa. I feel like it all comes down to trust. When you can connect with somebody, you get positive results. If you give a little, she'll give a lot.

The biggest misconception in any relationship is that the woman needs to be able to be in touch with her emotions, be able to articulate more and men feel that if they are in tune with their feelings they are less masculine. This is just ridiculous. Part of that comes with the connection. If you can build and give, then there's a major chance there will be new adventures and fantasies. Potential fulfilment in your sexual fantasies and your whole life. The vagina is not the only way inside of a woman. The people that engage in this lifestyle are deep passionate individuals that require more. Some people want your body and your mind, well myself, I'm greedy. I want it all. That's part of the control. As a man opens up more it will make her more comfortable to open up. You can explore so many possibilities together. After you fuck, where is your worth? Are you even worth a conversation? Can you hold a conversation? Waists expand. Beauty fades after a while. Are you worthy of seeing anymore? What are you worthy of being? Are you a being worthy of seeing? Once you have sex the relationship could very well be over. Most educated men desire woman that can stimulate them intellectually. 95% of intellectual men will correlate and incorporate with more intelligent women. At the end of the day, if you just have that physical connection with her, she won't keep your interest. You're on a different level. If she can't stimulate your brain as well as your dick, then she's just another number for the body count. Sapiosexuals require more intellectually. Once you develop yourself, you'll know what you want. Vibes and energy will talk louder than any words. You can be good and nice in life or you can take and be great at whatever you do. Men are many things, but masters of nothing. If you can understand people you can run a business, and that means you know how to influence people.

CHAPTER 13

Power

In beauty, strength, and intelligence there is power. One if not all three are linked with sex. When it comes to sex, sex is about power. What woman doesn't find muscles attractive, a handsome face alluring, tattoos a turn on, even foods like chocolate soothing? For example, let's go back to the tattoos, when you see a heavily tattooed man, what comes to mind besides great art? You haven't figured it out yet? Sex comes to mind. Sex pain, pleasure, aggressiveness comes to mind. Looks can be alluring, as it triggers curiosity. Curiosity becomes desire, desire becomes surrender, and surrender is now power, and power is sexy, and sex is powerful. Show me a woman that doesn't care to be lifted up, tossed around, pinned up against the wall, kissed roughly like you were the object of his unbridled lust. Protected and loved properly. Show me a woman that doesn't like to be Dominated, and I'll show you a liar.

Women are hardwired to want Dominant men. Forget women power, feminism, independence and all that bullshit. You go visit other countries you will see what I'm talking about. Visit other cultures, and different nationalities. Women love their men to be powerful and Dominant. While most men look for good looks and good bodies, women need reliable, independent and strong-minded men. They look for men who take charge. Women are subconsciously hard wired to respond sexually to men with higher values than themselves, and also to men with higher values than other men in their circles. You'd think women like men who are soft, weak, romantic but if there is one thing that turns women on, it is a man with Dominance and aura. Inequality beats equality. That's why opposites attract. Women can spot a man who lacks Dominance miles away, and adds that almost every quality of a Dominant male triggers arousal in the female psyche. These include Dominant scents, Dominant gaits, deep voices. Leadership DnA, Facial hair, muscles. Let's just say, anything that is big, or Dominant will always attract women. For a woman to feel womanly, she must be with a man who is manly. Masculinity inspires femininity. When she is with a guy who is not Dominant, she feels he is just another girl. Women expect you to know what to do. They don't want to teach, and they certainly do not want to be the person who's is making the decisions in the courtship. A true Dominant man has great self-control and will never allow the situation to get out of hands. When you communicate with women, don't gossip, speak only when you need to communicate something with real value and maintain strong eye contact when you speak to her. Don't get too emotional, stay in control. Lead the conversation and don't ever ask for permission for anything, tell her what you're doing and let her choose if she wants to be in or not, this also applies to sex. You want to know how to Dominate her? Find out what makes her tick. Knowledge is fuel for power; by being the Dominant, you understand the importance of power in one form or another. When you are in charge of guiding her through the correct path, understanding her primal needs is of high importance, and not as easy as it might first seem. First you have to understand that women, especially nowadays, have a lot of reasons to be dishonest about their true desires and needs. Society dictates mainstream social rules about what is and isn't acceptable, and it has been going on ever since the explosion of feminism. Basically a lot of desires and primal impulses that women possess have been shamed by such and similar ideologies. Being a Dominant man is basically rooting yourself into your core masculinity. But that's not all as in a relationship you also need to help her release her own repressed femininity. But how will you get a woman to communicate a need without feeling ashamed? This is one of the many reasons why and where you need to be fully trustworthy, as the Dominant male figure in her life. You need her to trust you enough so that she can feel free to leave you sufficient clues about what she truly wants, but cannot openly express. Be 100% trustworthy and only then be a good listener! Listen to her when she is speaking to you, ask questions and do not ever judge. I will not lie to you; this will feel more like playing detective work than an honest conversation with some of your best buddies. Why? Simply because that's how it really is with most women. Good submissive behavior must be rewarded. The best way to reward women without creating yourself problems in the future is by praising them and giving them more attention. If she has a good overall behavior, just express genuinely how beautiful she is when she does that or how proud you are to be with such a good woman who does this. When she is good, flood her with love and compliments. If she is disrespectful or starts showing signs of unacceptable behavior, immediately end the current activity and remove all the attention you have on her. She instantly becomes unworthy of being noticed by you. She is temporarily banished from your world. Do not react to her drama just calmly ignore her existence. This is like mental torture for women, because they crave attention. If she does not live with you, drop her at her place and cut off all communication for a period of 2-3 days depending on the gravity of the transgression. If she lives with you, or she is the mother of your child, ignore her totally and keep yourself busy. If you need to communicate with her for important reasons like the kids, go with a business tone and keep it short. A good Dominant figure doesn't need to raise his hand on women. Take responsibility for your bad choice, learn from it and move on with your life. Usually a man that knows he can get any girl will go with the flow, so he seems like he doesn't care. He perhaps treats her bad, because he knows she's not going anywhere. She won't find another like him so she needs him. Even though I understand women from experiences, don't stress out trying to understand them. For they all want different things, yet similar things. Women are not meant to be understood, just loved protected and cared for. Most people want control and to be in charge. They want the title but they can't handle it. They don't know how to utilize it efficiently. Dominant men are the most powerful men. Now when I say this it doesn't pertain to money or sex, I just mean power. Most want it but only a few can handle it. Very few people are able to be transformative. You go into a situation and you transition into something and are able to get positive results. Most people are scared of change. When you're use to something and asked to transition into something else, or given perform a task, you feel like you're out of your element or your comfort zone. Which you are. But the true strength of character of an individual is how they handle pressure. You've already placed this idea in your head that you are inadequate. So because you've placed this imaginary fear in your head, now this is what you become. Your body reacts to it. Your spirit reacts to it. You are unable to be assertive. Unable to proactively engage. The way you view this this may result in poor performance on your part, to be powerful. It's not about having a lot of money. It's not about being the most popular guy. Power is about influence. Power is about the people you inspire, and the impact you create. Take a shy closed off woman, she will gravitate to men of my caliber, because of the confidence and assertiveness and the measured authority, where she's hoping one day, I can allow her or help her bring out that assertiveness in herself. I will eradicate all those walls that you work so hard to keep up. You will never be the same or view ordinary men the same again. When it comes to me I have no need to worry about others, because I will ruin the possibility of anyone else. I know that when I touch you, that you will do anything for me. The type of energy I have is magnetic. A relationship and lifestyle of this magnitude is so difficult to find. Reason being, the passion, the connection, the Discipline, the intensity. My goal is to own the entirety of you. Cultivate your mind. Violate and claim ownership of your body. Ultimately, Dominating your soul. What I'm saying may frighten you, but even if you walked away you would return to me. Why? Because I am like a drug in itself and so powerful that, where even if you fought the desire, the urge would keep coming back. You remain here because, you do not want mediocrity. I will ignite this desire in your soul. No matter where you are. No matter what you are doing, your soul will be bound to mind. There is no need to remind you where you belong. No need to ask. My whip, my chain, my Dominance will reach far. I will fulfil a void you've had for so long. A void you were afraid to fulfil. Incomplete before me. Men in the past have never measured up. Why because they were afraid to explore the depths of your mental and soul. Places they never went deep enough into your body. Frightened to touch your soul. I will eradicate those fears. I will rebuild what the past or previous men have destroyed. You will never find better love, a deeper connection, immense Discipline or punishment, sex, power, protection, security, guidance, freedom, savagery, aftercare, Domination, than myself. Regular men can only dream of providing you this. But they pale in comparison. BDSM is just an acronym until a Dom and sub engage in such activities, and give it proper meaning. Psychological and physical. Women are inclined to be submissive. They are more emotional, more nurturing. Women correlate most things highly with sex. When a woman observes a man, she knows in 7 seconds of meeting him, if she wants him to Dominate her and if she wants to surrender to that man. It's all about her fucking body language. Women are kinkier and more adventurous. Women are more inclined to try new things. I've said this before…..They are subconsciously designed to be attracted to the stronger genes. Women are attracted to higher level of testosterone. High testosterone correlates with more stamina more sex drive. They love the following:

Assertive behavior

Dominate behavior

Risk taking

Strength

Confidence

Leadership

Facial hair

Muscles

The list goes on. Women crave to be Dominated. Women crave to be taken, desired, controlled. This is why most women gravitate towards powerful men. There is a lot of selfish lovers out there and women fall short of pleasure in these relationships. Most women are terrible in bed and it makes it more comfortable for them when someone there is skilled and knows what to do. It's a balance at the end of the day. A shy girl and a shy guy won't work. Two subs will never work. Two Doms don't work, unless one relinquishes control. Everything in this world is about power, balance and control. A good girl and a nice guy won't work. There's no balance.

Women love to feel wanted and needed. Power relates to:

Protection

Security

Aggression

Dominance

Assertive behavior

Everything women like, but will never admit to. In order for a man to attract these types of women, he has to first realize he has this power. If the lion is not aware of his power he will always be hunted, he is no longer on top of the food chain, now he is the food and the hunter will never fear him.

Normally a woman feeds off of energy. If she picks up on your assertive behaviors, strong character, how masculine you are, it will inspire her to be feminine. Motivate her to alter her behavior without you having to exert any type of force. This is why submission is beautiful. Because a sub has a choice to do whatever she pleases, but she would rather kneel. Your Dominance inspires her submission. I have been a greater Dom because of my subs. A man can learn a lot from a woman if he pays attention. Her mind, body, and soul. The biggest myth of Dom and sub, that one partner has to be weak. The best D/s relationship strengthens you both, that's what people fail to realize. So if the woman is normally the Dominant one in the relationship. Guess what – you're the weak one. Physically strong. But mentally weak. She picks up the slack and there is a power exchange. In order for the power exchange to take place, there needs to be an immense level of trust. In order to build that trust, you need not just conversing to converse, but efficient conversations, understanding each other, building and focusing on honesty, loyalty, devotion, dedication. Speak of hard limits and soft limits. Display emotions in public and in front each other. I love public affection, kisses and cuddles. Holding hands is a form of protection. Holding hands is a secret public form of foreplay. I'm over protective. At dinner, I sit next to her, to protect her, and also because I like to touch and feel my woman. Nothing about me is normal or ordinary. Not even my conversations. Why would you be afraid of showing people what's yours? Aren't you proud of what you have? I'm over protective – subs have to deal with that. Normally I test a sub. I'll take her out and see how she interacts in public. This is the biggest test, because if you do not behave as your Dom's sub at all time or you don't treat your Dom like a god in public, you don't deserve to have one. You are not sub, you are not owned, you are pretending. Feed me! Yes in front of everyone. Will you do it? I don't have to ask you, will you do it? If you're mine, what choice do you have? That's not a hard limit. Like myself, I don't care what the world thinks of me, therefore you shouldn't either.

My ideal goal is TPE(total power exchange). That's in and out of the bedroom. So if you don't appreciate and respect my Dominance outside of the bedroom, you won't inside of the bedroom. At least not 100%. We live in an "ob-sexed" world. Sex has been so repressed and demonized, that it comes out in unhealthy expressions. In it's most extreme and violent forms, the unhealthy expression of sexual and power dynamics show up as rape and sexual abuse, which are clearly more about power than sex. It is interesting that one of the most common verbal expressions of aggression in the English language, "Screw you!" and it's more colorful alternative, allude to sex. What's more, the word "fuck" is believed to originate from an Indo-European root meaning "to strike." In a more subtle sense, we often use sex to work out power dynamics in our relationships. Because we have not been taught about honest and authentic communicating or how to handle conflict, we tend to work out the power dynamics in relationships covertly, and frequently through sex. Navigating the power dynamics in the bedroom can feel like walking through a minefield. Whoever initiates risks rejection, which often takes the form of a power play: "Sorry, Honey, I have a headache," when inside what's really saying: "Fuck you! Hell will freeze over before you get any tonight!" Not initiating can also involve elements of power: we (men and women do this) relinquish power due to fear of rejection, and perhaps even in subtle ways. Like, manipulate the other to begin the process, thus minimizing risk. As our sense of self becomes stronger, we learn to more easily, ask for what we want without taking things personally.

Negotiating who's giving or receiving, as well as the logistics of sex—When? Where? How often?—can be fraught with danger. Sometimes it feels like walking on eggshells. Even engaging in sex for self-validation is about power in the sense, that we give our power away every time we look outside ourselves for acceptance or a sense of worth. and tragically, for many people the missionary position still represents an attempt to ensure the Domination of man over woman, who is relegated to being merely a passive incubator or instrument for the man's pleasure. Sex can be complex and complicated through sexual dynamics. Through fantasy and fetish, others learn to work out power dynamics more intentionally. Yes, sex is incredibly pleasurable and undoubtedly a powerful force, but it is more than that. Beyond the rush of endorphins and feelings of ecstasy, it is also a vehicle for deep connection, for transcendence, for momentary freeDOM. We have a deep longing to pop out of the prison of our minds even for a brief respite. When we open our hearts in lovemaking, it adds a whole other layer of emotional release and the sense of connection transcends the physical. The more in touch we are with who we are and with our soulful power, and the more that we learn to be congruent and communicate our needs and desires and emotions in a way they can be received. The less we need to resort to covert power plays in the bedroom. When we are established in our own power and realize that another's power does not take away from ours, we can allow sex to be a natural exchange of energy, of love—and of power. Women only want to be with a sexually confident, Dominant and powerful man but not Domineering. The reason that alpha male's are attractive to women is because they don't over think things and women get the sense that they're doing what they want to do. Because of this a feeling of attraction grows. The alpha male goes after what he wants, he doesn't sit around thinking and wishing. He figures out what he wants and creates his ideal scene. If you consider yourself to be a beta male then the only reason a woman is with you is because she's using you to fill a void just until she finds a man that is Dominant. It may seem counterintuitive to a beta male but attempting to do what the women may want, waiting for her or trying to say the right thing, will bring out a sense of insincerity. This may cause a woman to 'test' him just to see what he is really about since he's apparently showing her a 'weak' side. Unfortunately, the tests that women give are often very unfair. The reason this is done is to see if he can recover to prove himself. Alpha males are considered to be natures with women. Men want to be them and women want to fuck them. They seem to get respect everywhere they go. The reason that alpha males are who they are comes down to how they live their life, their values. The have cultivated certain values that have turned them into a confident, strong, determined man. That's full of energy, vitality and pride. Rejection doesn't affect them at all, it's like a drop of water hitting their shoulder. They demand respect and won't take anything less then being respected. By following these simple to live by values. They will crush all the bad habits you currently possess which make you into a loser. and replace them with good habits to possess that will make you into a winner. Don't be confused with the current dogma that an alpha male is this muscular brute that is rude and bullies people around to get what he wants. This couldn't be further from the truth. If an alpha is out at a club in a booth with his buddies but has no women with him or to his liking. An alpha puts his energy into changing his current environment into the one he wants. Therefore he must leaves his booth and goes find women that he likes and brings them back to the booth. Very simple. He doesn't sit around contemplating, he doesn't worry about fear or rejection. He figures out what he wants and decides on what the simplest and quickest action to take to get that thing. He doesn't think or theorize. The thought process from wanting-to-thinking-to-doing is very quick. The alpha doesn't blame others for what he doesn't have. He recognizes that the victim mentality is weak, and it's his responsibility to get that thing into his life. Alpha males are independent and self-reliant. You may have noticed that natural alpha males are social and Dominate that isn't necessarily because they're extroverted individuals. It's because they know that when they commit to the change they want. It's sometimes easier to bring in others to help you get what you want a lot faster. This is why alpha men will appear to be very Dominant it's because there's an intention behind their actions. and since most people just cruise through life with no intention or purpose to living. When an alpha male comes into the picture that has an intention or vision. It's easy for others to follow because naturally most people want to follow someone who appears to be a leader. Most people don't want to take responsibility for their own life, making it even easier to follow someone who looks like they have their life together. Later on in this book I will be showing you how you can take responsibility for your life. Getting physical: If you want to sleep with women, getting physical with them is the most important factor. From first approaching a woman, all the way to bedding her, touch is essential. What is most important, however, is that it progresses gradually. If you randomly try to kiss her out of the blue, without having touched her all night, she'll reject you out of surprise. If, however, she's used to your touch, progressing up to kissing and then bedding her is a much smoother process. So how do you get her used to your touch? By touching her all the time! Start out small, and as she gets used to you, gradually ramp it up. You can start by tapping her on the shoulder when you first approach her, to then lightly touching her on the arm to make a point or share a laugh. Slowly build up from there. You could then put your arm around her or rest your hand on her thigh. You could entwine your fingers in hers, or hold her hand and stroke her palm. Imagine you have a frog and you plop it into a pot of boiling water. What's it going to do? It's going to jump straight back out. However, if you put the frog in a pot of cool water, and slowly warm it up, the frog won't notice until it is too late. Similarly, gradually physically escalate your interactions with women, and they will get used to it. You can start with only a light touch on the arm when meeting a woman for the first time, and half an hour later have your arm around her and her leaning into your chest as you go about building a solid emotional connection with her. You can also use touch to communicate. If you're flirting with her, you can create sexual tension by stirring up playful conflict or creating a barrier to the two of you being together. You could tell her that she is too cute for you to handle and playfully push her away. If you are not being serious about something, a smile and light touch on the arm can communicate your playfulness. You can also just mess around and have fun by pulling her in, spinning her around like a ballerina, thumb wrestle, pinkie promise, or do whatever. Just have fun and be a cool, chill guy. Amuse yourself. Just keep in mind, if you want to get a woman to bed, start small, and work your way up. Nice guys generally wine and dine women for weeks without so much as a single touch. The world's greatest seducers, on the other hand, simply can't keep their hands off women. As a result, they get physical with women very quickly. So take note, and get physical! In the end, the main thing is to do the exact opposite of nice guys. Do not be a nice guy. Nice guys seek approval and acceptance from others, at the expense of their true selves. Don't do that. Be yourself! Respect yourself and your desires. Prioritize yourself over women you barely know. Ultimately, it is that attitude that women instinctively find most attractive. Be shameless about your masculinity. Don't hide who you truly are. Show strength by overcoming our evolutionary urge to seek the acceptance and approval of those around us, especially hot women. If you want to do something, do it. If a woman isn't so keen, who cares? After all, there are millions of other hot women out there. Don't become so attached to women you barely know solely because of their physical appearance. Have confidence in yourself. Be confident of your value as a man and women will too. Be yourself. Follow your desires. Don't do things that you don't want to do (or otherwise would not do if it were not for a hot chick). Be unpredictable. Don't chase and be heavily invested in women you hardly even know. Ignore any shit that women give you or stupid things they say or ask. Show leadership by doing whatever you want to do. Women want to tag along with a strong man as he does as he pleases, they don't want to have to take charge of an indecisive wuss. Connect with women, play with them, tease them, build sexual tension, and don't be afraid of gradually getting physical right from the start. The biggest thing, however, is realizing who you truly are, and then shamelessly being that person all the time. Life is too short for trying to be someone else or trying to please everyone (no matter how long the legs or how hot they are). Be yourself and have fun doing it. It is the most attractive thing you can do.

CHAPTER 14

You Are Mine

Some women search the world for love. They will do anything, even manipulate and beg for love. They yearn for their significant other to say the words, 'I LOVE YOU', and it is supposed to be reciprocated. Then there are a separate portion of women that want to be called, 'mine.' They want to be called, 'yours', and that is good enough for them. The love is a bonus. You see a woman can have a title as you girlfriend, your wife, but do you claim her? Do you own her how she should be owned, is she with you or is she yours? Does she belong to you or is she just with you? Do you feel you deserve her, and she deserves you?

I'm not going to preach something to you and say I'm Prince Charming, because I am not. I wouldn't kiss you awake, but more like fuck you savagely to sleep, But with me you would get non-stop thrills like an action movie. I will eradicate those fears, gradually dismantle the walls and guards you work so hard to keep up; I will claim every inch of you. There is nothing more intimate than ownership, love is a verb at the end of the day, it's not like a cliché greeting like, 'How are you.' Some of us don't really care how you are; it's just a pleasant greeting or a good start of a conversation. But it's like a rhetorical question. Some men are too wrapped up in their work, games, toys that they forget they have a woman. A woman always feels like she is not desired, loved or appreciated enough. You have women that say they don't make love, they don't love, first of all, are you fucking him or is he fucking you? You are what you get, you get use to what he gives you or doesn't give you. Some women are into mediocrity, therefore they give mediocre. I refuse to settle for mediocre, I want all of you, mind, body and soul. Why? Because, I know what I bring to the table, I don't desire it, I fucking demand it. This is why there are so many unhappily married women out there, and they lie, saying they're happily married, or have a status up, stating, "hi, I'm happily married, look at me." Cut the bullshit, when you get married, most of the adventure comes to a halt. When you have children it's even worst. Only a few married couples still keep it spiced up. who cares if you have Chanel on your back, Louis on your arm, Gucci on your ass, money comes and goes, but hot sex never gets old. Passion isn't something you can teach.

Dominance is something you just can't emulate. When you touch her, fucking TOUCH her. Grab her, that expensive lingerie she bought for you, rip that shit off. What do you plan to do with all that body of hers? All that ass? Tits, thighs? Nothing, you scared she's fragile? Show her the reason for your high level of testosterone. Unless she uses her safe word that's she is granted. Unless she tells you that you are going too far, don't baby her, manhandle her. Yes, grabbing her pinning her against the wall, showing forms of aggression that is not the only way to claim her and make her yours. The way you truly Dominate her soul, cultivate her mind, and penetrate her body is the way you have her completely. Here is when you have invaded her every thought. No matter where she is, she will bind her soul to yours. She will get these butterflies in her belly when she sees you. Goosebumps. Don't be afraid to claim her body, her face, ass, tits, legs, back, thighs, feet, etc. Bite, slap, grab with no hesitation. Grab her body like you own it. Grab it like you mean it. Trust me she will know the difference. Penetrate her mind so she'll always be wet, especially when you fuck, and Dominate her soul. She'll always feels complete when you engage in sex. Violate her body and she will be yours for good. Baby girl no need to dwell in your own flaws, and not see the beauty I see in you. Don't ever doubt me, you will be reassured by the bruises you see on your flesh. The soreness you feel in the morning. The wetness that you experience during the day. How insane you become with the moments I give you. The moments we engage in. Lose yourself in my insanity, I want you obsessed with me. I will bury myself so deep inside you, that you will feel hollow when I'm not around. This is where you belong. MINE. This is what your psyche craves. MINE. This is phenomenal. MINE. Anything else will bore and piss you off. MINE. You are MINE. For as long as I please. Whenever I please. However I please. Wherever I please. You belong to a BEAST, a SAVAGE, a MASTER, a DOMINANT, a KING and don't you ever fuc'KING' forget it. Every calculated touch from my big hands, will heat your flesh faster than a sun against a barren land. Soon as my chocolate anaconda slides in your tight pussy, and your drenched walls will not help but close in on me. MINE. Screaming to cum all over me. I will make your body feel weak at the slightest thought of me. MINE. I know you feel me when I think about you. I will stroke your cerebral so aggressively with my words, and with my deep voice that you will beg me to mark your body aggressively, with my big muscular hands, with my whip, with my crop. All your life you were begging for someone like me to bring out the beast within you. Like an angel seeking a devil as you yearn to seek peace in my chaos. Begging him to please him. Yearning to serve and worship. Someone like me to fuck with your halo. A good girl like you, searching for a bad boy like me to bring out that improper, bad nympho, big chocolate dick hungry, loving whore that you are deep inside. I am a representation of what you couldn't, the things that frightens you. I am more than just breathing. I will be intoxicating. I will be your drug that you need a hit for everyday, and even if you fought the desire, you will keep coming back. Your mind will be a slave to my words. My commands, my voice, your body will be a slave to my lifestyle. You will feel like a virgin again as my big cock Dominates your pussy, and fills it like it's never been filled. Your soul will be a slave to my Dominance. A slave to all I am, and all I do. Ownership over the entirety of you. A captive only I can set you free. I am your guilty pleasure, I am your bad, I am your escape. Your favorite sin. Your 'everything' you are not. Safe in my presence. You're in heaven in my grasp, not hell. Uncomfortable when I'm not around, and you're hurt without my touch. I am what you need to breathe. The irony is, when I'm not choking you, you are suffocating. I am the air you breathe. When I'm not whipping you, you feel pain. Without Discipline you have no structure, no stability. I am your fucking balance. The void you so yearn to fulfil. Your submission is your strength. My control is your release. Re-fucking-lax when you're with me, you no longer need to think. You simply need to just 'be.' You yearn to please me. Because you are perfectly aware that pleasing me, pleases you. This morning, you were an angel. But, tonight you will be a slut. I can see the look in your eyes; the passion, the will, the desire. You are MINE. Most men do the minimum. Slap her ass, pull her hair. Afraid to go against the grain. To go over and beyond. Perhaps fear of breaking, fear of hurting you. Fear of you 'can't handle it.' Fear of themselves going too far. I'm not most men. I enjoy breaking pretty things. I find gratification in hurting the fragile, and corrupting the innocent. Your body is like heaven, but I will put it through hell. If you are mine, then you know what that entails. I am not going to slow down. I'm not going to be gentle or adjust. This is why I grant you a safe word. It's up to you to know what your limits are. My job is to push those limits. Most men are fine with the minimum. Myself, when I own; I own the entirety of it. Especially your body, every fucking inch I will:

Slap.

Grab.

Pull.

Bite.

Devour.

Violate.

Ravage.

Destroy.

Annihilate from head to toe, when I please, however I please, where I please. Suck on your throbbing clit. When I grab and slap your tits. Nibble and bite on your neck, as I whip your clit. I will bite the meatiest parts of your flesh. You will be marked as mine, marked as owned. Branded with me. I will establish my Dominance all over your body. What you would call hickies, I call battle wounds. Brand you so you never forget who did it, who the fuck I am, what you are to me, and what this relationship is. Ultimately, establishing where you belong. Which is, in my zone, in my grasp, my touch will complete you. Destroyed by the extent of my sadism. Discipline is what you crave and WHO you crave. Beg for pain and pleasure will follow. I will ignite a fire within your soul where you will have no control over. Once you have had a taste of Discipline the rest will pale in comparison.

Then and truly then, you will belong to me. You are mine.

CHAPTER 15

Her Need

You are never the same once you've experienced a true Dominant man. They ruin any possibility of anyone else, and anything else. Everything you feel is intensified. A weak man cannot love a strong woman; he won't know what to do with her. He won't know how to handle her, how to love her, how to fuck her efficiently. You don't know a woman, until you understand what she's not saying to you. In the hands of the right man, a woman can be many different things. It is of his willing to allow her to feel safe and lead her. Be a man and take charge. Never let her question your desire for her. Don't just tell her, more importantly, show her. Take her aggressively, don't be gentle. You do that outside of bed already, allow her to feel real testosterone, allow her to feel your hunger. Grab her, don't hesitate, grab her like she's yours, grab her like you own her and trust me; she'll know the difference. Yes, I'm reiterating sentences, because that's how imperative it is. You may articulate you want someone, but the only way to prove it is, ACTIONS. Some want you to speak dirty, it intensifies pleasure, words are a woman's weakness, it is one of the major aphrodisiacs, and in her ears is one of the locations of her g spot. Try to stimulate her mentally, while you're physically stimulating her, and this will pleasure her immensely. Quiet activity is boring activity. Let's be honest here. Just like any successful team in today's sports, communication is imperative. Communicating efficiently, will allow you to achieve your goal. If you can't speak to your partner during sex or feel uncomfortable about it, it says a lot about your chemistry, and sexual mental, emotional connection. Most women do not feel comfortable telling you about their darkest desires, they feel a man should know what those desires are. Do they really care if you orgasm or you are just glad they got theirs? Does he care to pleasure you, or is he just pleased to be inside you? Does she even care what he or care what herself desires, does she care to give her trust? Are you a man worthy of her submission, where it should be masterfully taken? Would you meet her expectations, once you've reached an immense level of trust with her, you can take her mind, body, and soul places she's never even thought possible. Once you can read her pages, you will be able to master her book, pay attention to the hints, and the things she doesn't say. Let her eyes speak, there are so many reasons, why women are hesitant to not only tell their significant other their desires, but to display it as well. Most basic, traditional relationships are limited, limited trust, limited sex, limited openness, because of the fear of resentment and judgement. Why would your woman tell you, she desires to be slapped in the face with your hand? Taking the chance of you calling her insane, or having you freaking out? Perhaps you guys have been doing it in the same old position, same old style for years. Now you've put him in a position, where he feels inadequate. He's telling you, he doesn't want to hurt you. Perhaps the positions you both have been engaged in, and have for so long, why switch it up? You haven't been complaining. What's wrong with it? I'll tell you what's wrong with it. It's boring, and being bored traps desires. You as the man should take control, if you can take control and feel comfortable about being assertive, 95% of the chance she will always follow your lead. Feel free to do as you please. Bite, spank, mark, slap, she will appreciate that in the morning. Speak dirty, call her disrespectful things, fucking verbally abuse her, you have to understand, some women are afraid to speak in bed, they don't want to make the first move. It's like, when you like that girl and she's making eye contact with you, she's waiting for you to come over there and talk to her. So once you start talking to her, she's going to talk back, so set the fucking tone as the man. It will make her feel more comfortable and she will be receptive, and she will talk dirty back. Women love testosterone and aggressiveness, so when you're doing this add some spice to it, you can't be pounding her and saying sweet things, that's just fucking weird. It's like an oxymoron, biggie smalls, a nice asshole, calm storm, friendly argument, police protection, passive aggressive, safe or gentle sex, boxing ring, a submissive Dominant, you get the point? If she's not comfortable about this toughness, this roughness, this assertive behavior, grant her a safe word to be used whenever you engage in activity. Perhaps if she whispers "harder" that may mean a green light, or "pineapple", that's yellow for slow down or "apple", for stop. I don't use these safe words, but these are just examples. I give my sub safe words based on their personalities, off of our dynamics or our connection. They do not all have the same safe word, by doing this, this may make your woman trust you more and be open, to bringing more adventure into the bedroom. My advice as a man, always be in control, don't lose it. Even if the activity is so intense, and is so great. If she uses her safe word, respect it. If you don't respect it, next time you go to touch her, even though she is saying yes, her body may cringe, and pull away from you. She may be doing it subconsciously. I constantly meet women who don't know me, but want me to Dominate them. My character is so strong, they want to me to Dominate them and guide them. My guidance for these new subs are vital. They are knowledgeable about the life, but they need to know what I like, and how I want things to be done. The new subs that have never had a Dom before are the ones that need constant guidance, and reassurances for this life. Littles(a type of submissive) are very needy and clingy. There is no age bracket for a little – could be 27, 35, 40, 50. Littles have baby tendencies. Some suck on pacifiers, wear diapers, others just wear diapers on their attitude, and have brattiness tendencies. Some suck their thumbs. They have this habit in private as well, way more than public. I had a sub years ago, and after we would engage in intense sex, I would cuddle her, and I would constantly witness her sucking her thumb, while I held her. This woman was older than me, she was like thirty four. I put an end to that habit she had. These little ones need lots of guidance and tasks daily. If they are pleasing you, you can reward them with children's presents, like stuffed animals. Every woman has a little girl on her. Especially around holidays, and anniversaries. These littles, they require your attention every minute of the day. When they don't get what they want, they act bratty and you constantly need to put them in their place. They need more Discipline, and guidance on a daily basis. Be willing to allow her to feel safe and lead her. Be a man and take charge. When a man can take charge and he is comfortable in being assertive, it is a relief to a woman. When you have a leader that is strong, you are comfortable to rise and prosper. It is very tiresome when a woman is required to do everything. What she needs in the home, in life is balance, he should do the heavy things and fix things around the house, and bring in the heavy groceries, the yard work, fill up the petrol things women shouldn't have to do. Women should do the soft things in the house, like cooking, cleaning etc. I was raised by my grandparents, so I have an old school mentality. I know that a woman needs to know that she's desired, loved, and cherished. Don't just tell her, but show her. It takes a good woman to tame a beast. If you want sunny days, go through the storms. The whole need is a process, the need to feel loved and needed. I always appreciate someone that wants to work hard, or is working hard. She needs trust, reassurance, Discipline, and she needs to feel passion. Passion changes everything. A man should know what his woman's desires are. If you're investing time in someone, you should know them so well that the things they are not saying, is the loudest thing you hear. It says plenty about their connections, if there is no communication. With BDSM, we are already considered different. So we already have to go against what society dictates. When you act different, you become like a problem in societies eyes, like you're going against the norm. In order for her to be able to be open, and to be able to trust you enough to unveil secrets and talk about her desires, she needs to know your soul is open and trusting as much as she is. She needs to know, she won't be judged or ridiculed. She needs you to be confident. In any relationship you had, you feed off of one another. If we're talking about a sub; she needs to know that her job is being appreciated. That if you're pleased, then express words of encouragement such as, "I'm proud of you", or "good girl". These words motivate these women. Words of encouragement makes them want to do more, be more for you. At end of the day, they want to know, they are pleasing you. If you don't communicate, it will fuck you up. If she's constantly getting punished and not rewarded she will act out. You need positive reinforcements. If she's not being rewarded, what are you doing? What is the fulfilment? Why are you in this lifestyle? What she needs is protection and security. What are you doing that is conductive to what you two are striving to build upon? Once she has these things(security and protection), she will give you what you want. Trust means more than love. In order to get to trust, you need love. There has to be a balance between a 'want', and a 'need.' At some point, the need is going to take over. It becomes a hunger. A touch. A feel. A word. A gesture. She needs to feel wanted, she needs to please you. She needs to know that you're pleased. It becomes an immense habit. Routines turn into patterns and patterns turn into habits.

CHAPTER 16

Wet For Daddy

I had left a key for her with the clerk at the front desk of the hotel. I told her to mention "Mr. Discipline" at the front desk, and she would be given the key to the bedroom. I had told the clerk in advance that, he should be waiting for her arrival. The clerk gave her the key, and gave her directions to the room. She turns the key in the lock and opens the door. The first thing she notices, besides the massive bed in the middle of the room, is the note that is laid on the middle of the bed, and next to the note is a blindfold. She shuts the door softly behind her, making sure the door is securely locked. She throws her bag on the chair next to the door, and walks over to the bed. She opens the note, staring out the corner of her eyes at the blindfold still on the bed, and wondering what was in store for her. The note had 3 simple words.

"Strip yourself bare".

She turns the note over, seeing if there were any other clues, or instructions. But there were none. She dropped the note back on the bed and began to undress. Before her hands opened the top button of her blouse, she notices another note on the counter. She walks slowly towards the next note. She opens the next note and reads the next instruction.

"When you are finished stripping bare, lay on the bed, on your back and place the blindfold over your eyes, and wait patiently for me".

She looks up and around, certain that she could feel someone in the room with her, but doesn't see anyone. The room is large and spacious, but she was the only one in there. Nervously, she straightens her hair back from her face, takes a quick look around again, takes a deep breath and finishes off unbuttoning her blouse.

What she doesn't realize is that, I am watching her every move. From the second she walked into the hotel, I knew every step she took. Behind the security of the second bedroom door, which was cracked open slightly, I could clearly see everything she was doing. I was enclosed in darkness, so while I could see her, she could not see me. Bird's eye, I had a clear view. Oh you can't see me, but I could see you. I watched her every move with a hunger deep in my eyes. I could smell her scent; feel her nervous vibrations, see every delicate hair on her head. My body was already turned on, knowing what I was going to do to her. All my muscles were tensed, and I was ready to pounce, but I didn't move an inch. Instead, I devoured every move she made with my eyes, my arms folded across my large torso. Tonight, I was ravenous, and she was exactly what I wanted to consume. I watched as she continued to unbutton her blouse, and laid it on the chair beside her bag. She started to remove her skirt, she found some rare form of confidence. If he was watching her, she was going to make a show of it. She stood there with her blouse removed, and only in her dainty, very feminine lace bra and tight knee length skirt, she remembered the feel of my hands, as I ran them through her hair. She sighed as she remembered how beautiful she felt, when she saw herself in my eyes. Tugging the memory close, she grabbed onto it to help her with the removal of her skirt. She slowly wiggled her hips as she pulled the skirt down, showing me exactly the outline of her plump delicious ass. Tight material was pulled down over it, revealing of sexy, sheer lace nylon panties that her ass was already eating up. Taking her time, she carefully stepped out of the skirt, bent from her hips very slowly and picked up the skirt, folded it and placed it next to her blouse on the chair. From that angle, I was tantalized with the most delightful view of her pussy. I continued to watch, enjoying the show. She left her heels on and with just her panties and bra on, she walked over to the full-length mirror next to the bed. She gazed at her body, and then met her reflection in the dark glass. With another deep breath, she unfastened her bra and watch as her breast sprung free from the lacy confines, her beautiful breasts so firm, so sensitive. Her nipples were so erect from the sheer anticipation she felt. She was aroused. Her hands went to stroke her breasts, but she faltered mid air. Did she dare? She knew the rules. She was forbidden from touching herself, from pleasuring herself without my permission, without her Dom's permission. But she could feel him; she knew he was in the room, somewhere watching her. There was no way, he would not be here watching her, stalking her, protecting her. Knowing this, gave her even more courage, she was so turned on right now that nothing could stop her hands running up her stomach to grab, and squeezing her breasts. Her pussy was throbbing now, she could feel the heaviness of it, and she could feel the wetness seeping out onto her panties, she was already wet for Daddy. She played with her nipples, knowing it would be his hands playing with them soon. Her head fell back in pleasure, her long gorgeous hair almost touching her ass. She ran her hand over her hot pussy, rubbed it slightly before pulling the panties off. I had contemplated leaving her something sexy to wear, but to me, nothing is sexier than the human body, it truly is an artistic masterpiece. She looked at herself in the mirror again; all she had on were her stilettos. My instructions were to be completely naked, and this slight disobedience did not go unnoticed. Even though she was in trouble, Daddy loved what he was seeing, and it turned him on even more. But she would pay for her disobedience later. She wanted to rub her pussy again and went to rub it and stifled a moan. But remembered where she is and whom she belongs to, and stopped immediately and continues to follow the instructions given to her. She walks over to the bed, picks up the blindfold, and proceeds to place it over her head. She's on the verge on placing the blindfold on her eyes, I stealthy walk up behind her. I stand right behind her, my hard body touching her soft body, and I whisper hotly in her ear:

"You seem set on pleasure tonight hey baby girl? Are you hungry for what only a Dom can provide?"

She did not move her face, or her body, the blindfold still in her hands, her quiet answer washed through me

"Yes Daddy."

I took a deep breath, satisfied with her answer, but also not fully satisfied either. You see her answer was exactly as I expected, but not what I wanted. I had a hunger of my own and it revolved all around her. From day one, I had made certain that there were no misunderstandings. This was far too important, so I immediately responded to her answer;

"Wrong. You hunger for what I, and only I can provide. You may not be aware of this, but no other Dom will do or provide you with what I can. It seems you need to be taught this lesson properly. Before we go any further, you will have to understand the difference between, just what any Dom can provide, and what YOUR Dom will provide".

I heard a distinct hitch in her breathing. I didn't know if she understood my meaning, but at least I knew she wasn't unaffected by my words.

She stood there, so close there was no space between our bodies, my big, muscular chocolate rock hard dick nestled in-between her big soft ass. I finger a soft curl of her long beautiful hair trailing down her back. Oh how I always loved her hair I thought, but to finally be able to touch it again, wrapping it around my hand brought me so much joy. I grab more of her hair and angled her hair with a firm grip. I could no longer wait.

"You won't receive the release you crave so badly, until you understand the difference that you're not a Dom's sub you're MY sub. There is a massive difference which you need to understand".

She doesn't say a word. I tell her to put the blindfold on. I watch her breasts as they move when she lifts her arms up to cover her eyes. I grab her upper arm and walk her towards the table near the mirror. I lean my head into her ear again and whisper

"Place your hands on the table and no matter what I do, don't fucking move".

She placed her palms on the table with no hesitation, no games, and no pretence. Just how I liked it. I stood behind her now; my view of her ass was spectacular.

"Now spread your legs".

She spreads her sexy legs, calves defined as her feet remained in her high stilettos, and it's all the motivation I have just to slap her juicy cheeks.

"Now baby girl, we've already gone over your hard limits in the past, but before we start anything now, is there anything you would like to add, because once we begin, there will be no going back, unless you use your safe word."

This whole time I still have my grip of her hair in my hands, so I release the handful of hair and straighten the curls down her back.

"No sir", she replies. "I want only to please you, I want whatever you give me"

My response came out angry: "Me or any Dom?"

I concentrated hard on keeping the beast inside me in check. Her shoulders rose on another stuttered breath.............

"You", she says

"Me? Or 'You Daddy'?"

"You Daddy", she murmurs.

I stand back to watch her for a second. Her long legs in stilettos, spread, her hands on the table and the blindfold on. A sight to behold and I drank in every inch of her luscious body. I had never mentioned it again, but when she decided she wanted to give me her submission, we had both agreed that I would choose her safe word.

She asked me what her safe word would be. I thought for a moment and then I told her.

"Band-Aid."

She was quiet for a second, and then asked me ever so softly.

"If you don't mind me asking, why would you pick that word?"

"I thought back to when we first had met. One of the first things I had noticed was the band-aid on your little pinky, the fact that I couldn't stop staring at the band-aid. So many questions ran through my mind, as I looked at it that night. How did it get there? Why the pinky finger? Did it hurt you? How you were hurt, and I wanted to heal you. How you were healed, and I wanted to hurt you." The memory flashed in my brain for a split second.

"Band-aid", she confirms.

and I reply, "Good girl."

I pushed her long hair over her left shoulder, and traced the long line of her delicate spine with my fingertips now. I continued to question her.

"Now baby girl, were you aware that I was watching you tonight?"

I could feel her heart race up; I could feel the pounding of it through her skin. She wanted to lie to me, but she knew I knew the truth; she quickly threw that idea out the window, because she knew the punishment would be worse if she lied.

"Or do you always put on a strip tease when you undress?"

"I was wondering if you were watching, but I wasn't sure. But I remembered how beautiful you made me feel last time, and when I thought you might be watching me tonight, that feeling came back and I wanted you to see how lovely I felt. I apologize Daddy, I'm sorry."

I stared at the back of her head and realized that she was far too rare a woman, to let get away from me. I had a gem in my hands.

"Do not apologize for that. Ever!" I said sharply, "In fact, from this point forward, any time you undress before me, you do it just fucking like that. Understood?" I had growled that last word, because the beast was coming out of me.

"Yes Daddy", she whispered.

I retraced the path back up her spine with the palm of my hand,

"Good girl", I said. "So do you like touching your breasts? You seem to have enjoyed it a few minutes ago…"

"Sometimes Daddy", her quiet answer is barely audible.

I step back giving her space.

"Stand straight up and show me. Touch your breast, show me what you like and how you like it," I demanded.

I crossed my arms over my chest, and my gaze drank in her whole body. I marveled over her graceful legs and the prize at the end of the trail. Oh how many times, I've imagined sinking my fat, long dick into her aroused slickened pussy.

I watched as her palms and fingers played with her flesh, and slightly wish I could witness the bloom of pleasure on her face.

"You like it hard?" I asked. In time, I will learn all her secrets I vowed.

"I do, but it's not the same" she answers.

"What's not the same?" I ask.

My eyes still on her breasts, I watched as she tugged on her nipples, making my mouth water. Like a alpha wolf, ready to devour a deer.

"Touching myself. Though I enjoy it, it's not quite as good as having someone else touch me"

"Someone else?" I asked, my eyebrow raising. Tonight, I would make sure that it was the last time, she thought about anyone else touching what was mine.

"Having you touch me",she said

"What about your pussy, when was the last time you touched it?" I demanded to know.

"The night after our last encounter Daddy, I'm sorry, I needed the release", her voice quivered. She knew she was in trouble.

"Lay on the bed and get comfortable, you won't be going anywhere for a while", I ordered. I was calm but angry, and she doesn't know how furious I was as my face is expressionless. How dare she pleasure herself without my approval? Without my consent! Tonight, I would make sure that everything would be revealed, both physical and emotional.

She lay in the middle of the bed and waited. I walked to the end of the bed and watched.

"So tell me, did you use your fingers or a toy when you touched yourself?" My quiet voice hid the fury behind the question.

"My fingers Daddy", she was panting heavily now, with fear, excitement and arousal. Her pussy was throbbing, and I could tell it was starving for Discipline.

"Did you play with your pretty little clit or did you fuck yourself with your fingers?.....

You know what, don't answer me. Spread your legs, and show me how you pleasured yourself", I growl.

She opened her legs and the sight of her exposed sex, made me want to thrust my thick long chocolate muscular dick inside her, and pound the fuck out of her. But, I knew that's what she wanted also, and there was no way in hell, I was going to giver her what she wanted. Yet..

She rubs her clit and I can see how tense her body is, like a string that is wound too tight, about to snap. I let her continue, enjoying the sensual play. Her breathing gets heavier, and my body gets harder. However, the lesson wasn't over and she hasn't learned anything.

"Spread them wider."

She opens them a little bit more widely

"WIDER", I roar, "I want to see everything!" Wanted? More like needed to see it more than I needed my next breath.

She bent her knees and spread her legs even wider, Her luscious breast rose and fell as her arousal increased along with her heavy pants. I was rewarded with the view of her womanhood. I watched as her graceful fingers continued to toy with the pink slick folds or her honeypot.

The dangerous question rises from my voice: "So tell me, what did you think about when you finger fucked yourself."

The site of her, on her back, spread-eagle and blindfolded touching her wet pussy was driving me insane. I knew what she was going to say, she wasn't stupid. Her reply was quick and expected.

"You Daddy", she was so turned on, she was struggling not to moan and squirm.

"Me? What about me?" I asked with bated breath cursing the power she held over me. I needed to hear the words.

"I imagined your hands on my body and..." she pauses as her index slips into her pussy and she starts to moan again. I watch her fingers move, my dick harder than it's ever been and forcefully demand.....

"FINISH your fucking sentence, leave NOTHING out." I move to stand besides the bed, on her side, close to one of her knees. She was groaning as she answers, her head pushing back into the pillow, her hips grinding around her fingers.

"I imagined what it would feel like when you…if you…if we…." she couldn't finish her sentence, she was getting too caught up. Her eyes rolling back. Dopamine, and oxytocin dripping from her brain.

"SAY IT!" I roar yet again.

I wanted to resist her, I didn't want to touch her, but I was unable to stop myself, to stop the beast inside me, as I pushed her hand away and used my fingertips to touch her clit. Then inside her drenched hole. She was wet. So wet. Drenched. Her lubricated pussy was vibrating and I could feel my big dick jumping, begging to plunge into her having her wetness bless all my sins away.

Her sharp gasp of pleasure rewarded me, and then she answered:

"If we had sex", she was grinding her hips into my fingers, her luscious body glistened with sweat. Her eyes were squeezed shut, as she welcomed the pleasure of my fingers.

"You mean, if I fucked you?" I was going to fuck her so hard tonight. Fuck her so hard, she would feel me in her dreams. Snatch her soul out of her body.

I traced a line from her clit down to her pussy. My finger dipped deep inside her, and I stopped at the knuckle. Her response wasn't much more than a breath, "please Daddy, yes." She was begging. Begging Just how I wanted her. "Was it a hard and nasty fucking or brutal fucking?" I watched her face as I inserted my second finger. Her hot dripping wet silky pussy, sucking my fingers in making me hungry for her and for what was to come, what I was going to do to her, what she would do for me. I stopped moving my fingers and she arched her hips seeking more. She moaned and grind her hips to make my fingers move again. I pulled my fingers out and rested the tip of my knuckle on the tip of her clit again, and completely stopped.

"Say IT. ALL of it. If you do not say all of it, I will not continue." I needed to hear the words come from her mouth.

"Daddy you fucked me so hard I saw stars", she panted her eyes looking directly into my hot hard starving gaze. She relaxed her hips letting them fall flat on the bed. I was pleased. I rewarded her for finishing her sentence by inserting my fingers back into her dark, and beautiful heat.

"Did that make you cum?" I growl into her face.

"Oh yes Daddy", she groaned as her hands went back to her breasts pinching her nipples for extra pleasure. The site was so lovely, I didn't dare to stop her from touching them, so I allowed her this. But, I was going to stop something else.

"This time baby girl, DON'T cum. Hold yourself to the edge, I know you know how."

She laughed a delirious half laugh, half cry. She was so far gone, she didn't know if she could. I watched the muscles in her hips tighten but she held them in place waiting.

"How do you know that?"

"Well baby girl, you're an extremely intelligent person, I know."

"You can't know me that well."

"I know you better than you think", I whisper face to face.

I thrust my two fingers back inside of her and she fought hard not to arch her body into my hand. Her need for more was so overwhelming. Her body was so tense and she kept tossing her head side to side. I watched her face as I kept thrusting my fingers into her wet pussy. I curled my fingers like a hook inward and kept penetrating her walls. She moaned and I felt a shock wave of pleasure run through her whole body, so intense that it neared orgasmic levels. She was a hair shy of tipping over the edge. In her I could see how crazy she was going, how badly she wanted to bust. But, she yearned to please me, and yearned to follow my every command. That desire was stronger than the one pulsating between her thighs. She couldn't imagine what it would be like to have a Dom, or more accurately, this Dom in her life every day.

Maybe it was immature of her to equate physical pleasure with the relationships longevity, but she knew enough about herself to know that she wouldn't feel complete, without certain aspects of Dominance, and submission in her life. She knew she needed it. The first night with her, I had taken something so seemingly simple and used it to train her. I had done it by using pleasure and obedience. She might be in over her head, as she was always known as the most practical one in her group of friends. The nurses always encouraged her to let her hair down and have some fun. If they only knew she was so nasty. If they knew she was so freaky, and that she was well and truly sunk by a Dom. A Dom who commanded her body quiet, literally with the crook of his fingers, and she didn't even know his real name. Oh the judgement that would present itself. "You're such a slut." The dirty looks she was receive. But, it was our secret. I had her pussy pulsating around my fingers, drenching my hand, I stop and pulled them out. I move and get on the bed in between her spread legs, and place my forehead on her stomach. I grip her hips in a gentle hold and I kiss the skin just above her belly button. My thick lips kissed her pussy very softly, and I nuzzle my face into her core. Her hands come over to cup my head, but I grabbed her wrists with my big strong hands, and pinned them against the sides of her body. I then began to lick her clit, as I traced the number 8 with my tongue. Back and forth I go. I'm driving her completely insane. I place her legs over my shoulders, giving me better access to my prize and hold her wrists again. I was flicking my tongue up and down her clit, side to side, up and down, around and around. Her moans were getting louder and louder, I know she is on the brink of her orgasm. I come to an abrupt halt and lift my head away from her delicious pussy. Her hips literally lift off the bed and she cries out

"Please Daddy, why did you stop?" Her question comes out like a whimper.

I smirked at her and chuckled, my sadistic tone comes out: "You will have to learn that, I am in complete control. Complete control of your mind, body, and soul. I control when you get your release and when you don't. You will never want to touch yourself without my permission again, because if you do, then this will always be the result. Do you understand?"

"Yes Daddy", she cries. "Yes, please..Daddy, please..." she begs. Knowing what she wants, I go back down to her clit. Soon as I start licking her, orgasms rips through her body and she gushes all over my mouth. I drink all of her up as if her juices are what is keeping me alive. I lay next to her and let her catch her breath, as I take the blindfold off.

"You are to adhere to all my commands and you are expected to obey always, do you understand?" My deep voice sends shivers down her satiated body.

I get up and I begin to bind her hands and ankles to the bedposts. Now completely restrained, spread-eagled once again and in my control. I sit on her side, at the edge of the bed with my hand on my chin just gazing at her. Taking my sweet time. I stand and walk around the bed, my gaze still on my feast. Stalking her like I was a lion and she was my baby zebra that I was about to pounce on and kill, waiting methodically and calculating before I devour her in one go. Not one word leaves my mouth. The only noise in the room is her deep breathing. After a few more minutes of silence, I warned her.

"When you came in tonight, you were yours. But when you leave tonight you will be 100 percent mine". I continued, "I intend to make sure you take better care of yourself, because if you don't, I will. You need a Dom and I intend to be that Dom. You're an incredibly intelligent and beautiful woman, you know what you need and you're not about to shy away from taking it. Because, that self-awareness is necessary and extremely sexy to a man like me."

"A man like you", she asks looking at me as I walk around the bed. "What does a man like you want?"

"I'm a simple man, I despise game playing, and life is too short for complicated bullshit. I want a good woman that knows herself. A couple can't have happiness until both partners know themselves, and only then can they know each other. In order for this to work there must be immense trust, honesty, loyalty, dedication and devotion between us."

"You think you know me?" Her eyes are wide as she blinks a couple of times with her question.

"I know that you're an incredibly intelligent woman. I know you have one of the kindest hearts imaginable, and that you always put yourself last. I intend to put a stop to that, you always putting yourself last," I gently tell her as our gazes are locked. My body is humming with arousal, but I have my arousal under control. I mean, what could she say? She lost her ability to speak. She was impressed. However, she was also in no position to negotiate anything physically or verbally.

"How do you know this about me?" She asks.

"Well first of all, you're a Doctor. There must be a reason that you decided to take that shield. You have a kind heart, you want to help people. You care, it's clear." I answer.

"I am a Doctor, yes. I took a oath to always care for my patients, that's what I do."

"And that is what tells me about your kind heart, but you're going to save some of that energy, and use it in taking care of yourself. When we get that under control, then you'll start taking care of your Dom", I advised.

"My Dom?" She asks. She didn't know whether to leap for joy or curse at my audacity.

"You will please me", I stared squarely into her beautiful lustful eyes. "You'll understand that pleasing me, will please you. Why? Because of the ultimate reward at the end. You want me? This is the price you pay for greatness. I will humble you. Even if you told me that you never done something before. You will for me. My presence, my energy, my Dominance will have you doing things you've never done before. Feeling and experiencing things you've never felt. You will constantly yearn to prove yourself to me. You will submit because of my confident, measured authority. You will be willing, ready and able. You will be an avid sub. Willing to prioritize serving me over everything else. If you're not willing to give me all of you mind, body, and soul, I will take nothing. You may as well leave now. Because for me, the only submission is complete submission." I stop and let her absorb what I had just said.

"And sir, what if I don't abide by these rules? What if I don't do these things you demand of me?" She asks.

"I will punish you."

"How would you punish me?" Obviously her curiosity is piqued and she starts to question me.

"You will never know what the punishment will be prior to the punishment, nor will you have a choice. It will either be physical or mental." I stop pacing the floor and stand at the end of the bed again, cross my arms and look at her delicate face. She looks so cute, so innocent, so fragile, and so precious. Her helplessness and vulnerability triggered my voracious appetite. I was on the verge of feasting on her. I moved in closer and closer, until my face met her face and my lips met the luscious lips on her face.

"I will not call you by your real name, from now on you will be known as precious, you will answer as, precious." I grab her jaw again between my rough hand, my thumb and fingertips grasping her whole bottom face.

I begin to kiss her lips roughly and aggressively. I wanted her to feel the hunger in me. To feel my intensity. I wanted her to experience my passion. It was a heated and sexy kiss. When her tongue tangled with mine, it set fire to my blood. I broke away just enough to see her eyes, then I went back to her mouth, letting my tongue explore the deepest recesses of her mouth in my complete Domination.

I tear my lips away from the kiss and growl at her. "You will belong to me and only me. I will ruin any possibility of anyone else." I looked deep in her eyes and asked her. "Do you understand all these requirements precious?"

She sealed her fate with two little words "Yes Daddy." She was still looking me in the eyes. My dick was throbbing.

"When we're in public, you are my Queen, and you will address me as 'King.' When we are in private, you are my dirty, little naughty slut, you will always address me as 'Daddy, and Master.' We clear?"

She replied meekly, "yes King, yes Daddy, yes Master."

I replied, "good girl." She was so fucking good. Memory like an elephant. Patient as a high school teacher. Eager to please, eager to learn.

I take her face in both my hands and held her gaze with mine. I then traced one hand down her chest, over her supple breasts, down to her navel and onto her pussy. I felt her dampness, fully aroused by my words, my kiss and my seduction. I took off my belt buckle and start to take off my pants. My big muscular chocolate dick jumped out. She had me so hard. Her obedience, her willingness, and her submission had me ravenous for more of her. She had been starving for this. Empty before this, and I was going to fill her up like a tall glass of cold water on a hot summer day. All her dreams were going to come true, and all her voids were going to be fulfilled. I slid my big long chocolate cock between her drenched lips. I put her on her knees, as my index finger pointed downward. I place my big strong thumbs on the back of her neck. My other four fingers across her throat. Shoving my massive cock down her submissive throat. Her eyes were watering. She was gagging on my big dick. The noises were like music to my ears. Tears running down her cheeks. Fucking her face to a whole new dimension. I could literally feel her throat expanding in my hands, every time I shoved my big chocolate cock in her mouth. Head bobbing back and forth. I made her lick, kiss, slurp, spit, and suck like my dick was the cure, and she was dying. I shoved my big dick into her mouth as far as I could, and held it there. I held her head. Then after 10 seconds, I pulled it out. I said, "you may breathe now whore." She gasped so loudly, catching her breath. Her pussy was so wet, as I reached behind her to feel her. Stuck my fingers inside, and brought them to her lips, and mouth, as she then tastes herself off of my big, muscular fingers. "Lay on the bed, and spread that shit open for Daddy." I commanded sharply. I tied her up. I slid in so slowly. I wanted to enjoy every inch. I wanted her to feel every inch of this 9 inches and ¾ length, and 2 inches width of this muscular dick. Her tight wet pussy sucking my dick right in. All and I filled her up, like a nozzle filling up her gas tank on her vehicle. It took all my control to hold back my moan of satisfaction. When she felt my dick enter her, she gasped so loud and her eyes rolled back in the back of her head. The sweet delicious depths of her pussy drove me insane! She was so tight!! Her walls felt like they were closing in on me. I felt her climax building up again, so quickly so fast as though she wanted to release again right away. I forced myself to go deep inside her. The deeper I went, the more she cringed. My big dick was stretching her walls. She was so tight and I was so large, that it had to be uncomfortable, but the deeper I went, the more she moaned. Her moans kept getting louder.

"Shut the fuck up!" I commanded sharply.

She tries to abide by my commands, but I could still hear whimpers, so I took my big strong chocolate man hands and placed them over her mouth. At that moment, her eyes pop open and she stares at me, her eyes wide like an innocent animal about to be slaughtered by a lion. I held her gaze, and kept my hand on her mouth and thrust harder. Bam! Slow and deep. Bam! Again, going harder and harder, holding her gaze with my deadly stare.

"Open your legs wider, don't tighten your pussy. I wanna feel every inch of you. Keep them open and remain silent."

She complies. She would do nearly anything to keep me inside of her. I removed my hands from her mouth. Our gazes still locked, but she remains silent as I keep thrusting into her tight fucking pussy. My fingers trail down her body with a feather like touch, barely grazing her skin. I flutter it down between her thighs and veered down to one upper thigh. In a slow glide my fingers moved over the sensitive part of her inner thigh. I could feel that the sensation was erotic torture and I could tell that her instincts were screaming at her to shut her legs and end the sweet torture. But it was impossible. Her legs were tied up. I had her right where wanted her: A gasping, desperate mess of need. I traced a path down to one knee, and then slowly returned the rough pad of my finger grazing gently, until it was mere inches away from her core. Her legs automatically tried to snap shut as much as they could. Immediately she knew her mistake and opened them to the former position but it was too late. I stopped and remained silent. But I knew that she knew immediately what her punishment was going to be.

"What the fuck did I tell you about your legs?" My voice was calm, but it was ferocious.

Her legs twitched involuntarily and she apologizes.

"I'm sorry Daddy, it wasn't my fault, it was automatic, I was just caught up in the moment, I'm sorry Daddy, please forgive me…" begging again.

I begin to untie her. I start with her wrists, then follow with her legs.

"What are you doing Daddy" she asks, worry seeping out of her face.

"Turn around, put your face down and your ass up facing towards me" I order. She does as she's told. I begin to tie her wrists to her ankles.

"Don't fucking move unless I instruct you otherwise, understood?"

"Yes Daddy."

With her wrists bound to her ankles, I use my fingertips and trace the line all the way down her spine down to her plump ass, and caress it before I slap it viciously. I climb up on the bed and get behind her. Without any warning, I slide my big dick inside her again from behind. A streak of hot pleasure mixed with stinging pain burst inside of her.Gulping back her pride, she held onto her whit's with a tenacious grip.The burn spread into tingles of ecstasy and she pressed her lips together to contain a moan. Her breasts throbbed until even a simple breath amplified the sensations coursing through her body. I began pounding into her flesh. Every time I thrust, my hand would slap each cheek. Harder and harder. Her composure evaporated and a moan escaped. Every single ounce of authority belonged to me. I can tell she is on the verge of begging me to allow her to come. I grab a fist full of her hair and pull her head back towards me. I move my lips close to her ear as I whisper and say:

"Not yet precious, I want you a little bit longer."

She didn't know how I knew what she wanted before having even asked me, but she held it in for me. She was so obedient, so 'precious', I know how hard it was for her to hold back from her release, and her obedience ran through my body with so much pleasure. After several more minutes of hard, fast, long, slow, deep and sensual thrusts, I pull her head back again and whisper in her ear:

"You may cum now", I grind my hips into her ass and with a final gasp of air, her body tenses up and spasms all over my dick for the next twenty five seconds. Her body spent. Violated. Ravaged. Taken. Conquered.

"Thank you Daddy", she whispers, her voice muffled by the pillow. "That was so amazing".

I don't reply right away, I pause for a few minutes but then I speak softly and say:

"You may have had your release, but I'm not through with you yet. It's only the beginning precious."

I was already planning on her next punishment in my head. While she was tied up, I turned her over to position her on her back. Hands still bound to her ankles, this position allows me so much access. My dick is still hard for her.

I place my big strong chocolate hands around her throat, and my grip gets tighter, as it is grounding her to the bed. I slide my big dick inside her very sensitive pussy again. She shudders.

"Now listen bitch, this time the louder you become the harder I will thrust."

I continue to penetrate deep, quick, slow, fast, hard thrusts. I had her bouncing off of me and on me, her tits moving in rhythmic motion up and down, back and forth like a ping pong ball. My grip tightens around her throat, her mouth wide open, her eyes looked as if she was in deeper love than ever before. My hands tighten, sinking my hands into her flesh. I grip her throat harder for more leverage to pound her deeper and more viciously. She was so drenched. I proceeded in destroying her. I didn't give a fuck. Her pussy was appreciating my girth, as her drenched walls begin to close in on my big cock once again. Within seconds she was gushing all over me. I growled at her. Didn't she know she had to ask for my approval? The audacity! The disrespect! My big hands whip across her face with a hard slap. Perhaps she knew, perhaps she just wants punishment? More punishment will come at a later time. I pull my big dick out of her glorious pussy.

"Open your mouth bitch" I order. She does. I straddle her stomach and explode cum shots on her face, her mouth, her breasts and wherever else I could aim. The ones that landed in her mouth, I told her to swallow each drop and to thank me for each one. I climb off of her and untie her arms and legs. She was like a rag doll. Gave her a warm, wet rag. I cleaned myself up as well, before we jumped into the shower. I gave her a bottle of water. She was half asleep, half in another world. I climb back on the bed and take her into my arms and stroke her hair. I cuddle her body.

"Precious, look at the mess you created. There's a large wet spot on the bed sheets." I gently tell her as she starts to doze off in my arms.

"Sorry Daddy", she mumbles into my chest.

"No need to apologize because you're sleeping in it tonight" I laugh.

This wakes her up "What? But…" she gasps.

"But nothing. You need to understand even if you don't respect me, you will respect this dick. Even if you don't worship or pay attention, you will for this hand. Even if you don't listen to me, you will answer to Discipline. You will be appreciative of my Dominance, you will be confident in my authority, completely unburdened by my decisions and trusting in my lead. Got it?"

"Yes Master." She whispers as sleep starts to claim her body once again.

"Good girl."

CHAPTER 17

Dope Dick

Crawl to me. Earn your thick, chocolate dessert. Beg for it. "Please daddy, can I have it? Can I taste it?" She was licking her lips. Salivating at any thought of having my thick, long chocolate cock sliding down her throat. I could see the hunger in her eyes. A hungry submissive, is an obedient submissive. I took it out, but I didn't place it immediately in her mouth. I whipped it across her face, back and forth. I wanted her to feel all that muscle. All that weight. "Obey me" I commanded. "Yes daddy", her eyes shut as she replied with a gasp and spoke softly. I put it in her mouth. Coaching her while she was blessing my girth with her warm pretty mouth. "Just like that, slurp, suck, spit. Open wider, you know daddy is a lot to handle." Amazing how she handled my girth. "Get crazy, go crazy. Devour, show me that beast you hide inside you so well, the beast others don't see. Faster. Open wider." I was going to stretch her jaws out. Give her mouth a workout. I still wasn't pleased. She was taking her time with this shit. Really? All this big chocolate beef cake, and she wants to make love to it with her mouth? Fuck that. I grabbed her by her jaw, yanked her hair back, my big strong hands left her jaw just as my strong fingers whip across her cheek. "Listen bitch. Because you're not listening. Show me why you're my good girl. Show me why you're my slut. Suck me how you would like to be fucked. Suck me like you're dying and my cum is the cure. Love it like a fat kid would love cake. Suck me like you've been starving all day, and you need this delicious thick long chocolate dessert. You want to show me why you're my good girl? Suck it like it's the fourth quarter and you're trying to win a championship. If you can't, you're not getting fucked. You can suck me all night. The choice is yours, now get on it!" I said so sharply, as my hand let's go of her face. She was an animal on my dick. Sucking and multitasking using both hands. One on the shaft, the other on the tip, twisting back and forth as though she was opening up a bottle cap of a drink. Just to think, what a little motivation will do. She has me groaning, moaning, gazing into her eyes. The deep steel in my eyes,

So she wakes up from a wet dream

She's like an addict

Dicking her down quick

Slow deep strokes

Long medium hard strokes

Tearing her apart

Taking my time with her

Telling her don't make a peep

Big dick stroking her until her body gets weak

She's soaking up the sheets

Get on your back I command

Missionary

Legs on my shoulders

I have her legs pinned back

Now legs wrapped around me

But I pin her hands down

Take all of my girth

Flip her over

Now in doggy style

As I take my big strong man hand

and whip it across her cheeks

Left

Right

Left

Right

Each time my hand kisses her flesh

She gasps and gets more wet

One hand on ass cheek

One fistful of hair

Anchoring towards me

Giddy up – commands roaring at her

Multitasking as if I was riding a horse

It hurts I don't give a fuck

You were good this morning but tonight you're my little slut

Now get on your back as I command so sharply

I'm going to make it hurt so good promptly

My big strong hands

Around her fragile throat

Thick dick continues to stroke slow deep strokes

Fast hard stroke

and keep going in that cycle

I'm working her like a shift I want her to earn her gift

Moan cry tear for me

As my big hands leave her throat

Just to slap her pretty little face

Hand back on throat

The tighter the grip the more she lets go

The tighter my grip her eyes go back

The tighter my grip her walls begin to close in

The harder I thrust the more she wants to explode

I can see it in her eyes hear it in her breathing

Ask me as I command abruptly ask me now

As I roar at her

She asks

Daddy May i???

You've been a good girl, you've earned it you may

There she goes she gushes all over me

Her submission is her strength my control becomes her release

Release like an eruption of a volcano

Busted like a fire hydrant

Drenched like Niagara Falls

Dope dick she's an addict a fiend

I ruined her

Her narrative

Sitting there at work

Begging me for your next fix

Drenched from the thought of it

Dope dick you will love me

But he will fuck you savagely

You're going to think I hate your pussy

Dope dick

Fuck you crazy

Make you sore make you cum

Make your body convulse

Make it hurt make it squirt

Thrust so hard you don't realize where you are

You don't realize who you are in the moment

You forget your name, but scream mine

Fuck you so hard you feel it in your dreams

Dope dick is like chocolate

Once you get a taste of it you get addicted

All this big, long, thick chocolate muscle inside you is going to change your body mind and soul forever. You will do things. Say things. You've never said. Never done.

Dope dick and in control

Your mind will crave my words

Your soul will require my strength

and your body will become use to me

and when it comes to anyone else

I will ruin any possibilities

I give you a gift and a curse.

Dope Dick will leave you convulsing. Pounded into a dripping mess. It will leave you drenched. You will replay the moments I gave you the next day in your head. and when you're at work, soaked, you will realized how I have invaded your every thought. You will think I've placed a spell on you. Every second. Minutes. Hour. Days. We spend apart your body will ache. Your mind will race. Your soul will ignite will flames. and you will suffer until you receive your medicine of Discipline once again.

CHAPTER 18

The Dangerous Kiss

"Dope souls need Dope souls." Until a woman, or a man finds themselves, they will ruin everyone they encounter. Or they will just not be ready. God gave us two ears, and one mouth for a reason. Listen, and pay attention more than you speak. Know when to speak, and when not to. Listen to a woman, and hear the things she doesn't say. Doesn't it feel amazing to be touched by a person who fully understands your mind? A person who acknowledges your flaws, and loves your soul anyways? When there is a deep and genuine connection, you will witness her doing things for you, she will not for another man. This generation is sex crazy, and think making love is crazy. He or she is drawn to you in a way that opens his or her heart in absolute vulnerability. Commingled with you in heart, body, spirit. They realize they have nothing to fear. Their flaws, insecurities and secrets are safe with you. They let down their guards. Let down their effort. Surrender in love with you for real without restrictions. It's like when you kiss....Kissing and sexual energy are linked. Erotic kissing involves the lips and tongue. That is part of love play. When couples kiss with their tongues, also known as French kissing or soul kissing. The tongue reflects and connects their hearts. While their lips give and receive affection between each other. I appreciate sexy lips. Kissing deeply is an exchange of energy. It is emotional. Sexual chemistry is powerful. Sometimes when you are angry with your partner, you may have rough sex to ease the frustration, and once you release you both think you're making up. But, I bet you're not kissing, and even if you are, it's not sensual. You aren't connecting. It's just all the anger has gotten you riled up, and you're disposing that off. That tension. It's not like you're making up, because I promise it will be a reoccurrence of the same shit you were arguing about. It's like a pattern. Patterns turn into habits. Now these habits turn into behaviors. Kissing her while you're inside her is a different level of intimacy. She is more than the pleasure. It is a ritual, where you exchange energy, emotions, thoughts, consciousness. That's why when you see women speaking or behaving a certain way, you can tell who she fucks with, or has fucked with. When you're both engaged in sex, you are one. It's important that your vibes resonate. Each pump and thrust is an affirmation. When a man enters your pussy, what type of vibe and energy is he giving? Is he happy or bitter? Is he a positive thinker? Does he love himself or love you? When a woman makes love to you, is she happy? Is she positive? Does she love herself, and you? She has trust issues? Is she blessing you? Is he cursing you? Is your partner refueling, healing and recharging your soul, or draining the life out of you? Are they dragging you down to low frequency energy, negativity, un-fulfillment, depression? Or are they elevating you? Empowering you? Into the high frequency of love, life and happiness, King, Queen, God, Goddess, immortality? I say sex is powerful all the time. You need to be mindful. Master how your energy is exchanged, received and returned back to you. Temporary forevers. Pleasures are temporary. But the side effects can last forever. Sex is a therapeutic medicine when done right. When two musical instruments do not resonate to each other's beat, the music is awful, really awful. And so is the sex. Engage in more cuddling. Love. Talking and conversing with one another before, during and after sex. Hugging. Holding hands. These things help with each other being able to orgasm. And when you orgasm, the body and mind starts the emotional well being. It's imperative to maintain a healthy well being for emotional strength in today's stressed and negative world. By you choosing who you have sex with, your building a bond to what is conductive to you, and what you desire. That bond becomes stronger through a creation of respect, love. That opens doors to intimacy, trust and loyalty. Respect and loyalty are not upgrades in relationships. They are requirements. Do I just fuck anyone? No, not only is my sex amazing, but I know what energy you're bringing into my life, and what I'm bringing into yours. It's imperative I know you, that's the only way I'll know how to work you. Physically, emotionally and psychologically. I always speak of the power exchange relationship, with Dom/sub, and a woman is the most powerful creature on this earth. Dominance is the most prestigious thing on this earth. Similar souls attract, inevitably. I enjoy kissing very much and because I enjoy it, I'm very good at it. Especially if you have nice lips, full lips. Kissing is the number one form of intimacy. You can make a woman cum from just kissing. A kiss is worth a thousand words. But to be honest, my kiss is very dangerous. It's the type of kiss where you grab her rough so she feels your intensity, your desire for her. Inhaling her face. Holding her head by her hair. Holding her throat with my big strong hands. Taking control of the kiss. Grabbing her ass so firmly her lips spread. Kissing while we are in missionary. Grabbing her breasts. I'm very affectionate and touchy, but I don't like being touched. I like to proactively engage in kissing. My kiss is very dangerous. It's tender. It's rough. It's aggressive. It's addictive. Powerful. I don't just kiss, I claim. I don't just taste, I fucking devour. It's like a magical spell from my lips. It's a curse and a gift. I'll kiss you like I want to write sweet poetry on your soul. I'll kiss you and bite you like I want to savagely tattoo my mark on your body. Your bottom lip belongs to me. I bite so hard. Pull it towards me. I bite to make it hurt. I thrive off your pain. I'll kiss you til you forget how to count. Even forget your name. I'll kiss you silent while you're upside down. Kiss you and make you turn your head to the side. Kiss you and make you forget where you are. Kiss you while my tongue dances and wrestles with your tongue. Kiss you and make everything else non-existent. I will leave my mark on your body. On your soul. Make fire where our bodies meet. Let's burn calories. I'll kiss you like I'm kissing your mind, and allow your thoughts to squirt everywhere. Kiss your lips so well, your other lips speak. Kiss you like the moonbeam kisses the sea. I told you my kiss is dangerous. I'll kiss you so thoroughly that you forget to breathe. Yes! Fucking forget to breathe, because the next breath you take fucking belongs to me

The slower the kiss, the faster the heartbeat. I mark my territory. I do not take, I Dominate. I taught her of Dominance, darkness, aggression, savagery, science, conversation, psychology, Discipline, the universe, sex, sports, logic, music, dancing. She taught me about history, passion, biology, Netflix, smart phone emoji's, tenderness, kindness and love. We could converse 'til the sun comes up, I could kiss her for hours, her lips are the greatest sin, taste so sweet like butter pecan. You can tell a lot about a kiss. It is the most intimate aside from eye contact and dancing. You can tell how someone engages in bed by the way they kiss. Whether it is rough or by pushing you up against the wall or slowly kissing you while stroking her hair. Grasping her throat, biting her bottom lip, tongue wrestling. When it comes to me, I only kiss one way and that's hard. "I am your guilty pleasure, but favorite sin. I am more than just breathing to you, I am intoxicating. I am your insane. This mixture of pleasure chocolate and pain, as potent as cocaine. I am your drug that even if you were to walk away, the urge for me would keep pulling you back. Your mind, body and soul react to me in ways you cannot control, because I control it. This escapism, this place that only makes sense to you. This freedom you have to articulate yourself, to be how society does not see you. To become lost in me for minutes before you come back to reality. Many couples do not do this enough and when I say enough, I am referring to kissing. I am the best kisser in the world with a mixture of technique, passion and intensity that can never be matched. A taste of vodka, pineapples, danger and chocolate candy. A woman can orgasm through my kiss alone. One look, one touch and she will give all her love. The chemicals dripping from her brain, panties soaked, she is ready. Eyes in deeper love than ever before. She is willing and ready to do anything, give everything.

My kisses are dangerous.

One touch from me, I leave you weak.

A kiss from me, your soul will love me.

Kiss where I want to explore the depths of your mouth.

As my tongue is in complete Domination.

As I bite your bottom lip.

I want you to feel my passion.

Kisses like this, sometimes I want it to hurt.

I want it to hurt, because I thrive off your pain.

The passion is so intense for me, that I need to release some of my pain onto you so you can understand, where I'm coming from.

Kiss so intense.

It makes your panties wet.

The type of kiss you say come here and shut up.

Grab her by her hair, as you place your hand around her throat or grab her hair. A kiss will determine how good you are in bed.

It is all about the passion in the kiss.

My kisses are dangerous.

One touch from me, I leave you weak.

A kiss from me and your soul will love me.

A kiss like this would make you want to give me everything and do anything for me. A kiss like this makes someone like me not do anything with my hands. Grabbing her ass so hard, her pussy lips have no other choice but to spread. Hand on neck, breast, and hair. Kiss so dangerous, I have you doing things you've wanted, have you doing things you have never done. Rough, aggressive, addictive. It is like a magical spell I am placing upon you.

Kiss you silent.

Leave you speechless.

A kiss so dangerous, you are willing to sign a pact with the devil.

Kiss you and leave my mark on your body.

Your mind, your soul.

Creating heat where our bodies meet.

Kiss your lips so well your other lips speak.

Kiss you as I take your breath away.

As you forget to breathe.

Because your next breath you take belongs to me.

Let us kiss and burn some calories as we create heat

Kiss you while you stare into my eyes.

Kiss you as our eyes are shut.

Kiss you allowing our souls to touch.

Kiss you like I had my big fucking dick inside of you.

The oxytocin, dopamine and serotonin dripping from your brain. Making your soul feel good, touching your heart. Now you need my kisses and without them, you go through withdrawal. You need them to fulfil every ache in your entire body. You need my kisses to calm you. To lower your depression, break your stress. Now look down at you panties... you made a big mess....

CHAPTER 19

Alpha Female / Dominant Woman

It never mattered if a woman made more money than me. It never mattered if she thought she was more Dominant than I was. Didn't matter if she thought she was more powerful than I was, or more intelligent. She was a woman at the end of the day, and it never made me feel like any less of a man. An alpha woman has no shame paying for a man. Has no shame bowing to a man. She actually feels empowered. Whether you go out to dinner, and she didn't mind picking up the check, or spoiling you with gifts. The biggest misconception of a relationship is, the man is required to do most of the spoiling. She may be a Queen, but I'm a King. She may look beautiful, but I look good as well. I am 25% ALPHA, 25% beast, 50% man, that's 100% KING. Everything in this world is about balance, Discipline and control. Without order there is chaos. Without structure, there is instability. I am a man that has the capability to handle any type of woman. I'm not talking shit either. Race doesn't matter. Idiosyncrasies do not matter. Even attitude whatever. All sizes as well. I have this intuitive capability to bring out the best in people. It does not mean I care to. Even when I'm not trying, it happens. Like I've said before, I motivate in all type of ways. Whether it is hate, love, envy, etc. Now back to the situation at hand. Two DOMINANTS will never work, as two submissives will never work. There is no balance. Someone has to relinquish control. Myself, I Dominate in all things. I exercise control in all aspects of my life. A woman that desires to be the man in the relationship would never get along with me and vice versa. I am not for everybody, but I can handle any woman. Shy, laid back, private girls, and women gravitate towards me more than I do them. Good girls love me because there is that balance I was talking about. Yin to Yang. No balance is like having the kush without the blunt. When it comes to "trust" and "loyalty", I don't just have those words tattooed on me. I value them significantly. I am adamant about it. I do not crave it, I do not desire it. I fucking demand it. It is a requirement. I don't just love being in control or a Dominant. This is not something that is cool. It is who and what I am. I can not hide it. I cannot transition in becoming a submissive. I'm not a switch. This is how I was born. I do not mind an ALPHA sub. She can be Dominant in her life and even have the ability to Dominate other people. But when she is in my presence, she is a submissive kitten.

That is not up for debate or negotiation. I do not believe women were born to be Dominant. Some had no choice but to be, because of men or circumstances. But, they won't be Dominant forever. They grow tired. They are nurturing and emotional creatures. When a Dominant force meets an immovable force, the Dominant force yields. It is inevitable. A Queen does not see shame in bowing to her KING. Allow me to explain it this way….The lioness is not submissive. She allows the lion to be king for as long as it pleases her, but she challenges him once in awhile. The lion does one of two things: slaps her back down to reality, and demonstrates to her, it has balls, and balls is what commands, or he backs down and bends over for her. Most submissive girls and women are shy. Not all of them, but most of them. They do not like being in control. They have a difficult time making decisions. They are laid back and quiet. They are reserved. You are not going to see them plastering themselves on social media. They think twice, three maybe four times before they make any decision. They are not very loud when they speak. They show you very little of themselves, physically, emotionally until they open up to you. Until you eradicate those walls and guards, they work so hard to keep up. Now an alpha submissive is the opposite. They're more confident. Bold. Assertive. Even if she is not a boss in her work or life. Her mannerisms show it. Most alpha subs are alone or in relationships that bore them. The reason is they find it difficult for a man to feed them. To find one that is stronger than them emotionally, physically, and mentally. A sub is just a stronger individual, seeking a stronger individual. But can you blame a man? Yes, a smart, strong submissive is a prize to a Dominant. However, it is a turn off when you are constantly trying to one up on him. Whether it is beating him in an intellectual conversation, argument or a board game. Calling him weak is just an excuse for your poor behavior. If you want to be a woman or treated like one, you must act like one, and allow him to be the King. To be the man. However, a true Dominant man is not going to Dominate you either, just because you are begging him, "please Dominate me." He has to want to engage as well. Dominant men, if you are begging or asking a sub to submit to you, or be yours then you lost. Lost power. You are the submissive. Subs, they tend to have the most innocent faces. But they don't fool me. A sexual submissive have the most artistic minds when it pertains to sex. What you people would call "freakiest" or "undercover nasty." They do not like to make eye contact so much. If you stared at them too long they get anxiety. "Omg, why is he looking at me, do I have something on my face, what is it? How do I look?" The list goes on. Shy females will always gravitate to bad boys or alpha men. Why? Because, they are the most confident, the adventurous and shy females crave to be like that. If you go through power struggles everyday, trouble letting go. Letting go of pride. Letting go what it is for yourself and please,then this isn't for you. You need to reevaluate yourself, and what it is you are actually looking for, because most of you women just want to be Dominated sexually. The women who are happiest in this life, have let go a long time ago. Maybe this life looks attractive, fun, intriguing, enticing, adventurous, phenomenal, a phenomenon, once in a life experience. However, so is a jet, it doesn't mean you can get on or afford one.

Why is it that MEN desire to Dominant women? Is it because they are weak? No... It is because they are so powerful and beautiful.

The true strength of Man in NOT measured by Dominating the weak. But by possessing, subduing, controlling and conquering that which is powerful. This is the true nature of man. This is what it means to be a Dominant.

An alpha woman is a bold, confident, assertive woman. She is assertive in her life, and even if she is not an authoritative figure in her life, she still has that assertive behavior in her.

She has the ability to Dominate males and females. Verbally, psychologically, or physically.

She is a prize. Most submissive women are shy, they are people pleasers

They love to please and make sure everyone is happy

and is happy with them. An alpha woman is a woman for a reason

They do not run in packs. They do not care about making people happy.

She stands alone if she needs to. This is what makes them special.

When you do break those walls down, make her 100 percent yours.

What's so special for a Dom is no other man has ever experienced this.

When you get an alpha sub to be yours,

she is only going to be submissive to you. She can be mean to everyone else, but supple to you. Like a female lion,

she allows the King to be King as long as she is happy.

Being hard to handle is like a challenge for a Dom.

Most alpha women like the challenge.

She may be able to Dominate men and women, and she has eaten men alive. She has walked over every man she can possibly ever encounter, until she meets Discipline. Not just me, but the act. Without structure there is instability. Everything in this world is about order, control, balance. A queen doesn't see shame in bowing to her king

and this goes back to lioness. She is not a sub but if it makes her happy, she allows it, etc. He establishes his position, and puts her back in her place. She is the epitome of submission. This is why she is the prize.

Because, if you have a strong alpha sub at your feet, you know you have won. Most alpha subs love a physically Dominant man. Because they feel a Dom has the ability to physically correct her, and put her in her place.

She is looking for a man to put her in her place. She is the apex predator. On top of the food chain. A leader amongst her peers

She is perhaps an authoritative figure in her life, her job

If she does not meet someone who is on her level or above, she will not be tamed. My masculinity will allow you to be feminine. My control will allow you to release. A man who is comfortable in being assertive.

A man who is comfortable in life, will have the power to allow her to just be her. I am mentally, emotionally and physically Dominant.

I will transform her, a transformation only I get the luxury to witness.

She was bold, confident, challenging, difficult and complicated.

She had the ability to Dominate men and women verbally, psychologically and physically. If you are not strong enough to handle her, emotionally, she will eat you alive. Like a lioness eating zebra. She walked all over every man she ever met. Every man until she met me. "I will humble you. That's non negotiable. The beast in me will feast in the entirety of you. Your pride, your stubbornness, attitude, your pretentious behavior. Get on your knees." Perhaps she has never knelt for a man before. Let alone crawled. I don't give a fuck, for me she will. For me she fucking would. I gazed into her eyes with my dark stare, I didn't even blink. I spoke softly, but forcefully. I grabbed a fist full of her hair. Just to anchor her towards me. I said, "bitch, do you think I'm fucking playing around with you?"

Are you deaf? I said, "on your knees"

She knelt immediately

"I am going to show you why I'm a man and you're a woman."

"The asshole in me will feast on the bitch in you."

She stares at me flatly, completely confused.

She said "excuse me."

"I didn't stutter."

She knelt right away

"Good girl."

"Beg me to give you this greatness."

"Beg me to give you something you have never had."

"The best you've always wanted."

"Beg me to give you something you have never felt."

"You want to be my slut?

"Don't you?"

She nodded yes

Then I said, "ask nicely, then fucking beg."

I was going to reward, I just wanted to see the length she would go.

I wanted to witness her passion, her dedication, her hard work.

I knew she had it in her,

I mean after all, she hasn't gotten to where she is by not displaying Dedication, passion or hard work.

I wanted to see if she wanted to earn it.

She gave me some of the cutest puppy dog eyes.

She stared at me squarely and begged me.

"Can I be your whore Mr. Discipline?"

"Can I be your good girl?"

"Can I be your bad, dirty, naughty little girl?"

"Please, pretty please"

She made me chuckle

Oh she was creative

She even added pretty please

I said "yes you can be my good, bad, dirty naughty little girl."

"But, now you are going to show me why you will be."

"I said after you take 20 spankings, and if you chose to use your safe word, we will stop and you will not earn anything."

I grabbed her by the hair and bent her over the bed

I took out my belt. The belt kisses her flesh one spank, 2, she counts one after the other followed by the spankings I delivered. Her face cringed

I spanked her ass, then thighs viciously as the belt claims every inch of her. I can only imagine what's going on in her head,

will he stop, would he have compassion?

Would he go too far?

Harder?

Faster?

Would I break?

How strong am I?

No matter her thoughts

She took it all

No safe word

No plea for stop

No tears ran down her cheeks?

I cuddled her face gently

Then I gave her everything she wanted, craved, yearned for

After all she deserved it

She fucking earned it

I cuddled her gently, I held her firmly and I whispered in her ear

You were definitely made for Me

You are Mine.

CHAPTER 20

Certain Beauty

There is more to pleasing a man than what is between your legs. I am a man that likes exclusivity. Nothing is more attractive than loyalty. Loyalty is everything to me. I do not desire this, crave this, ask for this, wait for this, or beg for this. I fucking demand this. I deserve this. I'm going to mention many different things right now and it is going to blow people's minds, anyway I'm going in....When I am emotionally invested, you can obtain all of me. Betray me, I turn my feelings off quickly. You could walk past me, and I would act like I don't even know you. That is the Scorpio in me. Once the chemistry is gone, the history does not matter. If I had an enemy, that's automatically your enemy. First, I am not friends with exes. I think that's fucking weird. Second, (jumping to another subject) if a person that I am not fond of is aware you associate yourself with me, they should not feel comfortable talking to you about anything. Especially anything pertaining to me. Unless you do business, then it's different. Business can be kept as business and personal can be kept as personal. My thing is, if I have someone I'm cool with, fuck with, am associated with, whatever it is, and they have an enemy... if that enemy thinks they can talk about the one I'm cool with to me, I might slap them. If not physically, then verbally and mentally. There is no way they should feel comfortable talking to me or anything pertaining to the person they are not associated with, but I am associated with or care about. Sometimes people love you because of the way many other people love you. Sometimes people hate you because of the fact that other people love you. Sometimes people gravitate to you because of the fact that many others gravitate to you. Women ask me all the time, "How can I be more submissive? Men ask, "How can I be more Dominant?" First, BDSM is not just bedroom play for me. Second, how you are outside of bed is how much he will give you in it. If you are talking or meeting for the first time. Do not resemble a whore. You may hint you want to work hard to be his whore, but do not resemble a whore. Where a man will pursue, only to lose interest in quickly. It's fine if you have an enormous sexual appetite or libido, but leave a little mystery. Be open. Communicate efficiently, do not string him along, play games or keep him on the back burner if you are not ready. Be honest, but expect him to be doing his thing. The older you get, you will witness the harder it becomes. You can't be upset about that. For me, I demand things from the get. I am rarely disappointed, because I know what to expect. I demand what I want, and I want what I demand. Therefore, Daddy always gets what he wants. I am not going to wait for you to communicate. That is your job. I am not asking for you to be open. I fucking demand it. I am not training honesty, dedication, commitment, etc, that's stupid. If you cannot provide these things, step aside, I'm sure someone will love to take your place. A woman that knows her place and has mastered it, never loses her position. I do not play, okay well only in bed sometimes, but you get my drift. The problem with this generation of men and women in relationships (especially women, where in this country has become a crazed, man-hating revolution) is, they are both playing games with each other. For you not being fulfilled in your relationship is entirely your fault. It is not his, it is not hers. You want a change? Fucking do something about it. Back to the situation at hand. For men, how can they be more Dominant? How you treat her outside of bed is how much she will give you inside of it. Share a little. Be straight up. The one who is more honest in the relationship or a potential relationship, has more control. It displays strength, and she will naturally follow your lead and gravitate to that easily. Does loyalty ruin marriages, relationships, friendships? Of course it does. Can you buy loyalty? No. Because even if a man is paying all your bills, you will still cheat and perhaps you're like, "I would if I wasn't in a relationship with him." You are not loyal. You have already cheated. That statement alone betrays your mindset. If you are married or have a relationship and you think of another man or woman at night, or when you fuck him, or her, and you imagine another, in your dreams even, you have cheated.

You are not loyal. If I walked into the gym and your weak boyfriend was doing a set, and you start fucking me with your eyes, because you're so in love with my tattoos, you are dangerous, and you just cheated on your boyfriend. Yes, in my opinion, you are cheating. I'm not calling you a cheater, I'm just calling the act. Loyalty is a delicate situation. It is fragile. As many want it, preach it, but it is difficult to maintain it, keep, provide isn't it? Reality is, we are flesh. Human beings. We are all on this earth for selfish reasons. We are with another being for selfish reasons. But, can you provide things that aren't so mundane? Superficial? Cheating is not just physical. Or mental. Affairs do not start in the bedroom, they start via conversation. Your body language, your soul betrays you as well. Money cannot buy love, submission, honesty, adherence, or hard work. You flirting, you're not loyal. You are too friendly with people who aren't in your circle, you're not loyal. I can go on and on. Many people think and have different definitions for loyalty. For example, if a woman just gives her body to a man. Take into account, she is only giving her body, and she feels he should be loyal to her. Remain loyal to her. Perhaps a man feels the same way. Yeah, this is how most vanilla (ordinary), not all, but most vanilla (ordinary) people think in my opinion. Why should they be loyal to each other if that is all they provide to one another? All of these are rhetorical questions. Sometimes you need to understand, people will use you for as long as you are giving them things. Squeeze you to get enough juice out of you. Ride you 'til the wheels fall off. People will stay with you for as long as you are giving them things, or how they can benefit from you. Because we are aware of this, it causes people to give less and less. Your relationship is not genuine, (I'm sorry to tell you this, well I'm lying, I'm not sorry to tell you this, you need to hear this. Matter fact, you need to read this) whether it is love, marriage, friendship, family, etc. Now let's talk about OWNERSHIP...You notice the chokers that the women have been crazed about and wearing this year (2017) alone? I do not view it as chokers, and women think I'm weird because they do not get it. They view it as 'cute', following of another, it goes with their attire blah, blah, blah. Me, I view it as 'owned.' Like a BDSM collar. Why? Because, it is a reminder of submission, because the neck is a very sensitive part of the human body, especially when groped. It is a reminder of place by uncomfortable sensation. Which brings me to my next point, where another portion of women love them because they love being choked, and that is like their sensation for that, which is to be around their neck. A collar can mean so many different things to so many different people, and it doesn't even need to be a collar either. That has proven to me that anyone can be into BDSM and you would never know. It could very much be the plainest person you know, because they would be the ones to have most to hide. Collar to me is like a wedding ring. Ownership. Complete submission. Loyalty. She is transitioning from a sub to a Queen or a Slave. You may have seen me use my collar in some photo shoots on my social media, but that's acting. If I ever give a woman my collar, she is to wear it twenty-four-seven. I will use the analogy of the dog. I hate cats. I'm a dog lover. Why? Dogs are more loving, more of protectors. Even if you have a dog who seems like a scaredy-cat, it's bark perhaps is so ferocious, it scares you. Cats are unpredictable and rub themselves on anybody. But when shit hits the fan and you need them, where are they? A dog will always let you know if a person has a good heart. Their sense of smell, their vision, and their other senses, they utilize so they are aware of this, and dogs trust their own instincts. One of the reasons why I love dogs and you don't need to believe me or agree with me, but them "boys" sometimes use dogs to sniff out narcotics. By "boys", y'all know who I'm referring to, I'm not going to write it on here. But the point I'm trying to make is, loyalty is everything to me. Submission is the same thing. Not half, not maybe. Nor uncertainty. Every-fucking-thing. Do you under-fucking-stand me? That's a rhetorical question. Vanilla (ordinary) people may view it as one thing. I view it as many different things. Above I have written of how friendly the pussy cat may appear. I do not take pride in Dominating the weak, yet friendly women. I take pride in Dominating what is strong. I am not fond of submissive women, I am fond of women who are submissive to me. There's a huge difference. If she is Dominant she can be loved. Alpha, she can be loved. Just because she is submissive, does not mean she is for me, or I want her. Just because she is an alpha, or think of herself as a Queen does not mean I want her. Doesn't mean she is a Queen either. Most submissive women are giving. People pleasers, hate going against the grain. Does what society tells them. But I have never loved a friendly woman. Ever! It's the little things that make a huge different and you won't even know, but i know. I watch the little things, maybe I don't mention it, but I keep mental documentations. I could never trust someone who is concerned with what people think about them, or a person who everyone likes. However, I can reform you. Help you build that courage, strength and confidence. It is impossible for everyone to like you. That means you play both sides of the fence. How are you trustworthy? Like I've said in a previous post, if you do not behave as your Dom's sub in public, outside of it, to his face, behind his back, you are not owned, you are not a sub, you are just pretending and quite frankly, do not deserve to have one. You do not deserve to be granted the most prestigious aspect in the world, which is Dominance as well. If a man feels you cannot trust him, you will never gain his love or respect. If a woman does not respect you, she will never trust you. No respect, equates to no obedience, no obedience, equates to no submission. No submission, equates to no loyalty. No loyalty, equates to no attraction. No attraction, means no relationship. Well, at least not a real one. So when it comes to your loyalty, I do not ask, crave, wish, hope for, beg, manipulate, trick, threat, or coerce for your Dedication. Devotion, Commitment, Hard Work, your Discipline, I fucking…demand it. If you are unwilling to give all of you, I promise I will gladly take nothing of you.

Twerking is attractive. As a man I can't lie, however it will get old and boring quickly. Dudes are funny nowadays. "If she has a hard time putting on jeans, wife her, if she rolls a blunt, wife her, if she can do a cartwheel, if she has that "good good", wife her." Really? Those are the only requirements? Most of you men are pussy whipped and the women do minimum to keep y'all and get your interest. Do not allow the fear of being inadequate inhibit you. A woman that can crawl has the potential to fly. You women will hate me for this, but honestly most women (not all) are followers. Especially of the social trends. People always say, "don't judge me on my social media, it's not my life." What is that reverse psychology? People are going to do just that. Judge you. What you post, what you say, and what you write. Some will post pics of their ass, using that reverse psychology, "don't look at my ass!" Half naked pictures like, "why are all these men in my dm, or thirsty?" If you are a model or fitness trainer, then cool. Other than that, why are y'all naked? If all you have to bring to the table is your body, don't even sit down to eat. After he fucks you, where is your worth? That is all you will be. This is why good girls are not getting fucked. They are in bad relationships. Wasting their life and engaging in relations that is not conducive to what they truly believe. They are single and the trash bags are getting wifed. This generation is backwards. The women that really put in work, aren't even appreciated. These twerk-ers, these banana or cucumber deep throat-ers, these trash bags are being glorified more than the real women. Like where are the real women? I know I'm young, but where are the women that were like back in the 50's? Where they catered, cooked, cleaned and knew their place? Self proclaimed queens? Listen up, a king crowns you at the end of the day. Y'all are not men, y'all are not animals, savages. More like savage cry babies. Y'all are not trash. Y'all are ladies, so behave as such. These women lack Discipline in their lives.(not me, but the act, the training). Just because you are independent or make your own money, does not make you a boss. Bosses, kings and Queens always lead by example. Always set the tone.

Submission is to be of use, not used. To give, not worry about what is being given to you. This is the true essence of submission. A man simply needs a woman or women that is truly his, who is at his feet, anything less is not his fulfillment. Weak men will never be able to understand this. Weak women will never be able to grasp this concept. A sub is free to do and be whatever she chooses. Whether she chooses to be your princess, your whore, your slut, your bitch, your good girl, and/or your baby girl. When she chooses to kneel willingly, this is what makes submission so beautiful. The purest level of submission is without bounds, without shackles. There is a certain beauty in obedience, nothing is more attractive than loyalty. When I am emotionally invested, you can obtain all of me. You want to be more submissive, you need to be more of a cheerleader for him. Encourage him. Don't break him down. Show that you trust in his decisions. Women only respect men that can Dominate them and men only respect women that trust them. So in order for him to Dominate you, you need to give him that respect and trust. A lot of men do not deserve your respect, they talk a lot and do little. Like many women do anyways. You do not have to respect any man that is not worthy of your respect outside of dating or a relationship. But when it comes to dating or having a relationship with a man, respecting a man matters. For the health of the relationship between you both. If you don't start off respecting a man in any way at all, he can not trust you and the foundation of your connection falls to pieces. He can not be the man you want him to be in a relationship because, you do not even believe in him. You are not giving him the gift and if you do not believe in him, he won't trust you or commit to you fully. He is going to doubt you, if you are criticizing him and if you are pointing out everything you think is a flaw. If you can not let him take you places and make decisions, he will automatically feel emasculated and he will not commit to you fully. If you do not respect a man, your eyes show it. Your body shows it, the words that come out of your mouth show it. So he feels it, and if he feels that you do not trust him, that is a sign to him that you don't see him as a valuable, respectable man. Then as a woman, you will complain, why you are not being fulfilled and you will never know why. I'm going to be frank, many women suck in relationships, no pun intended, but then again, plenty of men have no idea how to lead. Women are followers, its true, they hate going against the grain. Be honest with the type of man you want, that will cultivate your lifestyle and who you are as a woman. Give him the benefit of the doubt and when you do this, many men will step up to that plate and be that strong, powerful man for you. Earning your respect, in any long term relationship. Most alpha Dominant women, hell, most women that have been broken, they normally say, "if you can't handle me at my worse, you don't deserve me at my best." Or "you're weak, because you can't handle a strong woman." I am a man not a boy. For you women that say this, this does not make you strong, this does not make you appear strong, and you just think you are. Friends brainwashed you, you don't even behave as a strong woman, because strong women do not speak like this. You can not just call him weak and emasculate him, then expect him to be the man you want him to be. This is why it is crucial for you to not just go for any man who seems willing and available to have a relationship with you. You are hurting the both of you. Some women will be submissive to an extent outside of the bedroom because they want that reward. They manipulate, they scheme, they behave until they get what they want. Perhaps you are only able to control them with your dick. That sounds easy right? What happens when you're not giving her that good dick? A day or two maybe, possibly a week. I mean that lion remains your friend when you keep feeding it right? What happens when that lion isn't being fed? A hungry girl is an obedient girl. My question is, does your lady remain loyal in every aspect in her life for you, to you? Does she behave in a bratty fashion to get you to put her in her place? To receive immense pleasure? For the time being, you have lost her respect because she is not being fed. What you are teaching her? To fiend for dick. That sounds like a reward for misbehavior to me. If you want her to be your psychological sub, you must train her also. If she is constantly going through power struggles, brat tendencies, nitpicking, belittling you, making it seem like you answer to her, challenging you, always checking up, she needs to reevaluate what she truly wants in life and this relationship.

Communication is crucial. Perhaps she wants a submissive man who is Dominant in bed. You both need to discuss that. Therefore there will be no confusion moving forward. When you establish a strong dynamic, you will always keep a strong dynamic. If there are rules on the table, you abide by those rules. If you have both negotiated on certain conditions, then respect them. Everything should run smoothly. Only the submissive shows others what type of Dominant owns her. If a submissive does not behave as her Dominant's submissive, her Master's slave, her Daddy's little one, her Daddy Doms baby girl, her Top's bottom bitch, her King's Queen, at all times to his face or behind his back, she is just pretending, and she does not deserve to have that type of greatness in her life. Nor does she deserve to have the gift of Dominance which is the most prestigious gift on this earth.

Submission is difficult. It makes you the one that must let go. Submission, I mean complete submission, is beyond the body. What I want with my submissives is complete submission. Just because you have a desire to serve or please, does not make you mine. Submission is strength. It is not for the weak. It takes strength to stand alone. To give control to another. Courage to kneel for the one you trust. It takes honesty to open up, trust to allow someone access inside your mind. Body. Soul. Your secrets. Your doubts. Your fears. Your dreams. Your pains. Your pleasures. Your insecurities. Your imperfections. To be comfortable to communicate efficiently.

Articulate your emotions and desires. It's hard work, but once you let go and are accepted by the one you trust, love, yearn to please, it's invigorating. It is a heavy weight off of your shoulders. Nothing eases a woman's mind more than a man who is comfortable in being assertive. A man who can take charge without hesitation. A submissive requires more than the average girl or woman. More structure. Rules. Security. Focus. It's a lot to take on, but then again a woman give a lot. Once you are able to open all these hidden door within her, you have unlocked a door forever, where only you possess the key. Her wants become her need. Her breathing changes when I place my big strong chocolate man hand on her body. There is nothing more intimate than OWNERSHIP. It's intense, invigorating when one gives themselves to you. Or owns you. Everything feels massive. Physical gifts and objects are mundane but memories are a lifetime. Each sexual experience is not just craved. Each conversation is not just to converse. But is needed so badly that sometimes the body aches in anticipation. Each word either cuts deep or soothes your soul. I am extremely intense and passionate. I can manage different set of tasks efficiently. I love hard. I Discipline hard. I punish hard. I fuck hard. However, it is not always the biggest, flashiest that speak loudest in this lifestyle. When they come consistently and effortlessly, it is the little things that make a huge difference. It's moments where not just her actions or voice screams, "I submit", but whispers of warmth and softness that carries past your eyes and melts directly into your hard, cold soul. Times of hard work. Dedication. Devotion. Loyalty. Trust. Openness. Honesty. I have left my mark on you. I have left such an imprint on your heart, that anyone you attempt to entertain after me, will have to know me, to understand you. Once I've had you, I can always have you. The beauty in submission. Power given. Power is attractive. To own is precious. Her eyes have her own vocabulary. Her mind is quiet when you are around. Her begging pussy is wet as soon as you place a hand on her. Trust, it is very expensive. Money can't purchase this. When you have it from another, you can take them anywhere. Witness how the alteration of her mind, soul and body. The places it has never been will be breathtaking for you both.

Compliance

Obedience

Subservience

There is nothing more attractive to me than when a woman can listen

Seek direction

Execute with excellence and exceeds expectations

Most men love what a woman can do with their body

The beauty of her body is merely a bonus

But me I am not most men

There is nothing more attractive to me than what a woman can do with her mind

There are many different types of subs

But for the psychological sub her submission starts in her mental

The true beauty of a submissive does not come from the beauty of the body

But the beauty of the mind

Submission is not about pain, it is not about weak

It is about strength

Training your mind then your body to surrender to a Dominant that wants to meet your needs

A woman that can crawl has potential to fly

Submission is a will not an act. An emotion.

With no ulterior motive

Not doing to benefit

But if she were to receive something that would be a bonus

This is the beauty of submission

and how can a man not cherish or love a woman who is willing to worship the ground he walks on, who is patient, yearns to wait on him hand and foot, who is selfless and giving, who sacrifices, who is loyal dedicated, devoted and displays consistent hard work.

You can ask different types of subs

What fulfillments do they find in BDSM lifestyle/ relationships?

Some will say they don't know

Some will say they just like it, that it is a great feeling

Some will say the erotic breathtaking scenes or role play, some will say the punishment,the Discipline

Some will say it's about being controlled, restrained, being taken,

The surrender

But the special ones will say the freeDom to just be

The freeDom to please. The best subs in the world are the ones that willingly come to you and kneel

Knowing that they have the power to leave whenever they want, but they chose to remain at your feet

Not because they are expected to

But it is where they feel the safest

Where they feel the happiest

That is the beauty of submission

That is why submission is so beautiful

An alpha waits patiently. Knowing you are already his. You are his way before you realize it. But like a vampire, he can't sink his teeth into your flesh, until he had been invited in.

One of the greatest things in being an alpha is being observant and attentive, especially with your partner. He should be able to know what makes her body tick. He should be able to study all of her idiosyncrasies and patterns, the way her mind works is how you will be able to attack her body efficiently.

Different women have different orgasms.

Throat Orgasm

Women can have orgasms when performing oral, especially when deep-throating, or from having a finger or two rub the back of their throat. These orgasms are related to the arousal of the pituitary gland at the back of the throat. The experience of this orgasm might also be related to the physiological effects of holding one's breath and the suppression of the gag reflex. When stimulated orally, some women can excrete huge quantities of saliva and mucus that can be very viscous. Sometimes there is even a sort of white foam. The release of these fluids is considered to be throat ejaculation. A throat orgasm feels very pleasurable and is accompanied by convulsions and spasms and a need to make strong sounds. Some women need to pause if they are giving head because the orgasm is so strong they cannot continue. Although very pleasurable, a throat orgasm feels more transcendent. Some women go into a semi state of trance and experience a higher and more pure state of consciousness. Women's throat chakra is less open than those of men, and as a result women have more trouble expressing and asserting their needs. It is also interesting that many more women than men suffer from throat infections and thyroid problems. The frequent stimulation of the throat and experiencing these orgasms can lead to a better connection with your intuition and feminine wisDom, a deeper expression of your needs, creative and artistic abilities, and your higher potential. The common belief is that women don't enjoy giving oral sex; that they "give" head or do this for their partner. But the reality is that women can enjoy and benefit from this even more than men.

How to experience a throat orgasm: This is best done by another person. You first need to be sexually aroused, preferably after already experiencing a few non-clitoral orgasms. Have your partner insert his thumb, facing upward to your mouth, and rub the upper back side of your throat. Alternatively you can take his penis in your mouth and try to deepthroat him. In the beginning it might be quite challenging. You might be convulsing, feeling like you are going to vomit, or actually have some stomach fluids come up. Don't worry — it will get easier in time. Especially with his penis, try to keep him inside your throat for as long as you can without moving. Keep the stimulation for a few minutes and remove the fingers, or penis, if you are convulsing. Allow your body to go into spasms and convulsions and permit yourself to make strong sounds.

Anal Orgasm

The anus is an erogenous zone full of sensitive nerves. An anal orgasm will be earthy, raw, rough, physical, and will be generally localized in the genital area. It is also related to the root chakra. Some women might be more sensitive and open to anal stimulation than others. Some women need to have frequent anal stimulation to feel satisfied, otherwise they feel heavy, stagnant and stuck. An anal orgasm can be explosive, thus your partner should take extra care when penetrating you anally, as it might be more challenging to control his ejaculation. How to experience an anal orgasm: Use your own fingers or a dildo to stimulate your anus, first from the outside, and then venture inward. Make sure you use a lot of lube and that you completely relax your anus as you are inserting something inside. Make sure not to touch your vagina with anything that came near your anus, as this might cause an infection. You can also ask your partner to stimulate you anally, first with his fingers and later with his penis.

Cervical-Uterine Orgasm

A cervical orgasm is probably the most profound, meaningful, and special orgasm that a woman can have, at least on the physical level. The cervix is the entrance to the womb, the uterus. This is the pole or the center of the feminine energies in a woman's body. A woman's cervix is related to her feminine core, her sense of self, her heart, her creativity, and to her entire being. A cervical uterine orgasm will feel deeper, more intense and yet more "round" than the g-spot orgasm, and will be accompanied by strong emotions, love, oneness with self, partner and god, ecstasy and transcendence, tears, crying and a feeling of deep satisfaction on all levels. The experience of pleasure is deep and profound but at the same time, the cervical orgasm is perceived and appreciated as an experience that is beyond bodily pleasure, and is often perceived beyond the physical body.

A cervical orgasm is characterized by contractions of the deep vaginal muscles and uterus, while the pc muscle might stay relaxed. It effortlessly causes the sexual energy to move toward the higher chakras. It is related to the navel chakra (Manipura Chakra) but the energy easily rises to the heart chakra and beyond. This is why a cervical orgasm is a whole-body orgasm, as the energy moves throughout the body. A woman who experiences her first cervical-uterine orgasm will usually remember that day forever. One of my female teachers said that she could identify when and if a woman had this orgasm because she glows in a special way. How to experience a cervical orgasm: The cervix is located at the deepest part of your vagina, all the way in. It feels like a finger or the tip of the nose sticking from the back wall of your vagina. You definitely need a long dildo to reach your cervix. After getting yourself aroused, as explained earlier, and stimulating your clit, vaginal entrance and G-spot areas, use your dildo to reach all the way in. You will feel a sensation very deep inside you. In the beginning it might feel numb, tender or even painful. Repressed feelings and memories might come up.

Keep stimulating your cervix and allow yourself to go into and through whatever comes up. It can sometimes take 30 to 60 minutes of internal stimulation to reach a cervical orgasm, and allowing yourself to trust yourself and to surrender is a key aspect of experiencing it.

G-spot Orgasm

I call it the "Goddess spot" or the "Good spot". The G-spot is actually not exactly a spot but an area. Located just inside your vagina, near the entrance, on the upper wall under the pubic bone. When you insert your index and middle fingers into your vagina and curl or hook them towards your clit, you will discover that this area feels different than your vaginal walls. It's Like a ridged, soft, fleshy hill that feels like a combination between a hard tongue, and a soft palate. It will be much more engorged and swollen when you are really aroused. Some women's G-spot is located closer to the entrance, while others have their G-spot further back. All women have a G-spot. A G-spot orgasm feels like an overwhelming experience of intense pleasure, not as "sharp" as a clitoral orgasm, but rather more, "round," "expansive," and "expanded."

It takes longer to reach a G-post orgasm, it unfolds slower, lasts longer, and the pleasure decreases gradually and slowly, compared to the clit orgasm which usually crashes after the peak. A G-spot orgasm will be more emotionally intense, overwhelming, and meaningful and will be followed by a deep feeling of satisfaction and relaxation. There will be strong contractions of the whole pelvic floor, pc muscles and vaginal muscles. With continued stimulation, you could experience more G-spot orgasms, leading to an experience of multiple-orgasms or an intense orgasmic state, lasting for long minutes or even hours. Sometimes there might be an expelling of fluids from the vagina or the urethra, also known as female ejaculation. How to have a G-spot orgasm: Using your fingers, or better yet, a non-vibrating dildo, stimulate the area mentioned above 1 to 2 inches inside your vagina on the upper wall, kind of below your clit. Make sure you are wet or use plenty of natural lube. You might need to keep going for 20 or 30 minutes as this orgasm takes time, but it is soooooo worth it! While a clitoral stimulation is more technical, rub intensely for long enough and you will cum a G-spot orgasm requires that elusive mind-state known as "surrender." As you are stimulating yourself, keep an attitude of openness and acceptance toward yourself and the experience.

Vaginal Entrance Orgasm

There are many nerves at the entrance to your vagina, making it a sensitive and erogenous zone. Apart from clitoral orgasm, this is where most women experience pleasure and subsequent orgasm. But compared with the inner areas, the vaginal entrance orgasm is shallower and sharp, similar to a clitoral orgasm, and might also become explosive. If a man is penetrating you shallowly, at the area of your vaginal entrance, it feels very pleasurable on a physical level, but when he enters you deeper, the experience of the pleasure becomes deeper, more expansive and meaningful. Size does matter and so does depth. How to have a clitoral orgasm: Apply direct and indirect stimulation of your clitoris using your fingers, a shower-head, a vibrator or your partner's mouth. Note that some women love direct and intense stimulation of their clit, while others can only have indirect stimulation through the clitoral hood or sideways through the lips. Experiment with doing the same motion repeatedly for a while or with changing and alternating your touch.

Clitoral Orgasm

A clitoral orgasm is what most women know to be "an orgasm". Intense clitoral stimulation leads to a short peak of orgasm that lasts 20 to 30 seconds, focused mainly in the genital area, and feels intense, sharp, but a bit shallow compared to vaginal orgasms. The pleasure declines rapidly, your clit might feel hyper-sensitive and even a bit painful, and some women lose their interest and passion for a few minutes or even hours. Even with penetrative sex there are positions that stimulate the clitoris more than others. For example, if either partner is on top and leaning forward. A clitoral orgasm is not "bad", it just does not serve you and charge you like deep vaginal orgasms do. In order to discover the ecstasy and bliss of continuous internal orgasms, you can try avoiding having a clitoral orgasm for a while. However, after you learn how to turn clitoral stimulation into internal orgasms, it's great to have clitoral stimulation, as long as you can avoid having an explosive clitoral orgasm.

Nipple Orgasm

The nipples are an important erogenous zone. They are connected via energy channels to the clitoris, and thus, stimulation of the breasts will cause an arousal of the clitoris and the whole genital area. Continued stimulation of the breasts and nipples can result in an actual orgasm, or bring about more quickly and easily the onset of an orgasm when vaginal stimulation is applied. Women with small breasts tend to be more sensitive, but all women can develop sensitivity in their breasts, regardless of size. If your breasts are not sensitive, give yourself regular breast massage and/or ask your partner to do so, at least 20 minutes a day. How to have a nipple orgasm: Use fingers, a vibrator or your partner's mouth to stimulate your nipples. Touch, rub, pinch, pull, knead, and twist your nipples to explore different sensations. Your partner can lick, suck, and bite them. Try to do this for 20 to 30 minutes, even when they feel a bit sensitive or if the sensation has "plateaued".

There is a certain beauty pertaining to the woman's body and when you can master your partner's body you can take her to heaven and back.

CHAPTER 21

Fuck You 'til You Can't Walk

I had her face down, maintaining that impeccable arch for me. Face in the mattress, ass in the air. I was delivering intense Dominating thrusts from my thick long chocolate cock. The slapping of flesh sounds as though it is background music as her moans take over. She is lost in my insanity, but finds peace in my chaos. I trigger her fickle emotions. She will never remain one thing for me, not for long, she will constantly evolve. The endorphins kick in, the oxytocin drips from her brain, her pituitary gland is engaged, dripping of dopamine from her brain as she falls deeper in love than ever before. Her cheeks bouncing up and down off my pelvis. It sounds like a standing clapping ovation. A monsoon is due as I witness a raging river of her. I grabbed a fistful of her luscious hair and anchored her head back towards my mouth, I commanded sharply into her ear; "give me everything I own. Your screams, your pain, your lust, your cries, your body temperature, your orgasms", as I explored the depths of her body. "go ahead and beg me to allow you to come. I'm going to train you to take this big dick like the animal I want you to be. The nympho I turn you into for me." Fucking her like the filthy slut she is for me. The whore she wants to be. The bitch I bring out of her. She needs this Discipline therapy. I crave her flesh, the beast in me yearns to feast upon her. She yearned for my bruises. My marks, as a reminder of where she belongs and to whom she belongs to. She needs the pain. My pain, from my hand. She yearns for my Dominance and strength. I am her balance she has searched for her whole life. I am her most potent drug. I provide what she needs, and she never realized she needed. I quiet her busy thoughts. She does not need to analyze everything all the time, I am her escape. I make her feel like a real woman, I make her feel alive. I turn her over on her back. I did not command, ask or wait for her to be settled, I just flipped her over and took what I wanted. I had her legs pinned back, her heels towards her ears. Her delicious tight pussy spread open while I Dominated her drenched hole with my massive chocolate cock. Head swelled with power, as I further opened her flower. Walls closing in on me, we both drown in her pool of lust. We die together, reborn as immortals. Wetness sounds as though I were stirring macaroni and cheese. Her moans become louder, her breathing changes, her legs convulsing. My muscular hands grasping her throat, strong fingers squeezing the flesh around it. It's ironic, the tighter my grip, the more she let go. Now she is begging me to release.

"Daddy, may I please cum, please?"

I reply sharply, "no I want you a little longer"

Dominating her from on top, hips dancing in perfection, fingertips around her quivering flesh, moans come out from her beautiful soft moistened lips. My lust unabashed and bulging. The need to pleasure her overwhelmed me. My penetrating gaze left her breathless. Claiming every inch of her after several minutes, commanding her now, "cum for me, scream my name." She does and squirts all over. Now she is mine completely. Everywhere, I see fit. Fuck your public places, fuck your, "they might see us", "they might hear us" fuck your "shhhh" or quiet world. She struggles to get up from what I have done to her. Completely taken, used, owned, manhandled destroyed. Love and pain they go hand in hand. Like fighting a wave, no way to beat it. The choice is yours. You love the pain. You love to drown in it, It's hurt, it is the only exhilarating thing. The only thing that makes sense to you. So now you surf that fucking wave and enjoy yourself. Pain is now our language. We speak it fluently with finesse and a smile. We are made strong by it. We use it for our pleasure. In this there, is it strength. In your submission there is strength and in your strength you get a reward. This is Discipline's world now. Anytime, anywhere.

We are that anytime, anyplace, anyhow. We are not gentle. We do not have scheduled sex. We are not clockwork. We are that, when you walk in or I come to you, that "drop to your knees, and show me how much you've missed me." We are wrap my big strong, chocolate man hands around your throat, fist full of your hair. Pulled back and kiss you like I need mouth to mouth resuscitation. We are that passion, lust, fire. I am that instant wetness with only a look for you. We are that conversation with the waiter for your order and my hand touching your pussy under the table. Yes, act normal. Maintain your composure. Do not make faces. We are that vibrator in when you are out with your friends, and I control the vibrations with my phone. We are that hard, thick, long chocolate sliding in you, while you speak on the phone with your mom or dad. We are that, you gagging on me while I drive on the highway. We are that, you trust in me to get us safe to our destination. We are that, fingering you in the driveway because I want you now. We are that, me grabbing your ass so hard in public, your lips spread. We are that, I will grab your breast, or pussy, I don't care who is around. We are that, bruises on your flesh to remind you where you belong. You loving my Dominance. We are that, your beauty craving my beast. We are that, your eyes rolling in the back of your head. You squirting all over me. We are that, "Daddy may I cum now?" We are that, my rules and you obey. We are that, "thank you Daddy for my multiple orgasms." We are that,

"Daddy, I love you." We are that, "baby girl, I'm proud of you. You're such a good girl." We are that, round for round. Pound for pound, dick vs. pussy boxing match sex. We are that, I feel you from a distance. We are that, my deep bass in my voice, leaves you drenched. We are that, my tattoos make you want to misbehave. We are that good girl, bad boy. Bad bitch, good dick. I'm the blunt, you're the Kush. We are that, I break you, to heal you. Wrap you up in my arms. We are that pain and pleasure. Peace and chaos. This is where you feel safest. We are that no judgement. I do not give a fuck who you are. You will be whatever the hell I want. Leave with my essence all over you.

CHAPTER 22

Good Girls, Bad Boys

Not all Dominant men wear a suit. Testosterone, high levels with this hormone, can be correlated with Dominant behavior. With cave men in ancient times they would not speak to their woman. They would just bash the woman over the head with a club, drag her by her fucking hair, or lift her up over their shoulders, and take them home.

There is no gender when it comes to Dominance. There are female Dominants, Dominatrix and Domme, fem Dom also know as, "female Domination. However, the majority of them are Males. You have your different types of Dominance. Primal(who are your Tops or Alphas) your Daddy/ your Daddy Dom/even the non Doms that are ranked higher like Master or King, or Sadist. One thing about being a Dominant is self-development. BDSM is not associated with inadequate development. In order to develop one another, one must have control. One must have developed himself or herself. Self-development is the epitome of character. One of the toughest thing to posses in this world is patience with people and yourself in situations. Patience becomes control and with control you can take on anything in this world. I speak of this more in my future book, but back to the situation at hand.... Women need to be more honest with the type of man they want. Do not preach that you want a good guy, or a nice guy because you do not want to be viewed as a slut. When in reality you want a bad boy that will fuck your brains out like a slut. If you want an alpha male, if you want a high status man, do not pretend that you don't. Be honest with yourself, be authentic. Don't cheap out and go for a man you are not really attracted to, because you feel desperate for a relationship. If you are able to give a man, that you have chosen to date respect to begin with, then over time you will see and learn more about him, and you can make your decision from there. Your relationships will be more conducive and healthier with what you are trying to build upon. There are too many unhappily married women out there and too many women who do not feel desired, appreciated, wanted enough out there. But if you are a woman who is more masculine, that's fine, ignore this because you may not want a relationship where the man is more masculine than you are more feminine. Choose another type of relationship that is true to you.

Why do good girls love bad boys?

Women will preach they want a good guy

But for some weird reason they always tend to gravitate towards the danger, darkness and the mysterious

Good girls love bad boys

It is going to be like that 'til the end of time

Many women are like rescuers

It is like a challenge for them to reform an incorrigible man

These women think

Sure

He gets into trouble but I can change him

Ego is involved

It is inflating when a woman feels like she is the only one who can transform a man

Here is the biggest sentence of all

Women love to feel needed

Other women have an appetite for adventure

Other women like excitement, thrills and sense of danger bad boys bring

This is especially true for those who have been good girls all their lives

They perhaps grew up in a family with rules and restrictions

It is always some type of curiosity in the back of their head

To feel what they have been missing

and bad boys provide that

It is like opposites attract

Women are attracted to testosterone

High level of testosterone correlates with, assertive behavior,

Greater muscle mass

Risk taking,leadership, higher sex drive

and aggression

Most bad boys have high levels of testosterone

Most good girls have been good all their lives

Goody two shoes

Led a life demanded conformity and compliance with rules

So it intrigues them when they see men who do not listen to rules

How do these relationships turn out? Most turn out poorly?

Not all of them, but most of them

Because bad boys will not change unless they want to

No matter how long suffering their partner is

Or how dedicate their woman is to them

Women who sign on with bad boys are in this for endless conflict and turmoil

Here is the best part that I wrote

Ironically the very same that draws them together

Is usually their undoing

Many woman have learned the hard way

That bad boys make bad dating partners and worse spouses

However, they make phenomenal lovers

They make great lovers cos women love honesty. Now a bad boy, who is a good man is hard to resist. I don't care what any woman says, if they disagree, they're simply just lying. Now here's the thing with nice guys..

Nice guys do not seem genuine

No one is that nice unless you are a saint

Women instinctively do not trust that

Trust is very expensive

and bad boys keep it real

A nice guy is just a patient wolf in the mist

A bad boy unveils that were wolf tendencies straight away

A woman that craves danger and is afraid to explore or confront it

will gravitate towards a man who feels at home with it

A woman will not respect a doormat

Those get walked all over

Women will manipulate and walk all over a man, if he allows it

Women do not respect a man they can manipulate

A bad boy will put her in her place

As cruel as that sounds

It will turn her on though

To know she was put in her place

To know that he knows when to take charge

Women do not respect a man they can control

No respect equals no attraction

Women are inclined to nurture

Now instead of doing this with children

They often do this to bad boys

They think their love will save them

Nice guys rarely need to be saved

Women love to feel wanted and needed

Nice guys do not need fixing

Bad boys seem like a project to most

Now here is the biggest sentence of all time

Nice guys seem weak – women are subconsciously attracted to potential mates with stronger genes

Bad boys send out a subconscious message that they have more powerful genes

They believe their genes are so strong they aren't afraid of losing a woman because of bad behavior

Nice guys fear losing their women, send the exact opposite message, which is.. weak

Some women have low self esteem

Women do not feel comfortable with people who treat them better than they treat themselves

If they do not think much of themselves, the bad boys simply reinforce those negative beliefs

A nice guy is treating you in a way you are not familiar with, and that feels uncomfortable

If you are a woman and you are not bathing yourself in gifts and you get a guy who is constantly buying you stuff – you feel weird

Nice guys are not as strong physically

Historically, men have protected women

Physically and otherwise

Physically Bad boys give the illusion of being able to protect women

While with nice guys women are not so sure

See life is all about balance

Until men learn how to do that, more often than not, women will chose a bad boy unless they realize that his bad qualities outweigh his good ones

Nice guys play it safe

Too safe, it is boring

You can be good and nice in life, or take what you want and be great at whatever you do

Men are many things but masters at nothing, and masters of nothing.

Women and girls will always say, "I am really looking for a nice guy, but they are so difficult to find these days."

"I envy the women who will get you,because you are such a nice guy."

"Don't worry you're going to find a great guy

Cos nice guys like you are rare."

There is a fucking epidemic of nice guys

What are they talking about?

It is plain bullshit

They are just following the social trends

Their friends, families implemented in their psyche. Things they've witnessed on tv. Like every little girl wanted to be like the Disney animated movie, "Cinderella." She loses her slipper. He searches around town, she the woman that lost her slipper. To find her, and make her his wife. Now you're telling me no one in town has the same shoes size as you do? But, we are not thinking like this as we are younger.

Women are followers and they hate to go against the grain

They do what society tells them to do. That's fine, but as a man, at one point, when you want to be a real man, you need to stop taking advice from mass media, friends

Family, schools

and do what is best for you

My late grandma didn't raise me to be a nice guy

A good man but not a nice guy

My mother did not raise me to allow a woman to control me

and my father did not teach me to be weak

Born a King, raised a savage

A gentleman born to Dominate

Many children were privileged, catered to, hugged.

I was taught to be a man real early. I may attract everyone but I am not built for everyone

There is not enough cloth in the world for all of us to be cut from it

Some of us have that thing, or two you can't teach

This is Dominance at its finest

I feel like everyone wants a polite asshole

It is like an oxymoron

Someone who will hold the door open

But slap her ass as she walks in

The thing with good girls and bad boys

Sometimes a girl just wants to be bent over and banged like a screen door in a hurricane

and I feel like bad guys bring that type of nasty out of the girl

Everything that a man does – a woman correlates that with the bedroom

Like the aggression

The intensity, the passion

I feel like if a woman wants to be forcefully taken

She can get that with that type of man

Rather than the safe, by the book, boring, non risk taking individual

Every woman has a dark side, a hidden freak, whore, animal inside her

and a bad boy is the only one who can bring it out

Females love assholes

Because assholes know how to keep them in check

If I was fat and ugly I would be up for harassment

Assholes know how to make a girl try harder than she has to

While doing more of the giving

Than the girl just receives

Take into account

The harder you work for something, the more you appreciate it

Assholes know how to make a girl pay more attention to them

Than she usually does

While nice guys will spoil a girl with attention than they can handle

Anything that is unusual or different triggers the mind

When a girl gets lots of attention from a nice guy she expects it

But when that bad boy ignores her it will drive her nuts

and she will become obsessed

It's all psychological

So when that happens that automatically starts fucking with her psyche

So now it becomes "what it is about YOU that isn't attracted to me?"

It is almost like a power exchange, now she is focused on you

and now you become the target

That is going to engage in a race

and the chase is on

Assholes know how to make women miss them so much it hurts

While nice guys cling on so much to the point where the girl wants to be away

Assholes will keep a girl so deep in love that it feels impossible to leave

While nice guys give the girls too much freeDom

That they are able to explore into other options

Most women are not able to leave men

It is very rare to see a woman that makes the decision she wants to leave

It is rare

Most people do not want freeDom

That incurs responsibility

Most people are frightened of freeDom

I am the man

Because I am great.

Most women love a man to take charge, it brings ease to their mind

So most bad boys are alpha males

They do not follow the rules

They take what they want

They go for it

They do not question

Nice guys play it safe

They ask permission to behave in certain ways

It makes them feel weak

Women are strange emotional creatures

The same things that scare or steer them away, they gravitate towards

It is the thrill, the elusiveness

The thrill of danger

The unknown, the sexiness of the danger

The desire of the unknown

If you are someone that is of the norm

I expect you are going to do that

You are predictable

Unpredictable is exhilarating

You do not know a woman 'til you understand what she is not saying to you

In the hands of the right man

A single woman can be many different things

It is of his will to allow her to feel comfortable for him to lead

Never let her question your desire for her

Do not just tell her

More importantly show her

Be aggressive

Don't be gentle and at the end of the day that is the difference between to two male types we were talking about

You baby her outside already

Behind closed doors should be the opposite

Allow her to feel real testosterone

Allow her to feel your hunger

Grab her – do not hesitate

Grab her like she is yours

Grab her like you own her

See bad boys, they take what they want, they take risks and they do not mind if they hurt you or not

They will not hesitate to hurt you

and the opposite type of man will play it safe

and that suppresses her desires

Some women like to be talked to

Dirty

Aggressive

Disrespectfully

Mentally stimulating her

and nice guys just cannot do that

Most women do not feel comfortable telling you their darkest desires

They feel that they will be judged

They will be ridiculed

Resented and for a man that is already close to that world, it builds confidence

In herself in order to admit those desires

Unleash those slut tendencies

Give her what she is afraid to ask for

Everybody has different desires and fantasies

Most basic traditional relationships are limited

and the thing that bad boys bring is unlimited pleasure

Passion

Most ordinary men are boring

and the thing bad boys bring is breathtaking

Invigoration

Non stop thrill like an action movie

Why would your woman tell you she desires to be slapped in the face with your hand?

Knowing that you guys have been doing the same old position, style for years

The nice guy

"Baby are you crazy"

"Baby I don't want to hurt you"

"Baby the way we've been doing it for so long was wrong"

His feeling of being inadequate is kicking in

You as the woman feels he perhaps will not be able to fulfill your desires if it is not in him, it's not in him

All that romantic shit is fine

But sometimes you are going to have to take her down on the floor

O pin her up against the wall like the masterpiece she is

You think a nice guy is going to want to spank you, pull your hair

Go harder when you need it

Fuck her brains out to the point where the endorphin and the Oxytocin is released from her brain

She has no recollection of where she is

Who she is

She does not think

But feels

In that moment she yearns to feel pain

Some women are afraid of taking initiative so you as the man have to set the tone and this comes in with the bad boys that like to take charge and take control and engaging in the dirty talk.

Most men today have no clue what women really want. Many that think they do, give months of flowers, chocolates, and engage in expensive wining and dining but are actually completely wrong. There are four main reasons why so many of today's men find themselves struggling with women: Firstly, in recent times, society has increasingly made men feel that they need to impress and seek the approval of women in order to feel adequate and attract them. Secondly, today's men have been raised watching movies and television shows that depict female attraction in a way that is completely wrong. This has also made the first problem (above) worse by convincing men that they need to impress women. That they need to be a superhero and save the planet before they can "get the girl" as if a woman's attraction is a prize that is only unlocked by being a "nice guy" and impressing her. Thirdly, men often trust what women tell them when it comes to dating advice. That is, be a "nice guy" and women will flock to your side. Meanwhile the girl who gave that advice goes out and dates a jerk. The poor guy who followed the advice ends up in the friend zone. Fourthly and finally, men often find themselves assuming that female attraction works exactly the same as male attraction does, and that if you are not sexy, ripped, or a "10," then you have no hope. To create attraction there needs to be polarity. Sexual polarity. The masculine attracts the feminine and the feminine attracts the masculine. If you have ever seen two magnets, you know how this works. If you put two magnets of equal charge together, nothing happens. They just sit there. Likewise, when you have two androgynous partners together, nothing happens. Many couples complain of incredibly boring and unsatisfying sex lives, this is why. The man is too feminine while the woman is too masculine.

There is no sexual polarity, no magnetism, and no attraction. However, if you get two magnets of opposite charges such as "+" and "-" they attract. Moreover, the stronger the positive charge and the stronger the negative charge, the more intense the attraction is and just as positive attracts negative, the masculine attracts the feminine, and vice versa. At some point you might have noticed that in your friends relationships (or your own!) you can tell when there is a spark of sexual attraction. Likewise, you can tell when there is more of just a 'friend energy' rather than that of lovers. This 'friend energy' is the result of a lack of sexual polarity. There is no charge. There is no sexual energy. There is an absence of the polarity created by the interaction of masculinity or femininity. However, when there is a strong polarity, sexual attraction is inevitable. This is why the macho quarterback and the dainty cheerleader just can not resist each other. There is an undeniable force of attraction (i.e. polarity) between them. This is why some couples have sizzling hot sex every night and just can not seem to get off each other, while other relationships stagnate, become dull, and just seem to lack that "spark" and sexual energy.

Truth be told, women are into sex a lot more than men realize and they do not just want polite sex or demure sex or hotel sex. Today's woman is psychologically, socially and emotionally complicated and layered and her sexual appetite is just as intriguing as she is. Simple women with simple lives are a lot more rare than they used to be, so men would be wise to take this as a heads-up. Chances are you are with a woman who has at least a fleeting interest, if not a full-blown desire, to partake in a little rough sex. Nice Men are often surprised by this and wind up caught off guard when it is the women who are the ones who tell them that they want it rough. It is not always apparent when meeting these women, especially when they are baking cookies, playing with kittens and wearing floral print dresses, that they have got a dark side when it comes to sex. They just do not look the part! If they were slaying Wall Street while wearing leather and downing shots between stock trades, men might not be so surprised when these types of women want it rough. But, the women who do not seem like they would want it, but do, are the shockers and when it becomes apparent that they do, it is a definite game-changer. Sometimes, guys are so taken off guard by their women wanting it rough that they do not realize that it was difficult for women who do not live, looking as if they want it rough, to express themselves and come out and ask for it. They know you do not see it coming and they are afraid to scare you away, or get rejected, so they sometimes bite their tongues and hope you will bring it up. Having rough sex feels as if they have freed themselves. The intimacy that the bond created by rough sex created between a man and his partner is more than just a sexual connection.

It is a deep feeling that a partner has brought out in her man, his true self. Great rough sex allows a celebration of this part of a man's identity as well as of the sexual experience. Having rough sex does not have to be just a release or just a connection. It can be a way to learn about one's self and discover parts of one's personality and a partner's personality, that you had not realized before. Having rough sex can be just a hot romp between the sheets, but it also serves as validation for male feelings of self and the layered and complex feelings about a partner, and women, in general.

Nice guys finish last. It is true. Especially when it comes to women. So why is it that the polite and well-mannered men of this world, who always treat women like royalty, never actually get the girl? Why does it seem to be that desirable women always end up with 'assholes' or 'jerks'? We can break this issue down to two basic questions: First: What is it that women see in so-called 'assholes' and 'jerks'? Second: Why do women find so-called 'nice guys' so unattractive? These two questions form the basis of what I am going to answer for you today. Upon completing this book, not only will you understand the biological reasons behind why women find 'bad boys', 'assholes', and 'jerks' so damn attractive compared to nice guys, but you will also know how you can have the raw sex appeal of these types of men without actually being a true jerk. So, without further ado, let us dive right into understanding the inner workings of female attraction. Life is dangerous. To be safe and to survive, women needed strong, Dominant men. Women being physically weaker and more vulnerable are instinctively attracted to men who they feel can protect them. Why? Well, the women who were not attracted to such men died out. As a result, their genes were not passed on. The only genes passed on were those of women who were naturally attracted to men they felt could protect them. The result? Women are still instinctively attracted to men who they subconsciously feel would be able to protect them. Not consciously, but subconsciously. So the key thing to take away from here is this: women are attracted to the way you make them feel and how a woman feels around a man is dictated by his behavior. In other words, the determining factor of a woman's attraction for a man is how he behaves, as this influences how she feels around him. So, what on earth does this have to do with nice guys? Everything. The problem with nice guys is they do not behave in a way that triggers a woman's instinctive attraction. A woman's 'cavewoman' brain does not subconsciously feel that mating with a nice guy would provide her offspring with the best chance of survival. Consequently, as harsh as it might be, women are often repulsed by the idea of being sexually involved with a man she considers to be a 'nice guy'. Women will even flat out say "I don't think of you that way." So what is it about the behavior of nice guy's that fails to ignite that fiery sexual passion within women? Why are women so turned off by nice guys? When it comes to sexual interest, the word 'nice' can be a shorthand antonym for bold, strong, sexy and exciting. Instead, 'nice' can be a synonym for needy, weak, predictable and boring. Let us explore this. Men often make the mistake of assuming that a woman's attraction is the same as that of a man's. In other words, plenty of men assume that women are only interested in how physically attractive they are. This logic is flawed, however. A man's attraction is based on his evolutionary need to reproduce. In order to maximize his chances of successfully reproducing and having offspring that survive, men are attracted to qualities in women that indicate health and fertility. Why? We do not consciously think like this when deciding who we are attracted to. In fact, attraction is not a conscious decision. It is our subconscious caveman/ cavewoman brains pulling the strings. Okay, so let us get to the core of the issue. Why do women find nice guys unattractive? To discover this, let us have a look at some typical nice guy behaviors. The term 'nice guy' is a euphemism for insecure men unwilling to articulate their romantic or sexual feelings directly. Instead, nice guys choose to present themselves as their paramour's friend, and hang around, doing nice things for her in the hopes that she will one day pick up on his desire for her. If she fails to read the nice guy's secret feelings, however, the nice guy will become embittered and blame her for taking advantage of him and his niceness.

Nice guys are generally unassertive and afraid to express their true feelings. The nice guy does not just appear in dating, but in all aspects of life. Whether it is expressing their desire for a woman or having the courage to say 'no' to people. A nice guy's behavior manifests itself in all aspects of his life. So why is it that nice guys are unattractive to women? Don't women love it when a guy is willing to help them out all the time, and do whatever she wants? The simple answer is, hell fucking no! Women are not attracted to nice guys, because nice guys fail to ignite their attraction triggers. In fact, it could be argued, they do just the opposite. Remember, it is how a man makes a woman feel that matters, and how you make a woman feel is determined by your behavior. The problem with nice guys, put simply, is that all of their behavior is highly unattractive to a woman's primitive subconscious mind. Their behavior, does not push those attraction triggers that were developed tens of thousands of years ago. Women desire strong, Dominant, masculine men. They desire men who take charge, are confident and decisive. Nice guys embody behaviors that are almost the exact opposite of the attractive traits described. Nice guys are weak, submissive and feminine. They are scared of leading or taking charge, lack confidence and are indecisive. Sure, while nice guys might arguably be better for women in modern society than a 'jerk' or 'bad boy', that is irrelevant, because human society has changed immeasurably faster than the evolution of the human brain.

In other words, a woman's attraction is based on the same factors as it was back when, we were all running around naked in the bush. Unassertive men too scared to express their true feelings, display incredible mental weakness to women. Men who are too scared to stand up for themselves or do what they want to do because it might potentially upset someone else, display similarly undesirable characteristics to women. Women do not want weak, submissive men. Women are not attracted to weak, submissive men. If you want a simple way to be incredibly sexy and attractive to women, always do the exact opposite of what a nice guy would do. Let me say that again: always do the exact opposite of what a nice guy would do. If you are scared of what a woman might think about you, if you express your true feelings, who cares --do it anyway. If you are scared to do what you want to do, because of what others might think of you --or you just want to follow along in order to gain someone else's approval, who cares --do want you want to do anyway. The key to all of this is to be more invested in your own perception of yourself, than you are in other's perceptions of you. Try to impress yourself rather than others. Do not concern yourself with what other people might think of you, after all, they are most likely too busy being fearful of what others think of them. For women, the biggest aphrodisiac in the world is self-confidence. Confidence, confidence, confidence. One of the reasons confidence is so important, not just with women, but with life in general, is the fact that it is contagious. If you have confidence in yourself, you inspire others to have equal confidence in you. On the same token, if you lack confidence in yourself, others too, will question your ability. Men who show bawdy self-confidence --instead of an overarching fear of the world --appear as if they can handle anything. It has been proven time and time again by science. It has been proven that confident speakers and presenters are perceived to be more expert, knowledgeable and credible, even when they were not. Someone who displays extraordinary confidence and boldness, can say some of the most lame (or outrageous) things and get away with it. This is especially the case with women. A man who approaches a woman with great confidence and directness, yet says some pretty lame stuff, will be much better received, than a nervous wreck nice guy who says something Pulitzer Prize worthy. One of the problems with nice guys --apart from being unassertive, unable to express their true feelings, and using acts of ostensible friendship for the unstated aim of getting in a girls pants --is that they are (or at least come off as) needy and insecure. Nice guys tend to be clingy and emotionally dependent rather than, show strength by being their own independent man. However, having confidence is not the most important thing. It is the appearance of having confidence. If the world's most confident man pretends to be insecure and unsure of himself, he will be perceived negatively. If a man who is incredibly nervous gives the appearance of being calm, relaxed, composed and confident in himself, he will be perceived infinitely more positively. So, how do you give the appearance of confidence? Someone who is confident is comfortable with uncertainty. People who are super confident even embrace uncertainty. They put themselves out there and are okay with putting themselves in situations where they are vulnerable, like approaching an attractive girl or sharing an idea in front of an audience. Confidence is the appearance of being comfortable with uncertainty. Confidence also displays itself through body language. Confident people tend to move and speak slowly, take up more space with their body, have good posture, and so on. Display confidence in your interactions with women and watch their attraction grow. A woman's attraction to a man is proportional to his confidence. It is for this reason that women find carelessly confident 'jerks', 'assholes' and 'bad boys' so irresistible and attractive. Another reason that confidence makes you so sexy is because it makes you...unpredictable. Nice guys are boring, generic and predictable. Women are attracted to mystery. The unknown will always intrigue the mind. As a result, it is difficult for them to create that spark with women. The saying that 'girls just want to have fun' is true, and nice guys just do not do it. It is not just me saying this, there is science to back it up. Many studies have found that the brain releases more dopamine when rewards are unpredictable than it does when things go about as expected. In other words, women literally become addicted to unpredictable and exciting 'assholes' and 'bad boys.' Not only is the behavior of a nice guy an incredible bore for women, but the actual behavior itself is unattractive as well. Nice guys are predictable because, women know that they will go out of their way to cater to her every whim. Nice guys are all about seeking the approval of others and trying to make everyone happy at their own expense. As a result, it is obvious what they will do in any given situation. So-called 'assholes', 'jerks', and 'bad boys', however, stand up for themselves. They do not conform and thus everything they do is a surprise and a shock. They value themselves and say/ do whatever the hell they want. Women find this sort of behavior incredibly attractive. Why? Because it demonstrates confidence, and confidence is generally an indicator of everything else that women find instinctively attractive. Men who display strength and willpower, trigger subconscious attraction in women, and by disregarding what other people think and simply being true to yourself in your actions and your words, you are extremely attractive to women and display immense confidence and strength. So rather than being a nice guy and seeking the approval of others and devoting your every thought to ensuring the happiness of others, seek your own approval (impress yourself!) and think about what you want to say or do, and do it. Nice guys become highly emotionally invested in women, and this turns them off. Not-so-nice guys, on the other hand, are more highly invested in themselves. They stay true to themselves and do not really care what women, or people in general, think of them. So why is it that women find men who do not particularly care about them so attractive? Why will women run away from the nice guy who obviously likes her and instead chase the guy who treats her like shit? It is all because... the more you chase her, the more she will run. Words are powerful but actions say plenty about you. So, for example, by approaching a woman directly, you display confidence and boldness. Your actions sub-communicate that you are okay with the idea of rejection. Otherwise, you would not have approached her like that, right? On the other hand, consider a nice guy who is too scared to approach women, and so instead tries to get in a woman's pants by masquerading as her friend. What are his actions sub-communicating? A complete lack of confidence. This man is obviously terrified of rejection and if he is terrified of rejection, that means he has no other options. Women will work hard to obtain things from you when they witness how other people view you, especially other women. Because most women are followers. If you have intrigued her, she will chase you if she knows she can be replaced. Especially a woman who is extremely sexy and beautiful. She probably has a list of men, a line of men waiting. Waiting for a text, waiting for approval. A call back. A smile, an invitation. Assertive bad boys, do not give a fuck and they will let that be known with their actions. A woman of this caliber may view this and say, 'why isn't he all over me?' 'What does he have, who is in his life? All these other men like me, what is wrong with him?' Subconsciously she is now drawn to him because he may display he wants her, but he definitely does not need her. Everything you do with women comes down to what is being sub-communicated. When I say sub communicated, what is not spoken. Another reason women run from emotionally needy guys, they chase women out of fear that they will ditch them: women want what they can not have. If a guy is chasing her, obviously she can have him! He is no challenge whatsoever. On the other hand, a guy who is more challenging really piques a woman's interest. He is challenging. He is interesting. He is unique and once again, it all comes down to sub-communication. Think about this, what does a guy who is not super needy or aggressively chasing women sub-communicating? What is the likely cause of his actions and behavior? Perhaps he is of higher status than her. He might be more of a 'catch.' He could be slightly 'out of her league.'. Or, perhaps it is that he is preselected by other beautiful women and just is not quite as interested in her (and needy), as other nice guys who have not gotten laid in years. It could also be that he is simply high value. Most likely, a woman's subconscious will attribute all of the above to a man who does not chase her. As a result, she will begin to chase him. Why chase those other nice guys who are always sucking up to her, right? Obviously they just are not as high value or attractive as this other guy. As you can see, when you interact with women, everything comes down to sub-communication. You would be surprised at how adept women are at judging men, based solely on the implied reasons behind the way they act and behave. Another reason that women are not attracted to men who aggressively pursue and are over invested... A woman's attraction is generally proportional to the man's level of investment. In other words, overly invested, emotionally needy men are highly unattractive. Men who are instead more highly invested in themselves than they are in her, are much more attractive to women. Or, in the case of the jerk, well, they have women all over them. Why is this? The reason for women finding men who are less invested in them more attractive, once again relates to the difference between the inner workings of male and female attraction. Women are attracted to strong, powerful, Dominant men. Women are attracted to men that they respect. In fact, for women, the words respect and attraction are basically interchangeable, at least for the right type of respect. If we want to get into the nitty gritty, there are two types of respect. One of these types of respects create within women's intense attraction. The other, well, it sexually repulses them. So let us take a look at the two. The first is the type of respect that you would have for an emperor. The second is the type of respect that you would have for your grandfather. The emperor you respect for the man he is. He is a powerful man who you may even be a little intimidated by. Your grandfather on the other hand, he is kind of old and cute, like a puppy dog. You respect him, because, well he is probably friendly, nice and so on. However, the type of respect you have for him is completely different than that which you would have for an emperor. To consider this in a different light, think of a man who you have incredible respect for. He seems really powerful, strong, wise, etc. You might even be a little intimidated by him. This man could be a mentor, teacher, boss, coach, whoever. Would you ask this guy to do stuff for you? Would you nag and complain to him? Would you tell him to take you places? No, of course not. Now consider a cool friend you might have. You would not think too much of asking those same things, right? He is a cool guy and all, but, well, he is different. The first type is the type of respect that inspires intense attraction in women. Women desire strong, Dominant men who they have incredible, emperor-like respect for. Women are attracted to that feeling of awe-like and slightly intimidated kind of respect. The men they feel like this around are the type of men that they desire. These are the types of men that they most likely fantasise about. On the other hand, the second type of friend-like respect inspires no attraction in women. While the men that they hold this type of respect for, might make good shopping buddies and give her lots of expensive gifts, she has no attraction for them. The thought of getting sexual with these men would revolt a woman. So, what is one of the main differences between these two types of respect? Investment. Is that powerful awe-inspiring, slightly intimidating man you thought of before highly invested in you? No. On the other hand, nice guys are highly invested in women. They spend inordinate amounts of time with her, often while masquerading as her friend. They spend massive amounts of money on her, buying her expensive gifts, wining and dining her, and taking her on extravagant dates. They do not just become invested in her time-wise and materially either, they also become highly emotionally invested. All of this behavior is highly unattractive to women. Women are instead, more attracted to men who are less invested in her than she is in them. In other words, it is not your investment in a woman that matters, but her investment in you. The more invested in her you are, the more attached and attracted to her you become. The more invested she is in you, the more attached and attracted to you she becomes. The less invested you are in a woman, and the more highly invested she is in you, the more attracted to you she will be. This is yet another reason why jerks do so well with women. Jerks often get into fights with women, and women subsequently become very emotionally invested. They also spend a bunch of time and emotion being upset and fuming. As a result, they become highly emotionally invested in that jerk and her attraction for him subsequently increases. In addition, her subconscious concludes that her emotional investment in him must be indicative of his value. In other words, if she has spent so much time thinking about him, he must be worth it. This is well documented in psychology. The primitive section of the brain acts on It's desires and the logical part of the brain explains (or makes excuses for) why it did that. Women also justify that they should not ditch the jerk now, after everything that they have been through. After all that time, effort and emotional investment. After all those ups and downs. Nice guys, however, routinely find themselves being ditched by women. Why? Because women are not invested in them. They have no attachment to, or attraction for them. Women like to test their men. Often, it is a subconscious impulse, however, women can also be fully aware of what they are doing. A woman says or does something to 'test' a man's true character by judging how he responds. Tests can come in all shapes and sizes. If the guy appears to be upset by it or tries to explain himself, or reacts in any other similar way, the woman knows that the guy is not really the strong, confident man that she initially might have thought him to be. She will lose attraction for him. On the other hand, if the guy just does not seem to care, she knows that he is tough, strong, reliable and confident. All qualities of which women find attractive. Women also often test men by requesting that they do something they know they most likely do not want to do. If a guy submits to a woman's whims at his own expense, then she knows that he is not a high value man, who sticks up for himself and does what he wants to do.

Nice guys on the other hand attempt to keep their woman happy by telling her what she 'wants' to hear, which only serves to sub-communicate a nice guy's negative traits.

Why do women put nice guys in the friend zone? They do not view them as sexually desirable men. Why is it that they keep them in there? For security. But it is entirely the guy's fault. If you are a man that is trying to approach her as a friend and now you are trying to change that factor, it is going to be weird. The reason men are placed in the friend zone and kept there is because, he approaches a woman like he wants to be a friend. He talks to her like a friend would interact with her. So why is he surprised when he becomes her friend? Of course she is going to think of you as a friend if that is all you do. Once again this is what nice guys usually do. They interact with women in the exact same way they would with someone they would want to be friends with. Now you understand why nice guys fail? Now let's take a look at the guys who unfailing drives the women crazy and creates tangible sexual chemistry. The bad boy. The jerks, the assholes. So how do these guys create sexual tension or chemistry? They interact with women they find desirable. They are shameless about their desires, they do not hide behind false friendship. In other words, they make the fact known that he is a guy and she is a girl, obvious. They exploit the difference between the sexual roles to it's full potential. They create what I call polarity. It means being polar having opposite or contrary tendencies. A difference, opposites attracts. Like electricity, batteries or magnets. Polarity creates attraction. To create attraction you need polarity. To create attraction, you need to highlight sexual difference. This is the biggest sentence of all time......

This is why feminine women are attracted to very masculine men. The masculine men are attracted to very feminine women, all because of polarity. Bad boys, jerks, assholes unknowingly create polarity and it drives women wild. When they flirt, they role-play. He always takes on the masculine role. He might pretend to be an authoritative figure, put her in a position where she is overwhelmed, perhaps play the role of teacher and student. This approvingly tells her she has earned herself a detention. Or perhaps, he pretends to hire her as his secretary and then promptly fires her. He might also pretend he is not quite sure whether or not he likes her, and playfully accuses everything she does as trying to seduce him and get into his pants. He might even playfully tease her by awarding and subtracting points for ways she behaves. He becomes the selector. Playfully attempting to judge whether or not a woman meets his standards and she becomes one of many girls hitting on him. He might playfully criticise her for something that obviously is not true. Or is the opposite of what is true. For example, he might tell a really tall lady he is not into midgets. All of this flirtatious role playing intensifies a woman's attraction because, it involves you taking on the masculine role and her taking on the feminine role. Nice guys fail because, they remain neutral when interacting with women, so instead of ending up in a relationship that reflects the polarity of masculinity vs. femininity, they end up with the relationship that reflects their sexual neutrality for example lets just be friends.

Nice guys fail to build an emotional connecting with women. They ask question after question after question, just to ask lame question after lame question after lame question.

Such as 'what is your job?', 'where are you from?', and so on. They do not connect with her emotionally. They just find out heaps about her. Listen, you have to understand this is not a job interview or interrogation. Interrogation is not seduction. Nice guys can also fall into the trap of asking questions simply to keep a dying interaction alive, rather than have a genuine interest and women can sense this. So the best way to avoid the interview mode and connect with women emotionally is to, dive into the emotions behind things, rather than skimming over the surface when getting to know her. Dive into the emotions and feelings behind this. Not only does this enable you to connect with women emotionally, but also they would love it. I say this all the time, feminine women are creatures of emotions and feelings; women love it when you connect with them in this way. For example, if you find out a woman you are talking to is a nurse or surgeon, instead of asking, 'WOW, you must work long hours', get into the emotions. Get into depth and ask, 'what drives you to sacrifice so much for others?' Perhaps, 'what does it feel like to save someone's life?' You have to understand, she is probably going through this over and over again like a cycle on regular dates, so when you bring something different, it will intrigue them and get them excited. Another way to connect with women more powerfully, is to speak in statements rather than questions. In other words, turn any questions you might have into statements. Speaking in statements makes people subconsciously more comfortable around you. For example, people who know each other longer, friends and family, speak in statements rather than questions. Consequently, the feeling of familiarity and unfamiliarity have attached themselves to each style of conversation respectfully. So by transforming your questions into statements, you are creating a subconscious sense of familiarity. So instead of asking a woman where they grew up, take a guess where she grew up. Instead of asking where they work, take a guess. 'You seem like the creative type. I bet you work as….' Further more, if your guess is right, she will be amazed by your perceptiveness. If your guess is not correct, it makes it even more interesting, because she will ask you why you guessed what you did and you can explain. They are super interested in this.

Just as women love talking about themselves, women love hearing about themselves. Either way, talking in statements rather than questions is always better. It makes the feeling of familiarity and makes the conversation more interesting. It gets a woman more engaged in the interaction and gives you more things to talk about. If you decide to compliment a woman, decide to compliment her on who she is as a woman. Do not complete her physical appearance until you have taken her to bed. Women want to be appreciated for who they are as a person, by being indifferent to her beauty, you indicate you are not phased by her and are used to interacting with beautiful women, speaking of the physical. In conclusion, the main thing is to do the opposite of the nice guy. Do not be a nice guy. Be a good man, not a nice guy. Nice guys seek approval and seek acceptance by others at the expense of their true selves. Be yourself. Respect yourself and your desires. Prioritize yourself over women you barely know. Ultimately, this attitude, is what women instinctively find more attractive. Be shameless about your masculinity, do not hide who you truly are. Show strength by overcoming our evolutionary urge to seek the acceptance and approval of those around us, especially hot women. You have to understand most of these hot, beautiful women are constantly getting hit on by men, on social media or life. So, when you show you are not phased by them, it annoys them. Because, they start thinking who are you and what is wrong with them. It is a power thing – it is psychological. If you want to do something, do it. If a woman is not too keen, who cares, after all there are millions of other beautiful women out there. Do not become so attached to a woman you barely know solely because of their physical appearance. Have confidence in yourself. Be confident of your value as a man and women will as well. Be yourself and follow your desires, do not do things that are so obvious. You do not want to be unpredictable. Women love different. Do not chase and be heavily invested in a woman you hardly know. Ignore any shit women give you or stupid things they ask you. Show leadership by doing whatever you want to do. Women always want to tag along with a strong man, as he does what he pleases. They do not want to have to take charge or an indecisive weak man. Connect with women, play with them, tease them, build sexual tension and do not be afraid of gradually getting physical right from the start. The biggest thing of all however is realizing who you truly are, and then shamelessly being that person all the time. Life is too short trying to be someone else, and trying to please others. No matter how long the legs are or how hot they are, be yourself and have fun doing it. It is the most attractive thing you can do.

CHAPTER 23

Key To A Submissive's Heart

The key to a submissive woman's heart is through her pain threshold. Submissive women have tough skin, but fragile hearts. Fuck and hurt them roughly, but love them tenderly. Emotions and pain: women have twice as many nerve receptors than men. It causes them to feel pain more intensely. They have a high tolerance for it as well. Women are emotional creatures. Any way you touch her emotionally, she will gravitate towards you. Psychologically, emotionally or physically. This is one of the reasons why some women are attracted to funny guys, because it is like they are triggering an emotion. Danger triggers an emotion. Why is it most women cannot forget or they gravitate towards the guy that triggered her or broke her heart? That guy that emotionally had them bound and the nice guy that does everything she wants, has never been mean to her, she cannot give him the time of day.

The only person that can heal you is the person who hurt you. You are on her mind, body and soul. It is when we look at pain and pleasure, they are basically opposites in general terms. One feels good and one does not. However for those who engage in BDSM, this is often not the case. The pain the sub sometimes feel in the activity they pursue, gives them the pleasure they crave so much. What you do not understand is the pain from these activities are controlled pain. It is not something sudden or with no warning like for example; pain from an accidental injury. Within the realm of BDSM, there is most definitely good and bad pain. Mostly the things we choose to do are things that give us good pain. For example; good pain would be spanking or flogging. Bad pain would be a severe caning or needle play. There is different perspectives on what is good pain and bad pain, with different type of subs. For you to understand this pain, you would have to communicate with your submissive as to what would be perceived as good and bad pain. For me to get a sub's point of view, I usually engage with aftercare and connecting with them and conversing. It allows me to be able to perform well without hesitation, when I understand everything they need and the limits they can handle. We go through the negotiation process with the hard and soft limits from the beginning. I also evaluate the sub like I would a fitness client when training. I get their stats. When I engage with these activities with them, I can say they love all pain or hate all pain. The pain to a certain degree, they love. Majority of the time, this pain brings them pleasure. It sends them into subspace and then the pain goes away. It changes to a euphoric state as the endorphins kick in and they mentally float away. It is like getting a tattoo; at some point I do not feel the needle. All the good shit hurts in the beginning but then eventually you get used to it,(understand pain, therefore I am able to control it, and deliver it as well). For example, when you drive a stick for the first time, the first gear is the toughest, but once you get it rolling nothing can stop you. Once these chemicals are released from their brain during the activities, it is like an addiction; they now need it, compared to wanting it. This is where they need Discipline. The flogging and the spankings hurt us, but the pain we feel is what gives us the adrenaline rush, the adrenaline rush that we crave and therefore the pleasure becomes ours. Hence, the activity from our pain becomes our pleasure. Example; how pleasure and pain work: Nipple clamping. I do not use that as play. I use it as punishment. It feels nice but 'ouch', when they are put on. The sub may groan in pain but loves the pleasure, when the Dominate flicks and touches them. It increases the sensations in the nipples. Myself personally, I love to hear my subs moan, groan and whimper. It gives me pleasure to see the reaction to the pain. When the clamps are removed it hurts again, but the adrenaline rush is amazing for the sub. The rush is painful, but releases the endorphins which brings pleasure. For example, my dick is not average and when most women see my dick they freak out, like they think it is going to kill them. When I slide in, they gasp really loud and they brace themselves for the massive impact, and at that moment they have to get use to my size. It hurts at first, but once the chemicals are released from your brain, the endorphins and Oxytocin, the serotonin, the dopamine, you embrace the pain. The hair pulling, the spanking, the choking. The pain and the associated rush, brings the same release of endorphins, which in turn gives the pleasure your sub craves. I enjoy the relationship between pain and pleasure. It gives me pleasure to inflict controlled pain to a sub, knowing in turn the sub will also gain pleasure from the interaction between us. However, there is something to add to the whole picture and that is how the mind works. Without the mindset of a sub, a slave, a masochist, things like spanking, flogging, caning and piercing would simply hurt like hell. Like when I got my tattoos on my ribs, it hurt like hell, but I zoned out. I put my headphones on and watched a movie and did not think about the pain. I manipulated my senses, and my mind. It made the process so much easier for me. As a sub or slave you make a conscious choice to engage in these activities. Which is where the difference comes in. There are not many people who would have enjoyed being punished as a child, but here as consenting adults we have agreed to the same activity, although sometimes in more extreme ways. There are many reasons for pursuing the pleasure and pain side of things in BDSM. For many it is sexual gratifications. People get turned on with the activities they partake in. It fulfils a need. For others, it fills needs of a different kind. Perhaps someone needs to give pain or receive pain simply for the endorphin rush. Not connected to sexual gratification at all, but for the aspect of control and power exchange. That is where I come in. It is not just a sexual gratification. The rush of power and the control is where I thrive, and is where I excel. Power and control! That is the rush for me. Pain is pleasure and pleasure is pain. For a sub, it is the same emotion. For me it is the same emotion. Truth be told, women are into sex more than men. Some days women do not want to be taken lightly. They want to feel your testosterone. You as a man, sometimes they want to be pushed up against the wall and kissed passionately. To feel like they are the object of your unbridled lust. They love to feel helpless. Vulnerable. The late Bob Marley said, "being vulnerable is the only way to allow your heart to feel true pleasure." Simply meaning, when you open, your heart, mind, and body there are endless possibilities and blessing to enter into your realm. The thing about pain is, it demands to be felt. Pain becomes a requirement for the sub and the Dom. At the end of the day, I am a savage romantic

CHAPTER 24

Kiss Her Lips And The Other Lips Speak

Kiss her like you need mouth-to-mouth resuscitation. Kiss her like she is the object of your unbridled lust, and just witness how her pussy lips speak to you. Then take her. Do not ask, do not blink. Stare her dead in the eyes and take her. Lay her aggressively on the bed, pull up her dress, expose that pussy. Goosebumps cover her body, chills running up and down her spine. Whisper in her ear, "this pussy is mine." But do not just say so, own it, prove it. Eat that pussy like you mean it. Slurp on that clit, like it was the last Capri sun pouch drink. Tongue her clit, trace the number 8 back and forth on it, and flick your tongue up and down, side to side, if she is into it, multitask, stick a finger in her drenched begging hole. Use the come here gesture with your finger. Her G spot tail is on the top, trigger that. Have her singing high notes to you and it will be like music to your ears. Every woman has a freak inside her, it just takes the right man to unleash the beast out of her. "Kick back, moan and hold on to something. Do not hold onto me, but hold onto something and enjoy the ride." A well trained sub knows how to control herself. I do not want to have to get the spreader bar that would bind her ankles and hands to the bar. Not only that, I want to use my own physical strength to hold her on my own. I wanted to trust that she would listen. Listen to my commands, so that I would not have to tie her up. Just to witness how psychologically bound she was to me. Spreading her lips with my hands, as I dive in to feast on her delicious pussy. Her lips parted and the only thing to come out of her mouth besides her moans, was "oh fuck." I said to her, "oh fuck is right, I am going to fuck up your world." I grasped both of her luscious breasts, and hardened nipples, as I continued to eat. Slapping, pinching and grabbing them. I was succeeding in driving her insane. Her whimpering, whining, crying and begging to release. Climax, orgasm, squirming. I commanded sharply, "do not fucking move." She did not move, but her legs were shaking like she was nervous. She was cursing like a sailor. Begging me to allow her to cum. She begged me again, "please daddy, please, please, please can I cum?" I said no. I loved to watch her suffer and squirm. She did exactly as I commanded. She did not cum, she did not squirt. She waited for my command and she does as I tell her, just like a good sub. I tortured her some more, then finally allowed her to release. She gasped so loudly it was beautiful. Drenched like Niagara Falls, eruption like a volcano. I whispered in her ear "mine." She took a deep breath "yours".

CHAPTER 25

The Innocent Face

There is always a dangerous side to a innocent face. Normally the women who are laid back and shy are always the most adventurous. Every woman has a wild child in her, it just takes the right person to bring it out. You have some women that have authoritative positions in life. They are the boss in a company, but that does not mean she is not shy. She could be a realtor, a teacher, a lawyer and she is perhaps a homebody. By "homebody", I'm referring to, she doesn't go out much. She is a little antisocial. The shy girls, the innocent faces, the ones we love the most. The ones that look like church on a Sunday, but fuck nasty on Friday and Saturday. Good girls with naughty minds. Smooth criminals. The quiet, the laid back, the timid assassins. The 'secretly behind closed doors' loved getting slapped, whipped and choked out. The ones that enjoy screaming at the top of their lungs. The baby faces. The ones that make society say, "ohhhh she is so sweet, so cute", but the Scorpio that I am, I see right through you. I can look in your eyes and see through your soul. I see a beast begging to be unleashed. You gravitate towards a master like me for guidance. I can sense the tug of desire in your pussy. The throb of your clit when you peer at me. You run to a beast like me for savagery. You slither to an alpha like me for confidence. You come to a bad boy like me for adventure. Danger and corruption. You love and seek a Daddy like me for protection. A Dominant like me for strength. Who witness a King like me as perfection. Who seeks a Sadist like me for pain, who views me and thinks to themselves: "Ahhh freedom." Deep connection, extraordinary Dominant, passionate, beautiful greatness. The ones that yearn to love you unconditionally. Who knows I can give them these things and more.

Dominate them in a way a regular man could never, ever dream of. "Yes, you shy innocent woman you. This morning you were good but tonight, I am going to turn you into a loving, passionate, nymphomaniac, big chocolate cock sucking, hungry slut." To gaze into her eyes and think…I hope I scare her. But the question is, do I scare her away? Or do I scare her enough to come to me and desire to stay forever? When the desire overpowers the fear, when the desire triggers surrender, when her submission now becomes my power. That is beauty. It is okay, little innocent faces; you can admit it, you want it rough, deep, nasty and dirty. You want to see the steel in my eyes. To hear the bass in my voice. When I tell you how to please me, and you want to know that I will not hesitate to punish you, if you do not follow my commands. Yes, you heard me. I will punish you. I will not be gentle either. It will not be playful. I will bend you the fuck over however, wherever, whenever and spank your ass until it hurts, until it is branded with my big handprint. You will be out of sorts as you forget the line between pain and pleasure. You want to feel my thick chocolate cock pounding deep into you, until you scream for the man above to help you. Do not scream for him, he is busy. Scream for me. Scream for Discipline. Scream for pain. Most guys you have had in the past, did not get you, they think you desire the fake, and made up prince charming. The flowers, the candy, the roses. But, when you shut your eyes at night, whether it was a husband or a boyfriend you were with, or you were single, I am the type of man you fantasized about. Yanking your hair back and slamming you into me, shoving you down on your knees, fucking your face with my massive chocolate cock. Spanking you sore, while you drip, begging me for more. I know your secret, I can see it in your eyes, I can read it in your body language. The shameful uncomfortable, embarrassing things you cannot say out loud. Oh baby girl I know. But he is too worried about hurting you, ruining you or breaking you. "I love you baby, why would I hurt you? Why would you want me to hurt you?" But that is exactly what you desire. Because, your love is not just gentle. Your love is different from his love. You want that deep dick, can't walk, can hardly think, mind-blowing love. You want to feel the strength of a real man, an animal, biting, slapping and spanking. Shoving my monster chocolate cock so deep, you feel it in your chest or throat. Fucking you senseless until you forget your name. You want to be sore? You want to be sobbing? Gasping? Desperate for another taste? I know you do. Because what you really want is to surrender, and to give yourself to my every demand. To submit to me body and soul. However, I also desire your mind. The only difference with those other guys is,I really do not care if you are okay with it or not. I will make you beg. Scream. Crawl. And when you kneel and have earned what I think you should earn, you will get what you want.

Does this make me dangerous?

Of course it makes me dangerous!

One, because I know what I am and second, I know what I can do.

You do not know what to expect, but it does not matter does it? Even if you were a little bit frightened, it is still what you crave. I will not mislead you. I will make you feel alive. I will make you feel reckless. I will make you feel sexy. Secure. Wanted and desired. Safe. Loved. Protected and fucked senseless. The look in my piercing eyes will give you chills. I will do things to your mind, you will wish you had the strength to deny. Take you to heights you have never traveled, mind, body and soul. You will give me everything, you will give me all of you. But I only demand one thing in return......your complete submission!

CHAPTER 26

Listen Carefully

C oming back from the restaurant
    The drive back home
Driving home
She had liquor in her system
I am driving
Paying attention to the road
She is quiet
Now she is moving, body moving
She is slithering on her seat
Seat back
Doing all this stuff without my permission
Licks her lips
She is grabbing my thigh while I am driving
Which is not allowed
Don't want to be touched without permission
Becoming angry

But I am quiet

Main priority is making sure we are safe

Reach destination

No need to confront her while focusing on the road

She knows this – and wants to get into trouble

Feeling frisky

She is not fully aware of what she is doing

She is not thinking, she just wants to feel

As she grabs my thigh she leaves my hand

Starts rubbing down towards my knee

From pelvic area to knee

So now I grab her by her wrist

I have the wheel in my left hand

and my right hand grabbing her wrist

I do not say a word

Just grabbed

In that moment she knew to stop

To pause

To refrain from what she was doing

I placed her hand aggressively to her side

and then I let go

She starts touching herself

Rubbing her clit

Fingering herself, starts licking herself off of her fingers

Putting her fingers back inside her wet pussy hole

As she now starts to moan, she is commanding my attention

At this point I am so pissed off

Fucking pissed off

Fucking turned on

But kept driving

My fury is stronger and more potent than my lust right now

Discipline is my greatest asset

It does not matter about lust

Because that will always fade

More so my integrity, my rules, ethics and my Discipline that I stand by

This is what enforces me to be who I am and what I am

Fierce

Untamed

InDomitable

She moans extremely loud as she takes a loud gasp of air to cum

3 strikes and you are out

1. She touched herself without permission

2. Touched him without permission

3. orgasmed without permission

So that is out

This is narrative

I am playing it cool

But I knew that as soon as I got to our designation safe

Not only was she going to hear me

See the anger in my eyes, witness the anger, feel the anger

She was going to know what she did

and how we were going to correct it

Get to her house

I parked the car

I go to her side, open her door

I put out my hand

She takes my hand

I shut the door

I walk her up to her door

But I do not say good night

I go all the way inside

I shut the door

I push her up against the wall

So hard she gasps

My hand is pressed against her chest

and slithers up to her throat

My big chocolate man fingers

Squeezing the flesh around her throat

I gazed into her eyes

As she witnesses my menacing stare

I spoke softly but forcefully I said

"Listen carefully,

I told you prior that I own you

While you are here

With me

In my presence in my zone

You are mine

Your soul, your body

Whatever you have outside of me

Leave it where it is

Because whatever it is – that is irrelevant

In my presence you are on my time

I will reiterate

I own your mind, body and soul

I will have you and you are to do whatever pleases

Whenever, however

No question marks

I am not asking

I do not need to say, 'do I make myself clear?'

You know why you are here

You made 3 mistakes

You have violated 3 of the rules"

Then I explained what those 3 rules were that she violated and then told her this will never happen again

Why? Because tonight you are going to be punished at the highest degree. I turn her around

Grab a fist full of hair

Towards me

Head yanked back

I took her arms and clasped them together behind her in these big hands

and made her walk

She said

I'm sorry daddy

For violating the rules

and I say, "why are you apologetic now? because you are on the brink of being punished?

Where is your smile?

The licking of your lips

Where are your noise/moans now?

Oh you are going to make noise

But it will not be moans

Sorry? Sorry didn't violate the rules

You did, therefore you will be held accountable

What do you plan on doing with me?

Where are we going?

"Shhhhh, silence

In this moment no more questions and no more talking for you

You will speak when I say you may speak."

So In that moment I start to suspend

*****instead of dropping her off to her house – I take her back to my place instead. At my place, she was overwhelmed, excited, nervous.

Scared because I am furious.......

CHAPTER 27

Dominated / Punishment

I am furious. We walk inside my place and I push her up against the wall, and I mention her 3 critical errors tonight. I tell her now she will be punished. I tie her up. Her ankles, her hands, and I gag her mouth, with a gag ball, and blindfold her. I strip off her clothes and make her stand in the corner with just her heels on. "Don't fucking move from where you are until I get back. I don't give a fuck if you need to use the restroom. Pee on yourself, then I'll fucking make you clean it up. I left her standing in the corner of the room for an hour, before I come back with my whips. I went to make myself a sandwich. I boiled asparagus. When that cooking oil hits that pan, all I could think of, was what I was going to do to her. I fixed up a salad, lettuce, tomatoes and onions, with grilled chicken cutlets. Watched a little sports(football, basketball, and wrestling were ones I was fond of) on my television. I finally came back....she didn't move from where I ordered her. Didn't complain, or nag.

I mean even if she did, she was blindfolded, and gagged. I spoke softly, but forcefully…."Tonight you violated 3 rules", I said. "Touching what is MINE without my permission is a violation over the top. I am going to punish you in a way you will never forget." I brought out the whip and started to unravel it. "Listen to me carefully", I whisper.

"Every time I strike you, I want you to say that, "this is YOUR pussy Discipline." I advised close to her ear. I lashed her 25 times. The back of her thighs, her delicious plump ass. I told her she was entitled to use her safe word, however, if she used it we do not stop completely, we just take a brief recess and then we start counting from the beginning. After every lashing, she repeated everything I that I commanded she to repeat. She did not use her safe word. She took everything I was willing to deliver. I thought to myself, why would this woman go through all this? She is not using her safe word, she is enduring all this pain.

Is she falling in love with this pain, I wondered? After the 25th lashing, 'this is enough', I thought. No more. I released her. There were so many bruises on her flesh. This is what she signs up for. This is what she deserves. This is what she needs, or she forgets who the fuck I am. Who she is, what she is to me, and ultimately, what this life entails.

When a man has a true sadist that lurks within his soul, every now and then, he is blessed to find a person he can make whole. One whose face he can kiss and tell her she is pretty with no lies, but then push her to the wall and release everything that is inside. She fights a good fight, but he overpowers her but it is not the scar that she craves, it is the act. I grabbed her and put her over my shoulder.

CHAPTER 28

Aftercare

I carried her in my arms and I placed her on the bed, gently stroking her luxurious hair. My fingertips traced the bruises I left on her flesh softly and slowly. I then kissed her. I cuddled her in my big strong arms. Held her tight. Stroked her hair like a comb. This is where she feels safest, this is home. Even though she disobeyed. Even though she was punished. Her heart is still fragile as are her welts. Her bruises will heal quickly, her heart will take time. Holding her in my arms, allowing her to feel my appreciation. Love. Protection. Security. The type of comfort that encourages her serenity. Respect. No judgment, only acceptance. Feeling at ease, mentally, emotionally and physically. Granting each other access into a psychological, emotional and physical space. Allowing her to feel free to express herself around me. To discuss anything and everything. My sub will experience this life, and I do not except her to be or feel the same as to when she first came in. When you engage in this activity and live this life, you will start to develop very strong emotions. That is inevitable. All you see is the savagery. Brutality. Discipline. Sexual sadism. Punishment. This is what they do not show. This is what no one talks about. I think aftercare is extremely imperative. It is like a freshly done tattoo. The needle beats up your flesh, now you must work to heal it. In order for it to heal properly, you must engage in aftercare. Just like a submissive. A sub is an investment at the end of the day. Just like a home, a vehicle. She is your most prized possession. She may have tough skin, but her heart is fragile. Constant reassurance thy she is safe, protected and cared for is imperative. Especially when she goes into subspace. Give attention. Give affection. Aftercare is displayed in many different ways and forms. Most of the time during physical sexual activity, there are these chemicals released from our brains. Like oxytocin. Endorphins. Every sub reacts differently once she is in subspace. If she goes into some type of anxiety, you as her Dom, needs to be aware of that and transform into Daddy. You have access into a psychological space of your sub. An emotional space. Some Dominants may experience Dom burnout or Dom drop. In order to understand each other and the dynamics, each must communicate. Not just communicate, but efficiently. Do not just Dominate her roughly. Cuddle her roughly as well. If a Dom will not cuddle you, he is not really a Dom. BDSM is not some cheap thrill. Not some cheap no feelings attached. Friends with benefits dynamic. Re-evaluate and rebrand. I am just saying, I like to cuddle my subs and communicate after. It is a form of me connecting more with them. Building more trust, building more of a bond. It is not just about "fucking", it is about sex, it is about intimacy. A Dom wants to feel needed, and a sub needs to feel wanted. Aftercare is not just cuddling. It depends on the sub and Dom. For example, her temperature may drop and she may need a blanket. She may need to be held, as your body heat blends with hers. Fluids, etc. BDSM creates strong emotions. If you choose to skip after care, it is worst than abandonment. Fucking her up psychologically, in a negative way. After care is a great investment in your sexual future. Why? Because the more you show you care for you partner, the safer they feel. The safer they feel, they tend to bring new sexual experiences to new levels. Once trust is established immensely, you can take her to the moon and back. Give her millions of orgasms without trying. Take her mind everywhere, and you can take her body anywhere. Subspace is a state of non verbal ecstasy. Cuddling literally kills depression. Relieves anxiety and strengthens the immune system. Some essentials you may need in aftercare is water. When you perspire you need to replenish your fluids, baby wipes, some fruit close by to strengthen immune system, because they are high in vitamin C. Shower. For myself, I like a blunt. A massage from her, love a good conversation, and be ready for round two. When conversing….It is essential to be close, know where they are, how they felt from the experience, where their mind is, and their feelings. The safer both parties feel, the better the relationship. The healing and bonding is quicker. We cuddled on the bed. We conversed. She was constantly meeting these men and they could never measure up. Especially to a woman of her calibre. Accolades. Etc. She was everything a man could want. A fox to a lot of hound dogs on the hunt. The kush to a lot of kush, rolling the blunt. But because her mind was so beautiful, she was limited with certain tastes she desired. Requiring a different substance. Today, I was going to show her a different perspective. She was not just educated, she was wise. Intelligent. The world was overpopulated with stupid people. There wasn't a law requiring her to associate with them. She was forced to deal with them enough on a daily basis. She damn sure did not want to be in a relationship with one. No matter how handsome he was. She met some fairly dumbness in men from college. She said, "There appeared to be an asshole

ratio proportion to their dumb-assery and handsomeness."
She said, "the cuter and dumber they were, the more they
expected any woman to give her left nipple, and jump into
bed with them." She said, "it was fun to mess with them,
then turn them down. If you're going to be handsome and
an asshole, at least back it up." I said sarcastically, "like
how dare you say no to their chiselled bodies, good looks,
and boudoir skills. With the "z" being all unfortunately
visible in the way they said it, or spelled it." She sighed. "If
I would use an overused word to describe your situation,
it would probably be, the dumb is strong out here. The
struggle, for reals, with a deliberately iconic 'z.'" She
giggled. She sighed again, "oh my god, you get me! You get
it!" I smirked discreetly. "Oh you're making fun. Ha ha",
with her sarcasm right back to me. "Relax, it's slangs. Did
you take the time to get to know them?" I called her an
"intellectual snob." Her lips parted in shock. "Hey!! I like
to consider myself a sapiosexual!" I smirked once again
prior to shaking my head, "yeah, intellectual snob." She
shook her head at me. I said to her, "so before me, where
were you then with men?" She paused and I said, "exactly,
meeting guys locally, via online, Fetlife, etc. Hasn't worked
out so well for the snarky, creative woman with a borderline
genius IQ level." She laughs, "I can't help that I'm
Sapiosexual." I moved closer to her earlobe then whispered,
"I think the term you meant was, intellectual snob." She

squints her eyes at me. "You're so mean Daddy, I'm not a snob. I can't help that I'm choosey. There's a big difference." "You want a creative, intelligent, preferably employed guy, who has some charming quirks, strong, who can stimulate your mind, and has a wild side. Who isn't a Domineering asshole. Preferably black. If you shoot one of those out your ass, you can take that act on the road, and make some real entertainment." Her mouth parted again, "you are quite fresh tonight Daddy", saying it with a smirk on her face. She is an intelligent woman. She allows her imagination to run wild. You are enticing her because you seem like a challenge. In a world full of the liars, small minded, the pretenders, the under performers, the weak men who cannot keep up with her ravenous passions. Her intellectual thoughts. Her beautiful mind is flowing with sensations. Deeper than the ocean. Where most would drown in. She has arousing cravings for her aches to be filled. Her mind races. (Thoughts to myself while I stared at her) To crawl inside her cerebral and tame it. Dive my fingers into her rawness. Shove my intellect into her pineal gland and thrust, entrap, demoralize, Dominate, entice, ravish, choke hold her soul, making her die a thousand deaths. Just to bring her back to life, a brand new woman again. "Am I right?" She gasped, "yes, fine, yes you are right, are you happy now?" I shook my head, "no, I want to know more. So what will happen when you meet this guy?" She replied,

"I met you already. I smirk, "let's keep me out of the picture. Let's say you met this man of your dreams, hypothetically speaking? She pauses before replying... "Perhaps, I would marry him." I laughed, and she asked me, "What is so damn funny?" "Well, I don't mean to laugh, but what makes you so sure he will be fond of you?" She stared at me, "because he will be!" "What makes you so sure? So confident?" "Why are you being so pessimistic?" "I'm not, I am being realistic. The epidemic of alpha males in this world, you need to take into account the odds. Unless you crave all these and desire a submissive man who is a warrior in bed?" She said, "no I will get bored." "Then an intellectual alpha male, who isn't going to fuck your brains out?" She replied, "no"? "So what about he's that psychologically, physically and spiritually being, then would you want him? He can stimulate your mind as well as your soul and body, however, what happens if he isn't fond of you? You're going to force him? But, you don't want a Domineering man, but you want him to be the man? As much of an intellectual snob as you are. As much of an alpha woman as you are. Will you allow the man to be the man?" She stared at me again. "I am....not.....a....snob." I laughed, "I said all that and all you heard was snob?" We both stared at each other and smiled. "You know you're a little funny. When you're not so serious, you're intriguing. Something about you. I'm so curious." I said, "careful, curiosity killed the cat." She said, "that's fine, because I think everything that kills a person, makes them feel so alive." She was so fucking good. I craved to turn her so fucking bad. Enticed to see what more the future holds for us. She spoke softly, "I would love to know about you. Your family, life outside of this, if you have a middle name. Your real name. If this is all we will be, Dominant/submissive. If this is the type of relationship we will have forever?" "Hey, calm the fuck down. I will answer the most important thing and that is this relationship…yes, this is your life now. No, we will not always be Dominant and submissive. My goal is for you to one day be my slave or Queen. Where you will have no limits, no safe words and you will be, take, whatever. Do whatever for me. But that will be your decision down the road. It will not be coerced. As far as the other questions, you will have to earn those. I told her, "I would be more than addicting to you. You would need me like you need air to breathe. If I kissed you, then you would always need my kisses to be complete. I will take your breath away. The next one you take will belong to me." In my head all I could think about, when I said it to her, was giving her nasty, wet kisses. Biting her juicy bottom lip, while I tug on her hair, tilting her head back, while my hand was placed around her throat. Squeezing the flesh around it. Dominating her mouth, but there was so much more she needed to learn. So much more she needed to be aware of. So much more she needed guidance on to please me. To be a better sub for herself and I. "I will teach you everything I know of this lifestyle, and you will eat my words, as I feed them to you. Utilize my commands as guidance and direction. My intentions have been set from the beginning...you are going to fucking please me. Your only job is that, and that is it. My job is to make sure you focus on nothing but. You will have a memory like an elephant. Listen carefully, pay attention.. So I will go over a few things with you and first things first, your name is changed. As we discussed this prior, but I'm reiterating. As my name has changed as well. You will only refer to me as, Daddy, Papi, Master and/or King. Nothing else or I will punish you. You are never to call me 'baby.' My mother is the only woman in the world that can address me as this, for I came out of her. Do not address me as, "boo", it is not Halloween. Do not address me as, 'bae', I do not know what that is, is that an acronym for, ' bacon and eggs?'" She giggled, "Ahh, cut that out, you are lucky we are having a vanilla(regular) conversation or I would punish you for giggling and cutting me off." "Sorry Daddy." She said so meekly. "Good girl. Now if I say 'good girl', that means I am pleased with you. I am proud of you. Now, do not address me as 'sweetie, hun, love', or any of those silly ridiculous nicknames. Do you understand everything I am telling you? Everything I demand of you?" "Yes King, I am here to serve you and only you. You lead and I follow." I smirk. "Good girl. Now we will go over some rules............

CHAPTER 29

My Rules

There are things I demand from the beginning. Your loyalty, your dedication, your devotion, your hard work, your Discipline, your openness, your honesty. I do not crave, desire, hope for these things. I fucking demand them. Dominance comes with a price. In order for you to obtain greatness, you must be willing to give parts or a part of yourself. For a psychological sub, I require your mind. As a emotionally intelligent Dom, I require your soul. As a physical Dom, I require your body. I do not want one and not the others, if you are unwilling to give all of you, I will take nothing. Once a sub has earned my trust, we pursue to engage in physical activity. I conduct what I like to call a negotiation process. Here is a negotiation of hard and soft limits. These are the only things I will negotiate. Hard limits that are too far, off limits, things that are grotesque or you never desire to fulfil. Soft limits are the opposite. For example, some soft limits may be mild or severe spanking, with a hand, crop or paddle. These are the things you agree upon, these are the things you welcome, these are the things that you do not mind. These are the things you love or you desire to fulfil. For example, hard limits can pertain to nipple clamps, clit clamps, choking with a hand around the throat, blindfold, electric play, water sports, gun play, knife play, threesome just to name a few. This lifestyle is predicated on trust. If you do not communicate efficiently and there is no trust 100%, it is extremely difficult to fulfil any of this. Once trust is established, you can go places mind, body and soul that transcends parameters beyond any basic traditional relationship is willing to offer. Some of the things on my list I give to my subs prior to starting a sexual relationship, I will ask questions such as, if they are interested in nipple clamps, clit clamps, water sports, facials, cum shots, spankings, bondage, worship (cock, hands, body worship like massages) kneeling, blindfolds, handcuffs, hair pulling, anal, covering mouth during intense penetration, face slapping, food porn, phone sex, breathing control, electric play, gun play, knife play, name change, hot wax, wrestling, biting and scratching, this is just to name some. The better I know my partner, the better I am able to pleasure her efficiently. Knowledge is power. The more I am aware, the better it is. I am a Scorpio that takes pride in being the greatest you ever had. Especially when it comes to sex, I take it seriously. The most powerful and intense of all signs especially in bed, lovemaking is an all or nothing mentality. I thrive off of foreplay. My body reacts to connection. Without any connection, I would just be a selected Dom to restrain you. We would have no relationship beyond that. You will not know what side of the bed I want to sleep on. How I like to tie my ties. If I drink coffee in the morning, and how I like my coffee. For the minimum I would provide, it would be the greatest thing ever in your life. However, for me I would be bored easily and if I am bored, the relationship will be temporary. I do not play for fun, I play for keeps. This lifestyle is a lifestyle that is special to me. Anyone coming into my lifestyle should have a goal in what they desire to build upon and what is conducive to our dynamic. If you are not trying to build a connection, you can look past me. In this moment I will not hold your hand. I will not guide you. I do what I want. I want what I take, and when I take, I fucking Dominate. I feed you my energy and corrupt your sensibilities. I will challenge every notion of pleasure you have ever known. I will shatter every boundary you thought you would never cross. If you come here to just fuck, I will make you fall in love. If you come here to just love, I will make you a chocolate addict. If you come here to just give, I will leave you giving me everything with no limits. You will come to me then you will cum for me. I am your first of many things, last of few. I am the Alpha and Omega. The beginning and end. You are a submissive of mine, you are a full time submissive. Not part time submissive. Not a weekend submissive. Not a holiday submissive. Not a vacation submissive. Your submission for me is not part time either, or half obtainable. I will protect you like you are a piece of fragile glass. Cherish your heart like a gift but I will destroy, devour, Dominate, gradually dismantle your body like it is unbreakable. Savagely. The fact that I love you, will not save you tonight. I am going to fuck you up. Every touch, no matter how rough or how tender. It is a reminder of how much you need me. You are appreciative. I show you how I appreciate you...to be stuck. Slapped. Kissed. Fucked. Made love to. Caressed. Used. As I choose to use you. Mine. A man who ruins you perfectly in every way you have ever secretly desired. A powerful MAN. A Chocolate KING. A Dominant BEAST. A Sadistic DADDY. A prominent MASTER who shows you love in many forms. Kind and unkind. All for you. All needed. Now smile for me...so I can fucking slap that smile off your face and grab it. Muscular hands grasp ahold of you. Breathless. But breath for me one time. As I make all your dreams come true, I want you to whisper, 'thank you.' You will always be humble to me, no matter how long it is, whether we are here, there or not there, because you respect what I can do. Which makes me the best in the world at what I fucking do. You will always respect me because of how I Dominate you. How I have Dominated you. You will respect my Dominance for as long as you live and when you do not, you know I can always take it away, for a short period of time to punish and control you. The way I leave you in a trance. Put you in subspace. Punish you emotionally, physically, or psychologically. For as long as you live, no other man will ever love you or fuck you as passionately. Dominantly. Forcefully. Roughly. Powerfully. Properly as I do you. Two lovers you will ever remember... Number one, your first love, and second, myself, and even then it will pale in comparison to me. I will pleasure you with pain. Spoil you with bruises. Those are your gifts. Wear them with pride. I will bite the meatiest parts of your flesh. Meticulously. Methodical. Calculating and taking my time. You are my main course meal. I will savor every bite, as you become momentarily dazed by my Dominant behavior. Enjoying you to the fullest. Your body and my body. Skin to skin. Flesh to flesh. Soul to soul. My mouth and your mouth. My thick, long chocolate Dick, your tight, drenched delicious pussy get along famously. Stern Dominant. On top of the fucking food chain. Now I show you why I will always be on top of you. With knowledge comes trust automatically. One of the reasons you confide in me. One of the reasons you give yourself to me. An inexperienced man will always leave a level of uncertainty for you. To you I am everything. Beast incarnate. Daddy. Sadist. King Kong. You will never forget this sharp mind, big ass morphine, demon dick, and tornado tongue. I know what to do with all three to you, and I do it extremely well. To be mine you will be giving up many parts of you. When I take, I take completely. The psychological and physical abuse I give you will either make or break you forever. Give you a case of algolagnia. Pain without sex and sex without pain, will never make sense to you. As you will need both to be fulfilled. You will witness the alteration of your entire being. You will evolve into a strong woman or deteriorate and become a weak one. You are worthless until I make you priceless. You are nothing, until I make you something. You know nothing, until I have shown you everything. I will fuck you to every song, so when you hear them when I am not around you will think of me. Grab your ankles, as I command you, "bounce on that shit like you mean it slut!" Staring down at that, whispering softly but forcefully in your ear, "oh you are fucking nasty, aren't you? You love bouncing off Daddy' big chocolate dick I see." Maneuvering my muscular, big hands to her waist. Mastering her curves. Controlling all her movements. Her love handles, I handle just to handle. Spreading her ass cheeks hard, just to get in deeper. Grasp a fist full of her hair, with one hand, other hand slapping each ass cheek, hard! Receiving every impactful delicious slap. Love how my hand print looks on her, branding my territory. She screams with every delicious, impactful slap. "Yes, you whore, get my big chocolate dick rock hard with your pain. With your suffering. With your cries. With your moans. Your whimpering. All that shit belongs to me. I create it." Thumb in her butt. Double the pain. Double the pleasure. You hear and feel every impactful, delicious slap. Hair pulling can be essential. When the endorphins kick, it can be extremely pleasurable. Women have twice as many nerve receptors than men. Causing them to feel pain more intensely. They have a high tolerance for it as well. When pulling her hair, pull more towards the scalp. It is an intense feeling. As the few chemicals released from our brains during intercourse, that Oxytocin now turns her pain into pleasure. Now it becomes addictive. The endorphins kicking in. What would normally hurt, is soothing. "You now need consistent Discipline. "There will be pain involved, but only if you ask nicely. Now beg bitch!" Now I guide her into my world, after all that activity was over. "Follow my rules and in my eyes, no matter what, you will always be good. Good girls get rewarded. However, if you deliberately disobey me, I will hold you personally accountable for your actions. Bad girls get punished. Disciplinary action will be in order. Punishment will not be fun. It will not be of your choosing, nor will it always be physical. Some do this for fun, I do it to teach you. Allowing you to thrive and excel. I own your soul as well as your body and mind. Therefore, it will be emotional or mental Discipline at times. Only excuses are family or work, but when I say "now", that means, "right now." Immediately. No cigarette smoke, I do not kiss ashtrays. Weed is acceptable. Do not drink excessively or on a daily basis. Once a week or bi weekly. Always say, "Please and thank you." You earned it, that means swallow it. Every drop.

The proper position is always on your knees, you shall kneel before me naked and unashamed. Unless we are in public. Then you walk to the side of me. Jealousy and insecurity will be left outside the door as you come into my world. Never, and allow me to reiterate, I mean never, be ashamed of getting too wet. That is inevitable when I am around or when you think of me. Embrace your beauty. If I say you are beautiful that is the truth. Never doubt me. Only thing you should assume anything is the damn position. You must ask permission to touch yourself. I own every inch of you. You must ask when you are about to gush, explode. Thank me for each one. Hair, nails, not only do I want to know about it, but you must ask my approval on styles and colors. Always tell daddy the truth. If you are sad, angry, whatever, I want to know about it. Come to me. Do not talk back. If you do, use your lower lips, because the ones up top I will slap. I hate to speak twice. If I do, get ready for a spanking. Unless we are having a vanilla conversation, then it is acceptable. Correct response to most things should be, yes King, yes Master. Only things I will negotiate with you are your hard and soft limits. Other than that, daddy is in complete control. Are we clear? Fuck the rhetorical question. Of course we are clear. You are mine. What choice do you have? No choice. You yearn to please me. I am not asking. Obey me at all times or else. Just as I give good things, I can withhold. Why? Because I can. Do not test me. "Yes daddy." GOOD GIRL.

One thing about a Scorpio, it is best to stay on our good side because we can make hell look like a prize compared to what we can give you, and take away. "The Sadist in me lurks. The beast is fighting me to come out. I hear voices in my head, and by pushing my button, you now answer to them. So let us all show you, why you are here. Who you are, who I am and what this is, because you seem to have forgotten. This will not be fun. This will not be pleasurable. You will not enjoy this, but I promise, you will learn today. Your pain belongs to me, your suffering belong to me, your tears belong to me. Your cries belong to me, your hurt belong to me, your marks, whether it is psychological, physical or emotional belong to me. One of many things I provide. But when you lose track of what we are, disobey, misbehave, I give you punishment. You get what you deserve. You earn it. Your behavior determines the results of everything I give you and do not give you." I am going to list a few punishments from my experiences. They are not all the same and I will explain why. In my opinion, punishment should be the last resort. I rather use positive reinforcement. However, in my lifestyle, in a D/s(Dom/sub) relationship, it is essential. It is definitely a part of a Dom/sub, Top/bottom, a Master/Slave, and even can be one in a King/ Queen, or Sadist/Masochist dynamic. However, I never look for punishment. It is the last thing I want to do to my Slave, sub, alpha-sub, bottom, etc. But, punishment offers closure. It puts an end to the problem that caused the punishment to begin with. I take no pleasure in punishing. Punishment is not playtime. Punishment is not, I am going to fuck you rough and choke you to the brink of asphyxiation until you burst like a gushers leaving puddles on the sheets. No!! Punishment is about self-Discipline. For example, I had an out of state sub (currently I have out of state subs) she was 26 and whenever we would FaceTime or video chat, she would suck her thumb. Now that is a subconscious habit and I could sense when she was doing it when we spoke, so I always demanded to FaceTime. So I warned her once, verbally, to eradicate this notion of you needing to suck your thumb. That is some anxiety you have created from your mind, you get physical responses to that. So one night, we were facetiming and she did it. I told her to put hot sauce on her thumb and that was done every damn time we spoke, to the point where she no longer needed to put hot sauce on. This habitual behavior never occurred again. Take into account, she hated hot sauce and it worked. This is where my intellect plays a factor and creativity comes in. There were times I would have her perform self flogging while I watch and we count together. Early bedtimes. No social media, no television, no radio, and I would choose the duration. Whether it was a short or long one. The punishment has to fit the crime. I do not punish to just punish. My goal is to obtain better behavior from you and never to resort to that poor behavior again. I have a current sub where "baby", slipped out of her mouth. It was an honest mistake, but, "baby"? Who is that?"

I did not let that slide. See, the only woman that is allowed to call me baby, is when I go see her, and that is Mi Mami. Because I came out of her. No other woman is allowed to call me that. Ever. This has been my rules since I was a teenager. So when I punished my sub I had her repeat, "Thank you Daddy", after each spanking, lashing, pounding. She endured every toy, from the most powerful tool I had, which was my big, muscular hand, and it has not ever slipped from her tongue or slips ever again. I had a Dominican/Colombian mix once. She was not submissive at all, however, she was a masochist. One hundred percent #painslut. Now I have witnessed things via social media and have heard things through individuals, "when she is acting up, she needs/give her good dick. People do not understand when I say, "I am in total control." Here's another one, "I cannot be manipulated. Even to the point of you getting what you want." You will never learn if I give you what you want. So as her Dominant (because any woman that is involved with me, automatically has a Dom. This is my lifestyle, it is not going to change) and trainer of this lifestyle, it was my duty to punish her. My goal is to know everything about her in order to work her in every way and I do not demand anything less. Some women hate the thick belt. Whether you had a bad childhood. Your dad perhaps used one on you, or whatever it is. However, for a masochist, you need to understand her pain is different from a submissive's pain (take into account subs do have a little bit of masochist tendencies) or even a vanilla (ordinary, boring, normal) woman's pain. Perhaps after the first four lashings/ slaps/ poundings/ spanks, she will beg for more. Now, it is not a good idea to punish a hardcore masochist with a beating. That is what she wants. She could even challenge you, "that's all you got. You are weak, pussy", whatever to fuel you to satisfy her desires. You are falling right into her trap. She has complete control over you and you do not fucking get it. For myself, I withhold the physical punishment. However, if I know she does not like the belt, I will give her the belt. But I withhold physical punishment. Your mind and soul belong to me as well. But you have to know your woman because humiliation, verbal abuse, emotional punishment, all these, a masochist can love as well. Perhaps ignore her for a little bit. Let her mind wander. Not too long. But perhaps she adores your mind and your conversation so you take that away for a day or two. Cold showers. Do not allow her to masturbate and you choose the duration of time. Lock her in the closet, no light and I would not care if she was 27, 35, or 40, I will put her on her fucking knees in the fucking corner like a 5 year old if I want, since you want to act childish. I always explain and discuss why they are being punished. Then I ask them what they will do to better themselves. Do not be bitter, be better. Do not say, "sorry", say you will do better. Sorry will not save you. Sorry will not assist you. Now brats and masochist can be fun, if you are only one masculinity. Like a Sadist. But I am also a Daddy, a Dominant, a King and Master. I like to be catered to and served. I give as I receive and brats I lose interest in quickly. There is nothing and what I am is not conductive to what we would strive to build upon. Unless she is willing to transition, then that is different. Even littles that gravitate to the Daddy, constant needing of direction every minute. I love my women self sufficient. I do not do the daily task shit. When I have certain tasks I say so. I am way too busy to be on the phone with someone every minute of the day and my time should be valued and appreciated as I give it. Begging for attention, I am going to do opposite and ignore you. You want me or attention? You love me or attention, because I do not see attention giving you great things. Pleasure. Power. Knowledge, freedom, etc. The baby girl or little who is more clingy, affectionate, kinky, caring, and can not keep her hands off of you. That is fine because I am very affectionate, and touchy. So there is a good balance there. When we are in each other's presence, I do not see the world or care who watches, I just embrace your essence. I believe one of the most essential things after punishment is aftercare. Without it, is like abuse or abandonment. Your sub is an investment. You should take care of her as you do your house, car, etc. Cuddles, kisses, assurance of safety and allow her to know she is cared for, loved, desired. Subs, and I will even throw masochists in there, may have tough skin but they have weak hearts. Pound, beat, fuck, slap, spank them roughly, but love them tenderly. Reality for me is, my goal is to never punish. For you to always be a good girl. The biggest misconception of this lifestyle is, it is all about kinky sex, or pain and punishment. You are mistaken. BDSM is a peaceful relationship. I am a calm, peaceful man. For this calmness to be interrupted and the beast to unleash there must be destructive acts in the bedroom or disobedience or misbehavior. Other than that I am cool. My subs are treated like Queens, especially in public. Good aftercare is not optional, it is essential after punishment or play. Because loyalty is everything to me, and in order to have a strong connection there needs to be a foundation and without proper self and mental Discipline a Dom/sub have nothing conductive. Nothing magnetic and that weakens many things, like communication, trust, and respect and without those there is no attraction and with no attraction there is no real relationship, and with no real relationship even the sex becomes weak, no matter how good you are, or she is. Only the submissive shows others what type of Dominant owns her. The true character of a man is always displayed by the woman/women he chooses. Serenity is the pinnacle of submission. She said, "sir, you can have anyone you wish. Why waste this time with me. I have been through things you should not have to deal with." I said, "why not you? You will build more confidence and courage in yourself. This is my short term goal for you. Broken women have the deepest souls and love. Damaged women love the hardest. That love is powerful. When you belong to me, it becomes a responsibility.

To provide things you can not get elsewhere. In order to do so, I need trust. No hiding, no secrets, openness. Loyalty. Dedication. Hard work, willingness, all of you. Most men, well regular men, love the superficial and mundane shit a woman has. Money, body and especially love what a woman can do with her body. That is attractive, as I am a man as well, however, that does not keep interests. Nothing is more attractive to me than when a woman can listen. Take direction. Follow without hesitation, without question. Cater. Please. Worship. Please a man besides what is between her legs. Exceeds all my expectations and executes with excellence. Not every woman can give this or do this. I see great potential in you." She gazed at me, "now I understand Sir. I am ready to be yours." I gazed into her eyes and spoke soft but forceful, "be sure this is what you desire, once you surrender there will be no turning back. No end to the torments of pain and tenderness that I will inflict on your soft, wondrous body. How I will make love to you softly and roughly. You will enjoy it as I will as well. Your job is to please me, no matter what and that is it. My job is to make sure you focus on nothing but pleasing me. Granted, you have limits and those can be negotiated, but other than that. You are mine. At all times. Whenever. However. Wherever. Whatever the fuck I want you to be as well. You have the freedom to walk away whenever you please, but if you do. Do not ever come back. Forget about me forever. I do not just want your good, I want your bad. Your imperfections, your dark side. The things you want to get rid of. The things you are afraid no one will love you for. I want that frisky evil you are keeping inside your soul, hiding from society. I want to grab you by your halo and your horns and push my thick chocolate muscular cock between your begging, wet pussy lips. Drenched as your walls hug my cock tightly, in deeper love than it has ever been. Passionately. As I thrust into you roughly. While your eyes burst into flames with lust. We both burn in ashes. As we are reborn immortals.

CHAPTER 30

Mr. Discipline

DOMINATE....The verb........All my life, what was instilled in me, born to do. As a child it did not resonate, as I got older I understood. THE DOMINANT......The noun......Who I am. What I am. A man who is Dominant.... The adjective......Within me, when I look in the mirror, I see my soul. I know who and what I am, and what I am capable of. King is the life I have lived. I believe I am the best in the world at what I do.

I have never had a woman I was with that did not treat me like a king inside and outside the bedroom. All my life, not a wish, not a desire. It is what I fucking demanded. You see some men like to be Dominant, some men ask, desire, crave to be Dominant. It is not something that I need to wish upon, desire, crave or ask for. It is who I am. It is me. It is the blood flowing in my veins, it is the air that courses through my body. Any woman I ever was involved with, automatically had a Dominant. Because, there was no conforming to another person's lifestyle or ways.

I am not here to take part in what society has to offer, I am here to take over. Reign supreme, I am powerful, natural born leader tendencies

Everyone wants power, titles or to be in charge

But no one knows or wants to properly lead

Inspire, coach or motivate

You will witness the sadist in me, the cruel savage callous behavior

Punishment will be calculated, methodical, strategic

Slowly penetrated

You will witness the daddy in me

Firm gaze, firm grip, firm hand

Soft heart

The ones I care for, I am overprotective of

Love to give

As they see parts of me that no one else is entitled to

Parts of me others wish to see, but are not entitled to

The soft side of me, the caring, the loving, the gentle, funny and generous man I am

I am the beast incarnate, the conqueror!

To Dominate is what I do in all things

All my life

Not just sometimes

It is not something, it is everything.

It is not an act. I look back and realize all this was my calling

Just begging me to realize it. To recognize it

Regular traditional relationships were mundane

The limitations, the disappointments, dissatisfaction

The constant demands, the need for attention

The petty arguments

Power struggles

Passive aggressive behavior

I do not do anything you tell me

I like to move when I want

It is more genuine this way

If I gave you attention because you begged for it

Just to shut you up, it is not genuine

The more I am catered to, the more I will give you

I always found that, it is always conducive to be with someone that will always want to know how your day was.

To always make sure that you ate. To always make sure, you made it home safe. When it came to bed

It was things like….."Stop, get off, not so rough please

Wait you're going to stick that big huge thing in me?

You will kill me. You want to do what? Try what? Hell no! I'm not trying that or doing that." Not just the worse of the words. But the looks. Oh the looks of confusion. Confusing looks as if they drank spoilt milk

You're crazy you freak, this is not normal. What is wrong with you?

You must not have respect for women. Meanwhile, their crazy is my sane. Their idea of freaky is normal to me. I bottled up my darkest desires just to keep them from running away. Now I want them scared.

Run away it just keeps the wrong people away from me

and that is good. Run like scared kittens because the wolf is loose

The lion is on a mission. He loves the fear in your eyes. The look of nervousness on your face. The boring unadventurous the looks of just, "get on top, and just fuck me" looks. The fakes who call themselves freaks. But, their idea of freaky were two major positions. Spanking, pulling hair. Really?? That is not freaky. Your rough is different from my rough. Choke me, but not too hard. Spank my ass, pull my hair. She is getting the best sex of her life. Because, most women are terrible in bed, and men do the minimum, because they are lazy. So that is the most amazing thing for most women to experience. Most men just gave them perhaps the norm. But boring to me is phenomenal to most women

Boring is what they are use to. Familiarity becomes safe. Comfortable. But it is just really all mental. But for me there was no fulfilment

My creativity stifled

Passion sustained

Intensity bottled up

Like a painter with no paint

A sculptor with no clay

I am phenomenal. I am great, not just good.

Mind body and soul

Not ordinary

A bit unorthodox

So why settle for mediocrity

I found me

He was always inside me

No more compromising

No more settling

This is fulfillment

Forever

and vanilla was gone forever

I am an asshole, freak, savage

Beast

A lunatic

A maniac

I have accepted this a long time ago

In bed, "shut the fuck up and do as you're told"

Perhaps if it is a hard limit of yours

It may be thrown out the window

Depending on what it is

But overall, I am in charge

In and out of the bedroom

If I want you to speak, then you will

Otherwise, shut the fuck up or get gagged

This is my world, you just live in it

This is the best experience you will ever get

You have been cordially invited to the jungle

My hunger

You will be preyed upon

Devoured

Ravaged

and you will love it

So kick back and enjoy the ride

If not, there is someone else that would love to take your

place

Discipline and punishment does not adjust to anyone

We all adjust to Discipline

From pain to pleasure

Get with it

Or get lost

That is non negotiable

You can't stand the heat

Stay out the kitchen

It hurts? Too deep? I slapped your ass too hard? Tell someone that cares

I swear I do not. In life. In the gym. In bed. Go hard, or go home.

You know what my life entails and what comes with it

Passion, intensity, Dominance

Power

I fuck hard

Discipline hard

Punish hard

Train hard

Teach hard

Stare hard

Love hard

Dominate hard

Who I am?

A King.

Your king.

What am I?

Dominant.

Where am I from?

The land of Dominance.

What is my name?

Discipline.

What do I do for a living?

Fucking Dominate.

I am young, black, powerful, transformative

Magnetic

A Scorpio

The alpha Dominant male

The master of my Domain

King among kings

I do not conform in the mild pleasure society offers

I also do not offer mild pleasures that society condones

I am that different

That chaos to the fly

That is normal to the spider

Brutally passionate when hunger and thirst is in my eyes

If I want it

It is already mine

Men are many things but masters of nothing

I am your release I am your freeDom

I am he

I am Discipline

I have inspired books

I have inspired movies

I have motivated and changed people's lives forever

Changed their minds

This uncanny ability to make others around me better

Managing different tasks efficiently

What makes me great is not my technique

Not my physique. Not my look

What makes me great is my integrity

My passion

My intensity

Character

In this world you get things done by one or two things

Money or by force

Do not be mistaken I am not a bully, I am a boss

I am not just in charge

I feel in charge

Natural ability to take charge

I am authoritative

I evoke strength and strong emotions

Powerful

I can be overwhelming

Intimidating

I represent power, sophistication

Elegance

Formality

I am dark and mysterious

I exude Dominance and sexual

Resiliency

Sex

Sexuality

Endurance

I am muscular, chocolate and tattooed, proud

I am some rare phenomenon

I am the apex predator

The ultimate alpha male who just happens to be chocolate

Let's be honest

How many colored people have you seen that is proactively
engaged in this lifestyle? This leads me to this

I am every woman's dream – but their worse nightmare

My mannerism

My Dominant Dick size

My Dominant psychologic capacity

My aggression

Intensity passion

Tattoos

Character body

Skin tone

Great adaptation in dark and in light

Gentlemen in the street

Beast and master in bed

No matter the inside or outside appearance

I make a huge impact

Women look for qualities in other men that I possess

They compare

With that said,

It takes someone like myself,

Why I behave like I do,

Does what I do,

A high commodity

Women love different

I am a hunter not prey

Not a servant but a King

A lion and alpha

I fucking lead

I can make a grown woman feel like a young lady

A confidant alpha female shy and nervous

A powerful Dominant woman

Submissive

It is like a magical spell

I have this unique sexual energy

Capable of attracting

That makes you hot in an instant

It is like you are minding your own business when you feel
a sudden change in the air

You look up and your eyes snap into focus

and they fix on me

The person who has entered the room

You struggle with the urge to fix your make up or straighten
your hair

Secretive, seductive, and sexy

My eyes are soulful pools of magnetism

That truly see you

Cut right through you

Chill you faster than the coldest winter night

It might be the innate ability

That I have to attract extract the most intimate details
out of you

Which such subtly

When my energy is present the moment will come that
your brain wanders off without permission

Talking to me the conversation may be about the economy,
politics, sports or fine wine

But you are probably imagining what I am like in bed, or

How big my dick is

and how much Dominance I can give you

Discipline and Dominance go hand in hand

Just like power and sex

Muscles and tattoos

Pain and pleasure

Peanut butter and jelly

Big bad wolf, little red riding hood

My powerful presence has a mystery that can turn on at
will

To put anyone the fuck I want under my spell

What makes me really irresistible?

The ability to see beneath the surface and communicate
soul to soul

I can look into your eyes and open a door to forever

An intense and passionate combination

The fact that I am a Dominant is a bonus

I have this power and I recognize my power

I am a master of my craft

A master at whatever I do

I am desired by many, but built for few

Because of who can really handle me

You have never really seen or heard Dominance like this before

There is certain things you cannot teach

There is not enough cloth in this world for everyone to be cut from it

This is Dominance at its finest

I am a bit far from the ordinary

I see fire and it is beautiful to me

Guns and knives and I see them as art

I love bondage and the craziest thing of all is…..when I see pain from my doing

It makes me happy

You can look at a painting, and see one thing. I see 15 things

and will explain it in 1000 words

I am strange weird

Why would some woman subject themselves to this type of insanity?

For you question your own sanity for the love of these moments

Many want me – but do they know me

If they knew me, maybe they would be crazy for me

If they knew me

Perhaps they would not want me

They love the idea of me

My lifestyle that I engage in

For they know a Beasts and Dominance, but not as men but as characters. I'm not mildly rough, I am severely rough

Not just physical but mentally and emotionally as well

I am strict and cruel

I am desired by most but I am built different

Beyond sadistic, remorseless, heartless at times. I can be so loving when deserving. Tender and gentle, but physically I am an animal

This is why I give safe words

I will slap that pretty little face

Not because you love it

But because I do

I will pull your hair and choke you

Not because it is what you want

But because it is what I want

All the good things hurt at first

All big things take getting use to

The ones that can handle me

I will love and cherish forever

The ones who can not, you will never ever be a thought

It is not my Dominance or all these other amazing gifts I am blessed with that allows my subs to be bound by me, or their submission to thrive, and remain consistent

It is my character

My subs are clearly aware not to fuck around

Especially with me

They know I will not hesitate to punish them

Physically mentally or emotionally

I do not beat women, I teach

I Discipline when need be

Guide when need be

I rebuild what the past or weak previous men have destroyed

I provide freeDom and other things

In exchange of complete submission

Their number one priority is to make sure I am pleased

I implement teaching in their lives

I am not something you can possess. I am one you worship, not something you can obtain. However, someone you can earn, work for. I do not crave mediocrity therefore I never offer it. I penetrate the minds of others and unleash charisma so potent and long lasting. I have the mentality that, I am the best at everything I do, therefore I am. When

I step into a room my energy screams at you. It captures and commands your focus, no words need to be exchanged. I am the cerebral assassin. I have the right amount of charm, muscle, soul and mental capacity to achieve anything I chose. When it comes to a woman, I am every woman's dream, as I attract every type as well. That classy business woman, that CEO, that hood, the submissive, the Dominant alpha woman, the mean, the shy, the good girls, the sapiosexuals, the eccentrics, the nerds, even the ones that say they are not into chocolate men, but it is something about me. I attract all this because I am not one thing. My accomplishments are not one thing. I am chocolate, muscular, tattooed, hood, intelligent, talented, powerful, classy, gangster, bad boy, good man, sexual intellect. Adamantly Dominant. I am the most powerful entity you can encounter. The disrupter of the status quo. The most unheralded. What you witness is a man who constantly transforms. What I have over all others is the ability to distract a woman. Whether it is her mind, body or spirit. However, I am not attracted to every type of woman. We all have a power of attraction, ability to draw people in, and hold them in our thrall. Some are aware of their inner potential. Some have not mastered or acknowledged it yet. Whether it is a lack of courage or confidence, this near mythical trait that a few are born with, and the rest will never command, is potent. My character, my words, my energy, has an innate ability to radiate quality that attracts people and stir their emotions in a way that is beyond their fucking control. It is like you are hypnotized by my seductive character. My eyes have their own gravitational pull, abundance of sexual energy and I know how to use it. Insatiably adores the opposite sex. Innate ability to control the female libido with a look, a touch, a word. I am an ideal lover that has an ecstatic sense of ability that I apply to romance, can play and manipulate with my image. Creating a striking enticing allure. Straightforward, self sufficient. With the fascinating cool at my core. A charmer that wants and knows how to please. Charismatic. My confidence is contagious. Mysterious alternating heat and coldness to ensnare a target. The ultimate alpha Dominant male. Women feel the energy, they flock to it, they fight for it, they fight over it, the strength and power, they love to gravitate to, there is no point in being shy with a seductive quality. I hate being sexy but someone has to do it. You witness this Dominant character but fail to realize there is a second, third, fourth, fifth, sixth trait that I possess, adding depth and mystery to my persona. I have extraordinary gifts you are still unaware of. I have an innate ability to reach beneath the surface and communicate soul to soul. I know what you want, need and desire. I know how to give it to you. Hold it from you, before you even open your mouth to ask. I can control your desires, give and take how I want, where I want, and when I want. I penetrate your defense and create your surrender instantly. The unknown will always intrigue the mind. Curiosity will always trigger desire. Your desire will yield to whoever and whatever ignites it. Now your submission becomes power. I am love incarnate, I am sex incarnate, I am drugs incarnate, I am what you never read, seen or heard about. I am Discipline.

I have never had vanilla (normal) sex. Lost my virginity when I was fifteen. I was always engaged in some hardcore shit. Women I have been with had such weak men prior to me, that the boring shit I gave them, like hair pulling, choking, spanking (doing the same shit since I was fifteen) was the greatest thing for them. But I was never fulfilled. I was always proactive and would initiate growth. "Let's take our relationship to the next level." The weird looks, the fear, the "oh hell no, we are not doing that!" "That big dick is way too fat to be in my asshole." "You'll kill me." "Not too rough" "hold on, it's too deep." The "are you fucking crazy?" The "you are such a fucking freak." Insatiable. I do not do vanilla (regular) women, vanilla sex, vanilla conversations. BEAST. Conqueror. DOMINATE, it is what I do. All my life. In all things, forever, not just sometimes, it is not something. But, an emotion. The Limitations. Disappointments. Dissatisfactions. "Why didn't you text or call me? I need your attention, demand, demand, demand, blah blah blah." No "did you eat?" "Did you make it home safe? How can I please you?" Etc. "Hold on one second", click dismissed, cancel that bitch. Was this really life? When it comes to bed. "Ouch (that's not a safe word) stop. "You are not normal, you must not have respect for women." I bottled up my darkest desires to protect their feelings, their apprehensiveness. The boring, the unadventurous. I was a Dominant before I knew the term. I was always assertive in life. When I was in high school, this is where my confidence started to build. I played many different sports, was very outgoing, interacted with the jocks, the cheerleaders. Women just naturally gravitated to the alpha in me. They wanted to carry my books to class, stand and walk besides me in the hallway, stand next to me and sit next to me in class. When it came to bedroom activity, I have always craved control. I would find myself doing subtle things subconsciously, for example, pinning her hands down with my big muscular strong hands, as I grasped her wrist, and her helplessness would turn me on. I love to utilize rope, handcuffs, blindfolds. I just never had a partner that was fully engaged in this as I was. They craved mild things – the mundane things, like hair pulling, etc. I was with an Italian woman for a year and a couple months. After a year, I demanded we take this relationship to the next level. She said, "what do you have in mind?" I said, "hand cuffs, blindfolds, rope, restraints".. She bugged out, "hell no, I have to trust you one hundred percent in order to engage in these activities." So one day we are having sex, and we were in the missionary position. We would always engage in various positions. I would flip her over. I would stare at ourselves in the mirror during the doggy position. She was open to things. She had beautiful sleek, long black hair. I pulled it, every fucking chance I got. I would spank her ass, but when we were in missionary, I placed one of my big, strong, muscular black man hand around her throat, I did not even squeeze or add pressure, I was testing to see how she reacted to it. She literally, pushes my hand away. So we both orgasm as we are engaging in aftercare. We conversed and she then proceeded to ask me, "what made you do that? Do you know you can kill someone by choking them?" We literally were on the edge of the bed, and it was a 20 to 30 minute lecture. Meanwhile, we could have been going another round. All that energy wasted. I then told her I am not spending the night, I am leaving. Next day or two when I saw her, I told her it was over. She asked why? I said, "because of what happened last night", she asked? "Because I wouldn't let you kill me?" I said "this is not funny. Hold your sarcasm. This is about principal. You don't trust me and without trust, there is no respect and with no respect there is no relationship." The connection was gone for me and that was it for me. I never went back to her. No matter how good the pussy was, I looked at the big picture. She would never conform to my ways. The little boring shit that I provided this woman, she was head over heels for, but I was not fulfilled. Ladies, in bed allow the man to do whatever the fuck he want. Yes, discuss limits and boundaries, but if you trust him that means you trust he will be in control and never lose it. He will respect your boundaries as you respect his. When it comes to BDSM the foundation is mutual trust and respect. If you do not respect that man or woman, why are you fucking with them? When it comes to me, Mr Discipline, what you see is what you get. It does not matter if you viewed me as temporary at first or long term, I will give my hundred percent. Just as I would in bed, I will out. The type of security, assurance and protection, pleasures I provide mind, body and soul is unheralded. The type of connection and soul to soul communicative experience is unprecedented. Repetitions building in your pituitary gland. Leaving such an impact and imprint in your entire being that it is impossible to forget. Oxytocin dripping from your pineal gland, every synapse. Every crevice, igniting desires throughout your entire psyche. Coursing through your veins. A connection as potent as cocaine. Addicting. A want turning into a need. Now every word cuts deep, or melts the coldest heart. That need for that conversation. That need to be in each other's presence. The little things make a huge difference. Most people who are adequate enough to engage mentally, as well as emotional and physical, are the ones who are best in bed and are sexual.. The chemistry is what gives me the power to do what I do best, and I am the best in the world at what I "fucking" do. I am dynamic and I can turn it up or down, whenever I please. I am as balanced and controlled as a waiter serving a full house table at once. Loyalty is everything to me. I do not wish upon it. Ask for it. Hope for it. I deserve it and I fucking demand it. Part of being loyal is being consistent not only with me, but with who you are, and what you say. I perform well because of it. Give more because of it. Trust is about "us." but what is love without trust? What is trust without honesty? What is honesty, without respect? What is respect without attraction? What is attraction without chemistry? What makes a woman submit to you at the end of the day, and what allows her submission to thrive.? Many things.....Because all different types of women, love all different types of things. Whether it is money, big dick, materials, jewelry, shoes, etc can all attract her to you if you are able to provide these things. However, you do have other women who are sapiosexuals, and by that I mean, they are attracted to intelligence. They are beyond deeper individuals and require a connection deeper than the parameters that transcends beyond what the basic traditional relationship would have to offer and without that bond, without that connection, they are not attracted to you. No matter what you throw at them. So what makes a woman submit to you at the end of the day? What allows her submission to remain consistent? It is not my ravishing good looks that make her submit. It is not my fat, long chocolate dick that makes her submit. It is not the idea of me and my lifestyle or exquisite techniques that make her submit. Her/their submission is fluid, it remains consistent and it thrives, because of my character. Allow me to reiterate, MY character. How I hold myself to the highest degree, she is aware she will be held to the same or higher. She's/they're held accountable. I am Disciplined and that allows me to enforce their Discipline. Control, poise, serenity will always allow people to feel comfortable around you. That is positive energy. I am consistent at the end of the day and this is what allows her/them to always remain consistent. Everyone needs to know what and who is right for them. Stop settling because you are afraid of being lonely. This is why there are so many things detrimental to relationships and you need advice from friends, a psychiatrists and other assistance in your relationship instead of conversing with the actual person you are with. Beasts tame Beasts. Sapiosexuals should be with Sapiosexuals. Freaks with Freaks. Dominants with submissives. Sadists with masochists. Nymphomaniacs with Nymphomaniacs. DOPE SOULS with DOPE SOULS. KINGS with QUEENS. MASTERS with SLAVES. Niggas with Bitches. It's ironic. They say, 'opposites attract", but never mention duration. Never mention, "is it long term?" You never see Queens with niggas, and you never see Kings with bitches, ratchets, or hoes. Do I believe a man can love or have a strong connection with more than one woman? Yes. Your energy introduces you before you speak. Yes, I acknowledge your face, your body, however, I am really looking through you and staring at your soul. If your soul is ugly, then you are ugly to me. I have walked away from a lot of good pussy. Nice bodies, pretty faces in the past. Things regular men would never have the strength to walk away from, because in my soul, I was not into it. The most difficult force between two people, between misunderstanding, is not distance. It is non communication. Many people have an issue in articulating their thoughts and feelings, and they end up blaming significant others for their desires not being fulfilled. It is all your fault. You know what you need, you just do not care to elaborate. The hardest thing you can have with anyone is a conversation. Friends, parents, significant others, co workers, etc. I believe in order to communicate efficiently, you need patience. Many people listen with the intent to reply, however, not understanding. Understanding is the main objective. Who cares about perception. It takes patience to learn. Listen. Observe. Understand. How many people actually understand you. They know of you. Heard of you. They know your lifestyle. Your mannerisms. Your appearance. Your words. But how many actually understand you? We have a strong connection, because of that connection it induces other emotions. Amplifies other senses. Her inner slut is never more free to be released, than when she is safe. Her fear is confined. She is protected. Adored, loved and is claimed as "mine." This connection. This chemistry, it allows me to talk to her while I am inside her. When I am engaged sexually with a woman, before I study her. Mind, body and soul. I see what makes her tick. How her body moves. She is like a target to me. This way I am able to attack it efficiently. Not every woman orgasms through penetration, you can have the biggest dick in the world. Some love that clit action. You have to get down and eat that pussy. You can not be worshiped as a man if you never know how to worship. That is like you being a great boss and was never a good worker. It is not heard of. Thus, building our sexual chemistry. I whisper shit in her ear while I am digging out her stress and kissing on her breasts. I believe the most delicious thing on earth, is the hunger of a submissive and Dominant. The most powerful creature on earth is a woman. The most prestigious aspect in the world is Dominance. I have never met a bond, a connection, or chemistry stronger than a passionate Dom and a loving, giving sub. Show me another evenly, unequal match of a couple, and I will show you a liar. We are both busy. So when we see each other we make it last a lifetime. I know everything she is allergic to. Everything she is not allergic to. I track her period every month. I know her thoughts, that is why I am able to give her what she needs before she opens her mouth to ask. I give her what she needs, never what she wants. When she begs for attention I ignore her, just to let her mind wonder and realize what is conducive to what we are building upon. No one can ever call her a bitch or slut, Queen but me. Because she is all those things for me. I shove my thick, long chocolate Cock between her begging lips, filling up her tight pussy. I show her what real high levels of testosterone is about. As I get in and on that pussy. I show her why I own that pussy.. I Dominate her soul and no matter where she is, she remains bound to me. I stroke her cerebral. Thrusting her pineal gland. Throttling her pituitary gland and I watch her thoughts, desires, dreams squirt everywhere. When it comes to BDSM, I believe it is you and I. Him and her. No rules but the rules you create. Fuck what you have read or seen. Show me fifty BDSM couples and I will show you one hundred different dynamics, ways, styles of BDSM. I am the exception, and not the rule.

CHAPTER 31

Pussy Is Power, Dick Is Control

I want to clear this up. This has been the talk since the beginning of time. It has gotten out of control and people are feeling themselves. Especially women. Don't let him gas your head up Ma. Just because he said it was good, now you women have built some type of confidence, where it's making you are not act humble? Sit the fuck down, get out your notebooks, I'm going to teach you a thing or two. I am here to set it straight. Power and control are two different things. Power lures you in, and control keeps you in line. Power can change at any given time. Power does not make you stay. It can be given. Taken. It can not ward you. Guide you. Secure you. Discipline you. For example my lifestyle, BDSM(bondage,Discipline/Dominance, sadism/submission, masochism). The total power exchange dynamic. Control is consistent. If you have control, you will always have control. Once you have had it, you can always have it. Think of power like a leader of an organization. He/she can be bought out by the competition. Therefore new territory, new leader. If you are the CEO and you own the competition, you have people in place to control the competition and organization, you are in complete control. Now if we are talking about sex, the human reproductive organ. The human genitals, well, first and foremost, women have holes. Men enter those holes, and fill them up. Women have voids that yearn to be fulfilled in their lives. I am going to write some real shit right now and a lot of you women will not be fond of this, but I guess I have to be the asshole to tell you the truth. Pussy is power when you deal with a small or medium dick man. When you deal with a man who has no expertise when it is pertaining to sex. Most women, not all (about 95%,there are 5% who are sexual Dominants or sexually Dominant, in your term it would be 'freaks' or nymphomaniacs, are great at sex) but most women are terrible in bed, bad at sex. Women are comfortable, when they see other women having fun, or are comfortable. Most people, learn about sex, and how demonstrative there are pertaining to this is from watching porn. When it comes to a relationship, the ones that care less, has more control. This is one of the reasons women stick to bad boys so often. Dangerous maniacs. Lunatics. Most bad boys have good dick. (See how I did that right there with the oxymoron? If you did not, just stop reading from now on). Women don't want nice guys, they want Dominant men. One thing you must understand is, good dick is hard to find. Devil, bomb, phenomenal dick is rare. (You have never been crazy drenched. Body convulsing. Soul out of body experience. You have not had anything). Pussy? Well, pussy is everywhere. Women love dick more than men love variety. Women, all they need to do is pick and choose who they want to submit to. Sit there and look pretty. They will tell you all the stories of them getting free drinks. Free tickets. Being flown out of state, bills paid for, etc etc etc without them needing to do much. Why? Because of their pussy. None of them will admit that? Oh no, they are way too classy right? They've gotten away with shit, because of their looks. Because, most men are pussy whipped and the women do minimum to none to get and keep their attention. Pussy is the circle of life. Man's Seed is the Master. Oh it is powerful(by "it", I'm referring to pussy), see most men would go to jail for it. Kill for it. Friends turn enemies over it. Some men go broke over it. Some men lie to get it. What is good pussy? Clean, wet from beginning to end. Can a woman that has had 6 or more kids have good pussy? Yes. What about if she has been with 15-20 guys? No. See now, her pussy has mileage on it. Pussy is like a vehicle. Women are not built like men. The more we engage, the better we get at it. Women love experienced men, let's be honest. You can have the full package, and when it comes down to the bedroom, soon as you pull out your junk, if it's not up to her standard. If you can't physically satisfy her, she will be so disappointed. You probably won't even get a text back. Ladies, the more beat up your pussy is, the less desirable it is. Remember ladies. The tighter, the better. You can also do your Kegel exercises. Make sure we are clear. Good pussy is subjective. What is good pussy to one man is mediocre to another. Like for example, she may think her head game is flawless and she meets me, and I am just not impressed. What will whip one man will not make another man break his stride. If you are in a room with a mixed crowd of men and women, the women with good pussy will be surrounded by men. Women with good pussy, let it shine thru in every aspect of her life. She walks the good pussy walk. She speaks with the confidence of a woman who has good pussy. She poses, eats and laughs the secret laugh of a woman with good pussy. I am not talking about any regular old missionary loving pussy. I am not talking about hunched for 15 minutes and does not care if you cum poon. I am talking about the poontang pie that's so sweet and juicy he can not get enough. The kind he goes to work thinking about coming home to. The kind that is odorless, moist and hugs your man meat with the perfect amount of pressure. That pressure that busts pipes. That pussy that looks like, 'I like it rough type.' The type that makes you nut in 2 minutes. Humbles you. The kind that makes it her mission to milk you dry and leave you paralyzed. She gets extra points for being a Scorpio. However, a Scorpio woman is not submissive. If you can challenge her mind or fuck her to next week, she will be, but out of bed, not at all (we are the sex sign. Sexual Dominants. Sexually Dominant. If you do not know what that means, it means, we are the greatest at sex in all ways, if we are not, we study and then master it). What happens when powerful pussy or regular pussy, meets Control Dick? Dick is control. It can change a woman's attitude. It can make a woman obey. It can make a woman go insane. It can make a woman submit. Do and say things she has never done or said before. Kill. Steal. Cry. Lie. Betray others. Great dick will have a woman calling out of work because she needs it. Because she is sore from it. Heading to work late, because she stayed up late for it. You surrender your some of your biweekly paycheck to good dick. Good dick is savage. It commands loyal pussy. Good dick will be your muse. Good dick makes your dreams come true. It could make you take birth control. You keep your dignity after being whipped by good dick. It humbles you. Good dick makes you hate condoms (but always use condoms y'all, safe sex is great sex as well, there are thin ones, that you hardly feel like it's there. Scented ones, and they make them in magnums and magnum XL as well). Good dick will help you live longer. DickQuil….Put you to sleep. Give you an amazing glow. Build your confidence. Good dick will have you thinking you have great pussy. Good dick puts you in your place. It inspires. Motivates. Women get great dick and say, "I just want to love it with all my heart." A man that knows he has great dick is the devil. He gets extra points for being a Scorpio. Good dick puts you in a great mood. Lowers your blood pressure. It gets you chance after chance. It erases a woman's memory temporarily. It makes you forget what you really deserve in life. It makes women talk about it with their friends. Causing their friends to be the followers of good dick. Good dick, all her friends and family know you. Great dick, is kept a secret. Good dick will make you want to cook and clean, when you know damn well you do not cook or clean. Good dick will have you ironing his work clothes knowing damn well he is unemployed. Good dick gets spoiled. It hardly does the spoiling. Good dick makes you walk funny. Good dick makes her text you like, "did your dick make it home okay? I mean, did you make it home okay, after you left?" Good dick will have you up late, knowing damn well you work in the morning. It will alter a woman's personality. Style. Ways. Attitude. Her mindset forever. With great dick comes great responsibilities. Good dick could ruin your life. If he has a big dick, she might let him. Great dick confuses a woman's heart and makes her think she is in love. Good dick could make a woman that is in a relationship with another man, resent him, or her husband. Good dick does the same thing as squats. Good dick leaves your pussy throbbing and drenched just thinking about it. Good dick will knock out that Dominant, alpha Amazon Wonder Woman. Good dick is when you let him drive your car when you know he has no license. Great dick ruins all possibilities of anything else and everyone else. Good dick makes a woman that is angry with you, call or text you, puts her pussy on the phone because even though her heart is telling her no, her brain is telling her, "I don't love him no more." Her pussy is saying, "stop being selfish bitch, you and I think differently." Good dick will have a woman five minutes later saying, "I miss you, I love you, I'm sorry." But five minutes prior, she was saying, "I'm done", and you both were having a full blown out argument. The reality is, most women are terrible in bed. Even if they have good pussy. But, when you are fucking a woman well, giving her great dick, great tongue, passionate and intense thrusts. Great stroke, moving your hips in all directions, a great mouth, with stamina, powerful energy behind it, going the distance, all she wants to do is give you the world. Treat you better than a King. Because good dick isn't shit, if she is not climaxing. Good dick makes you feel it when he is not there.

Good dick is healing. Good dick gives her superpowers. Good dick gives her pussy power. It is an exchange of energy. Not just physical, but spiritual. This is when you can create a bond. A connection emotionally, the sexual chemistry and connection is just so fluid. You are able to orgasm many times. Engage in intimacy for many hours, even after. His character will rub off on you. If you ever happen to be lucky to receive great Dominant Dick, well Dick is control. Power in the wrong hands is dangerous, however, if you have sex with a man who possesses conscious Dick. Have sex with a woman who possesses conscious pussy, sex can be very enlightening, and healing, rather than detrimental to the relationship.

CHAPTER 32

Sexual Chemistry or Emotional Connection

Which would you rather have? To each their own, but for me, it is emotional connection. The emotional connection is what builds a strong, unbreakable bond, a strong sexual chemistry. The difference between fucking and having to lose interest in each other quicker, because there is nothing else outside of that, than having sex. There's no love making. There's no intimacy. You can't sit back, laugh, enjoy each other's presence. Most people when they orgasm, they shut their eyes. That is because, it is intense. In order to build that intensity, you will require a deep connection. When was the last time someone touched you other than your body? Good sex involves the body. But, great sex begins in the mind. Nowadays, no one knows how to converse anymore. Social media has taken over. Everyone is busy. No one has time or care to drown in another. Put in work to know another and it gets harder as we get older. A woman will always love a man more from what she has learned from him, versus the expensive shit he can buy her. In my time, I had rich, powerful women that wanted to spoil me. No, I will not mention their names. Sex is an exchange of energy. It is emotional. Sexual chemistry now becomes very powerful. Great relationships are built upon mutual respect, trust, selflessness. Where there is trust, there is respect, where there is respect, there is attractions. Without attractions, there is no relationship or at least not a real one. This is why there are plenty of one night stands. You could meet someone and your body reacts to them. Not your mind or soul, but your body. It is magnetic. Sexual chemistry can be short term or long. It all depends what you have outside of that. By 'that', I mean an emotional connection as well. The person might just fuck you so well, that is all you allow him or her to do. There is no talking. There is no conversing. There is no hanging out. Y'all just fuck. Meet and fuck. Like a friends with hardly any benefits. A fuckship. This is short lived. Some people have a sexual preference, perhaps race, built, physique preference, a appearance where they know they are more compatible with. This is what inspires "side pieces and bitches." This is what creates them. You really can't control who you find sexy. Who you find irresistible. You perhaps have a husband or wife, and you have a great emotional connection, but weak sexual chemistry. Perhaps it's the other way around. Perhaps none at all. Some people build this chemistry through, trial and error. Sexual chemistry. Reciprocated chemistry is the answer. This is what you feel when you are sitting beside them or even just gazing at them across the room. Sometimes the pheromones are so powerful, that it actually pulls you towards them like a magnetic force. There is a magic in the air and it is an unmistakable euphoric feeling. How often does it happen? Not as often as one would think. What are the signs? There is an overwhelming urge to be close and touch them. It is like an electric current that is pulling you into them. It is not always at the right moment, it can be with someone who is out of bounds, but it is an undeniable feeling hard to ignore! Nervousness that you are not used to feeling. An arousal in the loin area, an amazing urge to kiss them right there on the spot. That you are willing to sleep with them as quickly as possible despite your strong morals. Certain people that are in relationships require distance from one another, or this occurs. Their scent is overly alluring and draws you closer. You are drawn into their eyes and have trouble focusing on what they are saying. If you are both single this is great but if not, it can be the catalyst in many relationship problems! Due to the magnitude of the electrical current some people tend to step over their boundaries. Acting first and dealing with the repercussions later. Does age make a difference in how a person looks at chemistry? Hell, fucking yes! As a person matures, so does their awareness. They may become more selective or intuitive due to some of the mistakes they have made in the past, and now when they feel it, they know it! (Some people can have a sexual relationship without the love and passion which is a "friend's with benefits" rapport). In your younger years you are sexually peaking, everything is experimental and not so much about chemistry. Everyone looks good and feels good for a while, until you start to differentiate with new emotions. In high school, most crushes for myself were experiments with an attraction. No one is thinking about a future yet. Ask your partner what the word "chemistry" means to them? Keep that alive and work with it continuously. Many couples let it fade by allowing other daily forces to replace passion. Nurturing each other first should be a priority. Think back to when you first became a couple, everything else in your life took second place. Keeping the chemistry alive will keep your relationship alive! Many parents today think it is selfish to get a babysitter and have a date night. Many older parents fall into this trap, because they have waited so long to have a family and now make it all about the children. This is a big mistake. Is it better for the kids to come from a divorced family, because the couple who made the kids forgot how to love each other? Physical. Mental. Emotional. Spiritual. How great it is when you have it all. If you get lucky that is. In my life, I have never witnessed a bond, a sexual chemistry, an emotional, deep connection, intimacy stronger than a passionate Dominant and a loving, giving submissive. Sex is many things, but the main thing about sex is, it is about power. What I am about to say is fucked up, but real. Many woman say they want or crave a big dick. Some can not handle it. Some do not want it. Most love it. Most try it, because of what they have heard from friends or others. Let's be real, most women, not all women, but most women are followers. Anyways back to the situation at hand. Big dick correlates with power. See if you have a little dick, make sure you make a lot of money. If you have a medium size dick, make sure you can give great head and do other tricks in bed that are amazing. But if you have a big dick, you can always be a dick and she will always come back. Women have options and men have options, hell there are billions of people in this world, but when you can stimulate one immensely, it is like they no longer have options. Allow me to explain... a man can stimulate a woman either physically, mentally or emotionally or all three, and she will not see any other man. There can be seven billion men in this world, but not every single one knows how you like it, knows how to stimulate you whether you tell them, give them hints or not. A woman that knows how to pleasure and is aware of her talents will always have options. No matter how she looks. A good looking woman can be terrible in bed, (because looks are always deceiving) have a bad attitude or personality, and she will appear ugly in every way to a man. One man's trash is another man's treasure. Sex is a power exchange, and an exchange of energy (in my opinion). Whether that intimacy be physical, emotional or psychological. Sex is nothing but merely about power. If she can fuck you. If she pleasures you more than you pleasure her, she has all the power. Allow me to explain something to you…....I can get my rocks off when I want. Because I can masturbate. My goal when I am with my lover, is to pleasure her immensely. (My sex and techniques are amazing, this is why I don't give it as a reward for misbehaving. Because, it is a reward). Not only is it a stroke to my ego to accomplish this, I have no desire to release before she does. I know how to control myself around pussy. It is one of the reasons why I can go the distance. I know how to control pussy because of it. I know how to whip pussy because of it. Pleasuring the person I am with is power. I am given the power to do what I do best, which is Dominate and Control. Sex is everything, but the main thing is power. When you have sex and love as a combination things can be so amazing. Most of the things in this world reminds us of sex. Words, attire, scents, authority, gestures, a look into another person's eyes. Music, drugs, alcohol, money, exercise, foods,art, etc. The only thing that doesn't remind us of sex, is sex. Sex is about fucking control. When I was younger, like my early teens, girls would say things about, how they would have me strung. How they would have me clingy, and whipped. Mainly, because, other men perhaps were gassing their heads up. Little did they know, I am a man, that inspires their humbleness. They would say all this to me, and I used to say, "everything you are saying is garbage, because when I have you face down, ass up or cumin until you are convulsing, everything I say, do, and am will be attractive to you." SEX!!!! It can blind you. It can make smart women, stupid. It can make sapiosexuals date men that cannot read a paragraph out loud, or when they read they need to trace under each word with their finger to follow. SEX!!! It can give you temporary memory loss. It can become a drug and with the appropriate person, become addicting. Dominance and submission goes back to history. With the ancient Egyptians(who were black by the way). Attractive females became a commodity when Egyptian kings demanded beautiful servant girls from their provincial governors. Sex is a smell. An appearance. Actions. Words. Ownerships. Authority. The more powerful a man/monarch/ruler was, the more women he had sex with (this is not all true, but most of it). This goes back to the ancient times. Leadership has long been associated with sexual Dominance throughout history and within the animal kingDom. Why do so many leaders fall prey to confusing power with sexual charisma? Sex is power, but many men are or act like they are slaves to pussy. So does that mean, "pussy is always power?" I say, "pussy is power" to a man that cannot fuck properly. Or to a man that's never had women. Or a man that never masturbates. Power corrupts and absolute power corrupts absolutely. Inappropriate sexual conduct is a form of corruption. Power is sexy and people in positions of power often find themselves recognized in public, being praised and flattered as never before. It is hard for that not to go to your head. This is why basketball, football players, celebrities cheat on their wives. The seductive power of power. Power is the most potent aphrodisiac. Forget oysters, power is at the top of the menu when it comes to sexual arousal. Men, certainly, are not the only people who abuse their power sexually. Women exhibit the dark side...too, and can become accustomed to power and it's perks as easily as a man can. What more? Testosterone, a primal driver of Dominant behavior, is not the exclusive province of men either. Women produce testosterone just like men do, even if at different levels. Foreign women have higher levels of testosterone than American women. They use their seductive powers as well. You witness it in how they dress. How they dance. Their eyes, their lips.

That means women have testosterone-driven tendencies as well, and that pays dividends. You can tell when a woman is off her period and you can always tell when she is about to go on it. You can't? Well, you need to fucking pay closer attention. Dominant animals tend to be more reproductively successful whether they are male or female. Very few headlines highlight the sexual indiscretions of powerful women and no politically prominent female, thus far, has been accused of rape or sexual assault. But that may change as increasing numbers of women rise to positions of political power. Women have been seeking the same opportunities as men for centuries. All in all, sex is power. However, if you have sex with a man who possesses a conscious dick or a woman who possesses conscious pussy, sex can be very healing rather than detrimental to the mind, body and soul. A woman is not written in Braille. You do not need to touch her to know her. The little things you both engage in is intimacy.. I love to build a connection with my submissives, or Slaves/Queens. We will engage in vanilla (regular) conversations, joke, perhaps laugh, but we never forget who we are, what the dynamic is, or what we are to one another. Be careful who you bring into your circle. You embrace their energy. Their energy remains within you whether, it is good or bad. Energy is contagious, either you affect people or you infect people. For women, the best aphrodisiacs are words. One of her G spots are located in her ears and I happen to have a deep voice I have no control over.

The bass in it, I am sure, feels like it is vibrations on the clit. Until a man finds himself and understands himself, finds his true identity, he will ruin every woman he comes across. Never being able to elevate her or rebuild what the past has destroyed. When a woman is loved correctly she becomes twenty times more the woman than what she was before. Sometimes you have to go deeper and she will feel you after you are gone. Men do not understand, having a well fucked woman on your side and how beneficial it is. Her mood, her mannerisms. Her willingness to worship, all comes from her need. However, never allow sex to cloud your judgement, or change your character. If sex or being physical is the only way you know how to connect and build with a man or woman, your relationship is on the verge of turmoil. You all may have had sex, but have no idea what true intimacy is. Some utilize sex as a way to connect more. Do not allow good sex to confuse your heart and make you think you are in love. (I know, easier said than done, because once women get great sex, it is like they become dumb. They get extremely weak). How do you have a well fucked woman on your side? Keep reading...She will never truly fall in love with a man she can not learn from, a man who can not elevate her. Some women are too much for some men. Undress her conscious and make love to her thoughts. Drink from her water fountain and touch her intellect. Watch how she breaks down those walls just so you can be inserted through those walls. Beauty without depth is just decoration. A woman's beautiful face will attract a flirter. A woman's beautiful heart will attract a lover. A woman's beautiful spirit will attract a King, and a woman's beautiful character will attract a real man. A true alpha knows exciting and pleasuring her body is easy. The question is, can you quiet her busy and noisy mind? Can you lead her down, deep into the blissful stillness? Into the calm that she craves? Find and hit that special spot deep inside her... cerebral. Conscious women taste better. Women with a high emotional intelligence cum plenty of times. It is a gift and a curse to feel everything so deeply. Sex is an exchange of energy and power. When you fuck with negative energy, that is what you endure. But remove sex from a lot of relationships and you will witness and discover that many people have nothing to offer. When it comes to me, I will imprint something so deep in your pineal gland that anyone who wants to know you, will need to know me. Crave to study my skills in order to understand you. You can not be a sapiosexual fucking with niggas. That is like an oxymoron almost. Like 'big shrimp' or 'Biggy Smalls.' You speaking like them, behaving like them subconsciously, to be accepted and now you are settling for mediocrity. Without that mental connection, I would be that selected Dominant to restrain you, we would not have a relationship beyond that. You would never know which side of the bed I preferred or if I even drink coffee in the morning. You might be complacent and content because you are getting that good shit from me, but I will get bored and the boring that I provide is the greatest thing for you. But a soulful individual requires more. I know what I provide, therefore I fucking demand what I demand. I have no issues working for you, or your trust, but I promise, you will work ten times harder for me. Knowledge can make her moist. Give her a mindgasm by going down on her thoughts. Intelligence is the ultimate aphrodisiac. I do not fuck, I soul touch. That is why every woman I have ever engaged in any physical, mental or emotional activity is never the same and they will always remember me. A part of me is with her. Women look for attributes and qualities in other men that I already possess. The deepest penetration is of the mind. I happen to be the cerebral assassin. Words are a woman's weakness. I just happen to be the master of the seductive language. A Sapiosexual connects with me on a deeper level, because I have the ability to see beneath the surface and communicate soul to soul. Conversations may pertain to economics, politics, fine wine, sports, art, sex, race, slavery, BDSM, media, relationships, etc., meanwhile, her mind will wander off without permission, imagining how big my chocolate dick is, or how great I am in bed. I have touched her pineal and pituitary gland, that has now ignited smoldering desires within her soul.

CHAPTER 33

What Is It About A Scorpio?

Born November 7th, master of the mental realm. Many people say, "it is not about signs." Aside from race, nationality, background, signs also play a factor in understanding people. Being able to witness their idiosyncrasies. Signs make 65% if not more of a person's personality. Scorpio is a water sign. Most water signs get along.

Fire Signs - Aries, Leo, Sagittarius.

Earth Signs - Taurus, Virgo, Capricorn.

Air Signs - Gemini, Libra, Aquarius.

Water Signs - Cancer, Scorpio, Pisces.

Scorpio sign are detectives, experts at the delicate art of strategy. Operates on It's perceptive abilities. Feels things deeper and forever. Most Scorpios are deep individuals but love their privacy. Can be secretive, seductive and mysterious all at once and it intrigues you and now you think to yourself, what is it about him or her?

Sign: Scorpio.

Element: water.

We are the water sign.

Mythology: Scorpio was ruled by Pluto (Hades), God of the underworld and Mars(Ares) god of aggression in war. We (SCORPIOS) exude sex. Powerful, Passionate and Intense. You will witness it in my eyes, mannerisms, intuitive capabilities, our swag, body language, just to name a few. Many of the most powerful people in this world are SCORPIOS. Our greatest physical attributes or characteristics are our sexual organ. For a man perhaps it is his Dick. The girth and the performance behind it. A woman told me my dick was powerful, as well as my mind. I must have been 18 years of age at the time. However, you can learn a lot from a woman, if you pay attention. I never believed her. As I got older, I became a master at my craft. It is like this. You can be a King and be great and knowledgeable about one thing. Myself, I am a King of many different things. I started to find my identity. Once I figured that, it is like a cub. The inevitability is he is destined to be a lion. Once he realizes that and masters his craft, he is unstoppable. This woman in my past was right about me. For women SCORPIOS perhaps her ass, pussy, lips, eyes, her technique might be her greatest sexual tool/tools. SCORPIOS are wise. Psychic. Intuitive. We can see right through you. Not like "Superman", but you get the point. We value honesty greatly, for we are very honest, blunt. Once you have broken the trust of a SCORPIO, they are never the same with you. When it comes to Domination and transformation, SCORPIOS have a tendency to do both with usually positive results. Sex, getting it and keeping it, is a primary motivator for a SCORPIO. We are labeled as, "freaks or kinky", but I say we are exquisite individuals. Sexual intellects. SCORPIOS can be very demanding, but excellent teachers in all sexual matters. Passion and intensity, go hand in hand for a SCORPIO. When it comes to sex and love, both SCORPIO men and women have an intensity others lack. It is ironic how great SCORPIOS are, but I have never been able to have a successful relationship with any when I was younger. I never understood. As I got older, I did. SCORPIOS, can make great DOMINANTS. Sex with a Scorpio is a total emotional and physical experience, with passion and intensity. Amazing stamina. We can go all night, round for round like a boxing match. Serious into foreplay, as we are not into quickies, unless it was like an experience in the car, a park, a restaurant bathroom, etc. Most people talk about sexual fantasies, a Scorpio will proactively engage in it. Direct and forceful and an expert in whatever they do. Scorpios are dangerous. Best friends, worst enemies. Best lovers, best kisser, because we are nasty. We are not satisfied until we pleasure you immensely. We are the best at everything when we set our mind, body, soul into it. Passionate, intense, magnetic, transformative, Dominant, observant, high sex drive, most

POWERFUL sign of the zodiac, wise beyond their years. Wiser Than Most People, unforgettable, irresistible, love control, psychic tendencies, intuitive, savages, exude sex, eyes that pierce through your soul, elephant memory. Scorpios do plenty of great things. Ironically, as great as Scorpios are, the females are difficult. Not the sex, but overall relationship. It can be full of passion or full of destruction. Leo women and Scorpio women are difficult, most of them are alpha females. It takes a special man to handle them. Yes, they can be loved. Leo is the strongest sign of zodiac, because of their lion symbol. They really live up to the symbol as well. These women may not be submissive, but they are masochists. But overall, Scorpio is the most POWERFUL sign of the zodiac. Scorpio + Scorpio, only works if one is willing to relinquish control. Why? Because Scorpios crave it. They require it (control that it). From my experience, I've had great relationships with cancers, and Pisces. They are very emotional, quick to love, and they love hard. For they are water signs as well as Scorpio. However, cancer can be a bit Dominant, but their passion is well compatible with Scorpio. Virgo, Aquarius, and Sagittarius. Capricorn, however, Capricorn can be controlling, and they have short tempers, rigid, steadfast, stubborn, so watch out. Libras, have a high sex drive as a Scorpio, so the Sex is always great, Libras crave balance, like a scale. Two Dominants never work because there is no balance. It is like the female lion. She is not submissive, only to her king or an extremely greater power than herself. She allows him to be King, as long as it pleases her. She challenges him, and the end result is one of two things; one, he either brings her down a notch and puts her in her place (whether that be psychologically or physically), or two, he backs down. When it comes to a Scorpio, nothing about us is boring. We can bring out the fucking best in you. Scorpios have this look and powerful aura, that makes you simply get attracted to them instantly and you do not know why. Why are SCORPIOS (Men and Women) so sexy?? What is it about a Scorpio (man/woman) that gets your attention and keeps it? I will tell you. Scorpios have a unique sexual energy, capable of attraction that can make you hot in an instant. For example, you are minding your own business when you feel a sudden change in the air. You look up and your eyes snap into focus and fixed on the person who has just entered the room. You struggle with the urge to check your makeup or straighten your tie: a Scorpio is here. Secretive, seductive, sexy! There is just something about a Scorpio. Maybe it is those eyes... soulful pools of magnetism that truly see you, cut right through you, or chill you faster than can the coldest winter night. Or it might be the innate ability to extract the most intimate details out of you with such subtlety, that it is only days later that you realize they know your blood type, and you do not even know their last name! Perhaps it is the way they move, quiet and lithe, as graceful as a ribbon of silk caught in a breeze twisting, flowing and caressing the wind. When Scorpio energy is present, the moment will come that your brain wanders off, without permission. The conversation may be about the economy, politics, sports, fitness, art, or fine wine, but you are probably imagining what we are like in bed. We do that to people. I know I do. Scorpio Sun is ruled by Pluto and Pluto is the most powerful planet in the solar system. Power is sexy. Powerful people are sexy. Power and sex just go together well. It is really simple. Truth is simple. Scorpios are so sexy, because their ruling planet Pluto is so powerful. So why are you so attracted to Scorpio? The universe and it's high vibrations. Polarity. Magnetic, because every fiber in your being gravitate to that magnetism beyond your control.

CHAPTER 34

You Will Beg

"I do not have to ask and you do not have to say. I do not have to say, and do not have to ask. However, you will beg. Why? Because I say so. Because I tell you to. You will get every delicious bruise. Every impactful slap against your soft ass you've been craving for. You have been aching for. The consistent Discipline you fiend for. Addicting, as you need it, I feel that you need it, you know that you need it. My powerful hands and ruthless aggressive nature, creates a savage cocktail of this pain and pleasure you can not help but fucking drink down. Taking it all in, drinking of my Dominance. Hypnotized by this Henny thug passion." I silently and meticulously remove her clothes. Forcefully peeling them off, jerking at the fabric. Not even with the hint of sex at my approach. This is the slow climb to the mountain of the brutality she so desperately wants. Spoke softly, but forceful, "In this moment, I do not want to cuddle you, I do not want to make love to you. Not a soft word, nor sweet kiss. No beauty in the beast tonight. To claim what is mine. Take what I please. No question marks. For I am not asking. Whenever, however, wherever. You have relinquished control, I will have all of you. You….are…mine. Mind, body, and soul. You will come to me when I want you. I will use you for my pleasures. You will fulfill all of them. Whether you choose to agree or not, I do not care. The only things I will negotiate with you are your hard and soft limits, as you know. You will enjoy me. You will not want anything else. You will never be satisfied with mediocrity. You will be so eager to please me. You will exceed all of my expectations. You will become appreciative of my Dominance, confident in my authority, and trusting in my decisions of leadership. I will teach you patience. You will be patient like you have never been in your life. You need your fix. Your chocolate addiction. I am your medicine. It is your oral fixation. You are under the spell of my merciless behavior, knowing damn well how I will Dominate your body. Like it has never been Dominated before. When it is over, you will look as if you had been mauled by a bear. I will find great pleasure in that. You will find astonishing gratification in it as well. Your pain is my pleasure, your pleasure is my pleasure. I will soon make the pain your pleasure." Through the slapping of skin caused by my furious, savage thrusts into her warm wet pussy. My hand slithering up her body. As my big chocolate muscular cock slides in and out of her, hand grasps her neck, and my grip intensifies around her fragile neck. Her moans and the sound of her wetness being ravaged by my big black cock as background noise. Pussy so wet, sounds like kids smacking water as I stir my chocolate cock in her pool of passion. The sweet sounds as if I was stirring macaroni and cheese. Your walls are closing in. You are drenched. Your eyes become wider. Wider in deeper love than ever before. "Look at me when I fuck you." I command it as I roar it to your attention. Grasping my girth as if you want to explode. "Daddy?" She gasps. As I already know what she wants to ask and say. Can she cum? "I say, no!." So sharply. I wanted her longer. She was compliant. After several more minutes I finally allowed her to cum. All the build up, holding it for me, she released. A puddle of her lustful, delicious drenched work all on the sheets, and me. Such a pretty sight. At this point no need to ask, for I command it. As she drowns my cock in her pool of lust. "Yes, cum on daddy's chocolate dick." The last thing she remembers before the sweet kiss of suffocation overtakes and she explodes in a sea of squirming cum. The whip of my strong fingers across her face to remind her who she belongs to. Remind her who the fuck I am, who the fuck she is and where she is.. Completely in my zone, my grasp. Taking this big, chocolate dick of Discipline like the slut I want her to be. My grip begins to tighten and I can see it in her eyes. I can hear it in your breathing, the way her breathing changes. I can feel it between her thighs. I can feel her walls getting tighter. At this point before she can ask, I command her to cum. What choice does she have? Nada, none. "Tan Bella. Oui Monsieur Discipline. Escúchame ahora. Mwen lakay (creole)." In my element, in my zone, where I thrive, where I excel. Relieved as she release. Eruption like a volcano. Fireworks like the 4th of July. Her body motionless, trying to catch her breath. Her eyes shut, wetness all over me. Dripping all over me. Dripping all over the sheets, and on her thighs like a good girl. She did not even have to ask. Relieved for her, the look of uncertainty if I would give her the green light. "Say thank you." She replied so meek…. "Thank you Daddy." I'm pleased, "good girl, precious. It is one thing to enjoy the act… It is another to want to please….But the NEED to taste me courses through her veins like an addict going without her fix…it is at that moment when I know she has crossed into the proper mindset, where I need her to be, before I put my huge dick in her mouth. Before I bless her mouth with my girth and am baptized by the warmth of her throat. When she does not just taste, does not just go through the motions, does not just suck, but to devour..attack..engulf. "Your mouth is no longer just a tool for sex, but an experience and of itself. The hours, minutes, seconds you have spent not enjoying me in your mouth, making every moment of the now so much sweeter for you. Drenched. The moment your mouth closes around me, you are soaking wet from just being able to have me in any part of you. But to taste, to actually taste me. To be on your knees, looking into my eyes, hands on your head pushing your throat to it's limit with every bob of your head. How do you feel? New limits as I slide my fingers into your hair. Now these are your new limits precious. Now you taste me the way I make you taste me. Gagging and tearing for me but unwilling to stop, refusing to stop. The NEED has taken over. Good Girl. On your knees, hands behind your back. Open your mouth. I am going to fuck your face and Dominate your throat. The wetness of your pussy belongs to me." Placing my strong, muscular thumbs on the back of her neck. My other four fingers across her throat. As I shove my fat, long chocolate Dick between her sweet begging lips, as I instruct her, "stick your tongue out, like I am your doctor. Keep it out until further instructions." Thrusting into her mouth, fast, then slowly. Touching the back of her submissive throat. Gagging is music to my ears. Eyes watering. Mascara running. Shortness of breath. I could see in her eyes, she has never experienced this before. Perhaps she has always been in charge. The man lays on his back. She does her thing. Today, I take her. Every part of her is mine and right now, I am focused on her mouth. Tears running down her cheeks. Delicious pussy soaked from this behavior. I introduce her to my big 'choker', and it chokes her. "Sloppy, nasty, get all of that spit. Work it. I like it wet, just the way I like your pussy for me. Work your neck like you have never worked your neck before. Look me in my eyes slut. Let me see those pupils dilated." I grasp a fist full of her hair. I curl my strong fingers into it, inward. Enough until I have a good amount to hold onto as a handle. I take out my big chocolate 'choker' and I slap it on her face, back and forth. "This is one of your correctors." I spoke to her forcefully, but soft, "It will relax you. Elevate you. Change you. Shape you. Heal you, and hurt you. Break you and build you. Leave you sore, but you will be yearning for more. It will always overpower you. One of your addictions. Your chocolate bar. More potent than morphine. Cocaine. Take that shit", reaching over from behind her, *slap*,as I spank that plump ass cheek and stated, "good girl" after. "Open wide and be ready for your dessert. Filled with plenty of protein, just enough to make you strong. The need...now fucking beg for it slut!!! Fucking Beg!!

CHAPTER 35

Her Vow

I commanded her, "strip down for me." I Put out my palm facing her, indicating for her to pause. "Start with your fears, doubts, and insecurities. Taking your clothes off for me is simple. The most difficult thing a man can explore is the mind and soul. I want you naked on the inside as well. I could care less about your outward appearance, if I can not see your inward appearance. I stare squarely at her. We gazed into each other's eyes. I spoke to her softly, but forceful. "Listen carefully, now that you are completely mine in every way, mind, body, and soul. We have discussed your hard and soft limits. This is not just something in bed. Discipline is not exempt in good times and only present in bad times. Neither is Dominance. This is your life now. A life that consist of rules, guidance, punishments (only if you disobey or misbehave), safety, confidence, security, empowerment, love, trust, pain, immense pleasure and keeping you in line when you think you can fucking get out of it. There will be no secrets between us. The reason we will be able to be successful and have great pleasure, and a great BDSM relationship is because of high vibrations. Connection. If we do not have this trust, we will have a weak bond. This is not your basic traditional relationship. We will never link vanilla (regular) and BDSM. Loyalty is everything to me. I do not crave it. I do not ask for it. I do not beg for it. I do not hope for it. I do not wish for it. I do not manipulate for it. I fucking demand it. I deserve it. I will not train you how to be honest, consistent, dedicated, devoted, trustworthy, open. If you cannot provide me with these, step aside, I am sure someone else will gladly love to take your place. I AM..... NOT......ASKING. To abide by my rules. I AM NOT ASKING....to give me what is mine. I will take what is mine. I AM NOT ASKING.. To choke you. To slap you. To spank you. For you to bend at my will. To please me. To beg, to crawl, to do. I WAS NOT ASKING.. To cater to my needs. To worship me. To suck, to grab your ass so hard, your PUSSY lips spread. To spread and allow me to swim in your pool of passion. I WAS NOT ASKING..To do. To give. Now. Like fucking right now. I WAS NOT ASKING, but for Me, you will...do what I say. For Me you are...whatever the fuck I want you to be. My slut. My bitch. My good girl. My prize. My love and my hate. My passion. My lust. My pleasure. Wherever, whenever, however. This is not a negotiation. We have done that prior to all this. If you are unwilling to give all of you, I will gladly take nothing. Your Hard work. Complete compliance. Your body. Your mind. Your soul. I do not crave it. I deserve it. I WAS NOT ASKING. Once you have given me power, your power, your gift, you will obtain greatness and that comes with a price. As I work for the gift of submission, you will work harder for the gift of Dominance. As you will witness the total power exchange taking place. The total alteration of yourself as you are reborn a brand new woman. You will receive pain before pleasure and you will learn to appreciate both. I will not give you a fucking thing but only the things you have earned. Only complete obedience will be rewarded. You are my submissive and I am your Daddy, your Dominant, your King. I do not need to give you anything. But I love to give. Especially to those deserving and hardworking. Do not beg for attention. You are not in a relationship with attention. You are in a BDSM relationship with me, with Discipline. Your only job is to please me. Worships me. Cater to me. Serve me and that is it. Prioritize serving me, where only family and work is an excuse, to an extent. My job is to make sure you focus on nothing but pleasing me. I will know everything about you. Inside and out of your mind. If I am doing my job, I will know what you need before you even ask me. I will never give you what you want. Only what you need. Which is, love, Discipline, wisDom, guidance, strength, confidence, protection, empowerment. You will never kneel in public, but I will not hesitate to Discipline you in public if you think you can act up there. You are my princess and goddess in public, worthless whore in private. This is a peaceful relationship to only be interrupted by misbehavior or destructive acts in the bedroom. Do not ever overstep me, challenge me or play games with me. I will make hell look like a prize and If you play mind games with me like a brat, you will find yourself playing checkers with a man playing chess. Your behavior is what determines what you are able to obtain and what is unobtainable. Words are powerful precious, but it is how you use them that will cost you. I swear I will fucking tax you as well. When you are sad, if you have something on your mind, speak it. The worst I can say to you is, 'shut the fuck up and stay in your fucking place.' We are to have open communication. Efficient communication. That is not up for debate. Moving forward no more 'Sir, or Discipline.' You have earned the right to address me as, 'Daddy, Papi, King.' All acceptable how you choose and I will not ask you, 'do you understand?' Of course you do, you are watching me as I speak to you and you hear every fucking word coming out of my mouth clearly. So any questions or anything you would love to add?" My left eyebrow rose up in wait for her reply. "Yes, if I may?" I smirk, "the floor is yours." Her head was down. She supplicates, "may I kneel before I speak?" I pointed downward with my index finger. She knelt. "I would love to make a vow to you. I vow to be your submissive at all times. When you need me. Wherever you need me. However you need me. You are my

Daddy, my King, my Dominant. I am your sub and yours only. I will follow without question. I will not question, for Daddy knows what is best for me. You are always right and not wrong. I will conduct myself in a way to make you proud of me. I yearn for your approval. Your happiness is my happiness. My only desire is to pleasure you. Worship you. Cater to you. Serve you. I love you and I will love you until the end of time. No one will know me like you know me. My fears. My doubts. My secrets. My insecurities and I will not allow them, because I am so stubborn. I am good to you. For you and will always be. When I am not, I will take whatever punishment you see fit, with no objections. When you control me, I feel protected. When you restrain me, I feel at home. In your presence is the only place that makes sense. At your feet is the only place I feel the safest. When you call me 'good girl', it gives me goosebumps. When you call me, 'slut', or 'bitch' it turns me on. My pulse races in anticipation. I wait for your commands and utilize them as guidance. I come to you humble as I offer myself to you always, mind, body, and soul."

If a woman of her caliber could truly love a lunatic like me, a maniac asshole that I am, I would never let her go. That type of love was powerful. Unconditional. Healing. Invigorating. The mutual need of Dom/sub.....the need to own her. The need to belong to him. She made all her decisions. In her everyday life, past relationships, but with me it felt good to release. No decisions were hers, they were all mine. Exhilarating. Hyperactive to be owned by me. A powerful man. An impeccable King. A firm Dominant. An exquisite Sadist. Knowledgeable Master. I allowed her to give in to her desires. Her desires became her surrender. My control was her escape. Her freeDom. I spoke softly, "Crawl to me beautiful. So beautiful on your knees. Even if you could run, you would not. Why? My presence is the only place where you can thrive. Truly be you. Where you can excel. Where there is no responsibility. Where you feel the safest, like you stated. Your secret is, you are not the average woman. When my hand is around your throat, you feel desired. When you cuddle up and place your head on my muscular chest, and I hold you in my big arms, you feel protected. When I am slapping you or spanking your ass, you feel loved. You love the pain, as the endorphins kick you. You are in your subspace. When I punish, whether it is physical or psychological, you need to be held accountable for your actions. Punished for your misbehavior. You need to learn. You need to be rewarded for being good. You need to be taught. You need to be taken. Used. Man handled. You need to be mine. You need to please me. That is what you yearn for. My happiness is what you live for. I could bind your body with my rope. Bind your wrists with my hand cuffs. Place shackles around your ankles. Blind fold you. It is me. I am that force that has a hold on you. Even when we are apart, you bind your soul to mine. No matter where you are, you know where you belong. The purest submission, without rope, without bounds. It is my words that keep your mind captive. It is my strength of character that ignites flames within your soul. You know where you belong. Once you had a taste of this real King. A chocolate, Disciplined King. The rest of the world have paled in comparison. I have imprinted my essence, my Dominance, my character in your heart, that anyone else who tries to entertain you, outside of me, will need to know me well. I mean fucking well, in order to understand you. Pleasure you how I pleasure you. Control your mind. Calm your busy thoughts like I do. Love you like I do. Hurt you like I hurt you. Heal you how I heal you. Kiss you like I kiss you. Make gentle love to you how I do. Fuck you savagely like I fuck you. Penetrate your mind and body like I do it. Place their hand around your throat and throttle you like I throttle you. Tame you like I tame you, and you will never kneel for anyone like you fucking kneel for me. You are mine. My bitch. My good girl. My slut. My whore. My prize. My baby doll. My desire. My precious. MINE. Your mind, body and soul are MINE. Your hair, your head, your eyes, your lips, your mouth, your throat, your breast, your pussy, your ass, your legs, your thighs, feet. Your tears are mine. Every breath you take belongs to me. Your sufferings belong to me. Your screams belong to me. Your fears, desires, power, love, pain, joy, sadness, madness, your angels and your demons. I am greedy. When I say you belong to me, I mean it in all the sense of the fucking word." She said, "I am yours, I am your sub, and I will earn any title you see fit for me. However, I yearn to be more than a sub to you. I want to be your slave...... I grab her chin and whisper, "mine." She shuts her eyes and let out a gasp....."yours." I reached for my collar and leash. I said to her, "once you become my slave, if you ever do, you will wear this. You will earn this. This is a symbol of our bond. You will be owned one hundred percent. You will wear this at all times. With friends, with family, at work, etc., the only person to take it off is me. Your friends may know about me but not the extent of our relationship in detail. Your safe word is sacred. Do not tell anyone your safe word. It is a sacred word for you and I. You will only elevate moving forward. What some women see as degrading, others see as empowering......

CONCLUSION

Fear is great. Trying something out of the norm is phenomenal. It entices and awakens our senses. Nothing is too good for you in my opinion. No matter how great the thing may appear. No matter who it is. You are entitled to the best there is. It is your direct inheritance. Do not be afraid to demand, take and conquer. Most men settle for what they can get in life. I am not most men. I see it, I want it and then it is already mine. Men are many things but masters of nothing. If you are able to master self, mental, and physical Discipline, you can take on anything in this world. There is no such thing as chance. I do not believe in coincidences. Whether it is something you can obtain or someone in your life. Your mind is your biggest gravitational pull. Whatever you need at the time will find it's way towards you.

ACKNOWLEDGMENTS

I would like to express my gratitude to the ones that saw me through this book. To the ones that saw this vision before I did. For the ones that appreciate my art and my words. To all that love me and secretly hate me. To all that did not think this was possible and to all that knew this day would come. To all that followed my steps to this journey. To all that have seen my progression, and hard work displayed in front of their very eyes. For the ones that were not apart of this, at least you get to witness. I want to thank Mami (my mom), and Mama (my late grandma, RIP) for instilling the teachings in me and raising a Dominant man. I want to thank everyone for being apart of this project. You can learn many things from women if you pay attention. I am strong because of women.

When I was 15, kids in my high school were getting new outfits every week, the new Jordan's. I was striving to get a car. I obtained money however I could. By 19, I had my own insurance. When my mom had a breakdown, I was working two jobs. I was always giving my mother money, here or there. Just because I wanted. I never needed to. Hell, when I saw my first twenty thousand dollars, I gave my mother twelve thousand and kept eight. Most kids I grew up with had an allowance every week. Not myself. There is no substitution for hard work, whether it is mentally or physically. Hard work builds character. I am a fitness trainer and that is one thing I always tell my clients. I thank my grandfather who is still resilient at 98 years old. Papi taught me how to be strong physically. My mother taught me about confidence. Never think you are dreaming too big. Nothing is unobtainable. Confidence starts in your mindset. Whatever you set your mind to, gravitates towards you. That is why it is always great to stay positive. Whatever you desire to accomplish will be accomplished. You place it in your mind and it sends vibes to the universe and every cell, thought, emotion, physiological bodily responses is because of it. I want to thank myself. Many people do not thank themselves, and when you read this book, you will learn I am not many people. I put my soul, mind and body into this artwork and it is a true inspiration. I have changed lives of few and inspired many. I also want to acknowledge my secretary, Daphne Politis, and photographer, Michael Zinn, whose photo of me is on the inside of this book.

My social media: Twitter @mrdiscipline_07

Instagram: @fitnesseducation07, @Discipline_beast07 and @alphaDominant07

Snapchat: @Discipline07

My website: www.mrdiscipline07.com and email: rockaballa05@hotmail.com

Made in the USA
Middletown, DE
04 November 2019